opt out

opt out

CAROLINA SETTERWALL

Translated from the Swedish
by Deborah Bragan-Turner

BLOOMSBURY CIRCUS
LONDON · OXFORD · NEW YORK · NEW DELHI · SYDNEY

BLOOMSBURY CIRCUS
Bloomsbury Publishing Plc
50 Bedford Square, London, WC1B 3DP, UK
Bloomsbury Publishing Ireland Limited,
29 Earlsfort Terrace, Dublin 2, D02 AY28, Ireland

BLOOMSBURY, BLOOMSBURY CIRCUS and the Circus logo
are trademarks of Bloomsbury Publishing Plc

First published in 2022 in Sweden as *Allt blir bra*
by Albert Bonniers Förlag
First published in English in Great Britain, 2025

Copyright © Carolina Setterwall, 2022
English translation © Deborah Bragan-Turner, 2025

Carolina Setterwall is identified as the author of this work in accordance
with the Copyright, Designs and Patents Act 1988

This is a work of fiction. Names and characters are the product of
the author's imagination and any resemblance to actual persons,
living or dead, is entirely coincidental

All rights reserved. No part of this publication may be: i) reproduced or
transmitted in any form, electronic or mechanical, including photocopying,
recording or by means of any information storage or retrieval system without
prior permission in writing from the publishers; or ii) used or reproduced in
any way for the training, development or operation of artificial intelligence (AI)
technologies, including generative AI technologies. The rights holders expressly
reserve this publication from the text and data mining exception as per Article
4(3) of the Digital Single Market Directive (EU) 2019/790

A catalogue record for this book is available from the British Library

ISBN: HB: 978-1-5266-0811-6; EBOOK: 978-1-5266-0809-3;
EPDF: 978-1-5266-7045-8

2 4 6 8 10 9 7 5 3 1

Typeset by Integra Software Services Pvt. Ltd.
Printed and bound in Great Britain by CPI Group (UK) Ltd,
Croydon CR0 4YY

To find out more about our authors and books visit www.bloomsbury.com
and sign up for our newsletters
For product-safety-related questions contact productsafety@bloomsbury.com

Part One

Mary

She struggles to hide her elation when the family leaves her and heads off for the mountains on the first morning of the winter holidays. A little sigh of relief when the door closes, but that's all. From the kitchen window she smiles her warmest, most motherly of smiles, and waves to the children in the back seat. As the car moves off she continues to smile and wave. She keeps waving until the boot of the white Volvo disappears at the junction between Tallvägen and Eriksbergsvägen. Only then does she allow her arms to fall to her side and the muscles in her face to relax, as she feels a smile of a different kind spread across her face.

She makes herself a fresh pot of coffee. Clears away the crumbs and plates, the bowls and glasses. She rinses the chocolate dregs out of the cups before putting them in the dishwasher. When all signs of the children's breakfast have disappeared, she assembles a new one for herself. She warms the frozen croissants in the oven and puts out the marmalade and butter, the cheese and ham. When she sits down at the kitchen table, she congratulates herself: it was a good idea to tell the children in advance that she wouldn't be going with them this year.

She'd mentioned it for the first time quite casually at the end of the Christmas holidays.

'It's possible,' she'd said, 'that Mum won't be going to the mountains with you for the winter holidays. It's not definite, but maybe.'

The reaction from the children, particularly Fredrika, was almost instant. Her daughter had begun by weeping, then arguing with her habitual logic: but that's the way it's *always* been, we've *always* gone as the *whole* family, it won't be the same if you're not there, can't you come, *please*?

John had weakened immediately, as he always does when Fredrika gets upset. It was obvious from the pleading look on his face, the worry line between his eyebrows, the way he glanced at Mary with an accusatory question mark in his eyes. *Can't you see what you're stirring up?* His entire countenance signalled that they'd need to revisit the subject.

After the children had gone to bed that night they had a row. Or rather, not a row as such, because she and John aren't the kind of couple who row, but they'd talked it over. And reasoned with each other. They hadn't quite seen eye to eye. John had insisted Mary should go to the mountains with them as usual, if only to make Fredrika happy. Mary was adamant this was a bad idea, partly because she was desperate to get out of the trip, and partly because it was high time their daughter realised, once and for all, how things actually stand. Everyone can't always be together. It would be doing the girl a disservice to always let her set the agenda. With that, the discussion had evaporated, and John gave up. There had been no need for her to even mention the fact that it was John, and not Mary, who'd always enjoyed the weeks spent crammed together in the mountain cabin.

For the first few days of the winter holidays Mary does as she'd planned; in other words, nothing special. She savours the tranquillity that fills the house after it's been cleaned from top to bottom. Now that none of the children's toys lie strewn over the floor, there's nothing to trip over and stub her toe on. She can balance her tray of cheese and wine with ease, without having to watch her step between the kitchen and the living room. There's no hum from John's television news to disturb her when she reads her books, no children's voices from the neighbouring rooms to warn of fights breaking out, no one pulling at the door handle while she's sitting on the toilet or taking a bath. She can finish knitting the Icelandic jumper she started in the Christmas holidays, can take an evening walk to the video shop in the Helenelund centre and rent whichever film she likes: a chick flick, the kind of film John would have spurned and the children wouldn't have been allowed to watch. She takes the video player from the TV room in the basement up to the living room and she watches her film, even though it's the middle of the night. She drinks wine on the sofa, even though it's midweek. Smokes her cigarettes in any room she fancies. She smokes in all the rooms except the children's.

When the telephone rings in the evenings it's always Fredrika who wants to speak first and longest. This week Fredrika, who usually cares deeply about fairness, doesn't seem to think it's important for Victor to come to the phone. As though she thinks their telephone conversations are something private between herself and Mary, and the other members of the family should keep out.

Yet she has nothing in particular to say. After Mary has assured her she's fine and asked what they've done that day, Fredrika is quiet, as if she's waiting for her mother to say something else. But what's she supposed to say? That she misses her daughter? She's already said that, several times. But Fredrika hangs on to the receiver and in the end the strained silence makes Mary so nervous that she asks her daughter to fetch her little brother. Only when Victor comes to the telephone does she relax again.

Victor. He's so easy to have around, so...uncomplicated, somehow. When he was a baby, he was fat and looked like a little old man with all his cute wrinkles, but over time he grew tall and slender and very, very beautiful. His skin is a soft olive colour and his green eyes, which he seems to have inherited directly from Mary, are lined with thick dark lashes. You don't have to be Victor's mother to see that he is an exceptionally attractive boy. His voice is always slightly croaky, but the hoarseness is amplified over the phoneline between the cabin and Sollentuna. Several times during the week Mary has asked him if he's caught a cold on the ski slopes. One evening she comes straight out and asks him if he misses her. That question appears to surprise him too.

'Of course,' he says, with no trace of sadness in his voice, 'of course I do.'

His answer is simply a statement, not a reproach, and as soon as he's confirmed that he misses her, he hands the receiver back to his sister, so that he can carry on playing with his cousins. And Fredrika comes back. With her long silences and reproving tones.

Every time Mary tries to remember when it was her daughter started to be this way, she comes to the conclusion that Fredrika must have emerged from the womb like this. When the nurses brought the newborns into the postnatal ward at breastfeeding time, Fredrika was the only one who was always crying, and the shrieking pierced through Mary's ears. They stayed on the maternity ward for seven days, and for seven days Fredrika cried.

When they came home from hospital, John took over. He had a better touch with their daughter than Mary had, right from the start. He got Fredrika to take the bottle of formula, sang to her in the evenings, swung her over his shoulder, and walked from room to room for hours, rocking her to sleep. He soon took main responsibility for the nights too. The nursery, which Mary had spent months decorating during her pregnancy, stood unoccupied for many more months. The cot was carried out and placed on John's side of the double bed and there it remained.

By the time Fredrika was six months old, he'd taken on the parental leave as well. He had nearly been given the sack in the process, his employer considering it totally inappropriate for a father to stay at home with his child for as long as John intended to. But, to Mary's huge relief, John had stood his ground, and when he threatened to resign with immediate effect the dispute was resolved. John took over Fredrika's daily care, Mary could return to work as a flight attendant, and on the whole everything improved. Two years later Victor arrived and it was never as difficult with him. It was as if he came out in a more flexible form. Less complicated, easier to love.

On the fourth day of the winter holiday Mary is having dinner with her colleagues from the office at Arlanda Airport. They've been planning it for over a month, but at the last moment they don't know whether Hans will be able to come or not. One of his sons is in bed with flu and that means his wife wants him at home. Mary, on the other hand, would rather he went to the restaurant with them. He's her favourite colleague; she's liked him since the day he joined the accounts department. Apart from being good at his job, he's always friendly, always positive and provides lots of laughs in their meetings and coffee breaks. He has beautiful hands, too. And a dark, sensuous voice, and curly hair that looks like a perpetual bed head. Not to mention the fact that whenever they drink wine together, they have fun. Several times over the years she's laughed so much in Hans' company her sides have ached. At the closing dinner of the conference last summer, he'd even rested his hand on her leg under the table. Her entire body had quivered. She'd pressed her leg against his to show she appreciated the gesture, and they'd stayed in that position for over an hour. The warmth from his hand had spread through her and when they finally stood up, she felt quite dizzy. It was as if the impression of his hand had been scalding, as if it had left burn marks on her skin, and she could still feel it throbbing on the way home in the taxi.

That night she woke John and made him have sex with her. There wasn't even any need for foreplay. John had been so surprised that he suspected nothing, just woke up and let himself be seduced. It was the best sex they'd had for years, and she had Hans to thank for that. But on the Monday after the conference everything was as usual at work, and there were no more nights of passion with John, either.

After some back-and-forth on the phone with his wife, Hans tells them that he can come to the restaurant, or at least for a few hours. The news makes Mary happier than it should, but this she reveals only to her reflection in the cloakroom mirror when she adjusts her make-up before they leave.

The workmates are in high spirits on the airport bus from Arlanda Airport to Stockholm Central Station. They choose an Italian restaurant, close to the metro for Hans' sake, and lose no time in ordering their wine. Mary relishes the feeling of being pretty and free. Her colleagues laugh at the jokes she makes; the more they drink, the louder they become. Across the table she can see Hans' eyes light up admiringly when he looks at her. At least, that's how she reads it. He's sitting slightly too far away for any physical acknowledgement.

It's a pity he has to leave early, she thinks, that his only son should be ill on the very night she has the house to herself. Not that she would be unfaithful even if she did have the chance, but still. He would probably have accepted if she'd invited him into the house on Tallvägen for one last drink. And maybe, if they had taken that last drink and Hans had tried to kiss her, she would have let it happen. Just one little kiss. Just to get it over with. Does it even count as cheating if you've almost decided to get a divorce? If you hardly ever have sex with your husband? She's not sure. But now it's not going to happen, because at nine o'clock on the dot Hans stands up and excuses himself. He really has to go. Less than thirty minutes later Mary is on her train home too.

When she reaches Tallvägen the house seems emptier than normal. She puts a pair of woolly socks on top of her tights and wanders aimlessly from one room to another, switching lights on and off, unable to decide where to sit down or what to do. She tiptoes into each of the children's rooms. In Victor's room she sniffs his pillow, before fluffing it up and putting it back neatly in its place. In Fredrika's, she smooths out a crease in the bedspread, and then rearranges the pens on her desk. When she's finished, she goes back to the kitchen.

The answering machine on the worktop next to the oven is flashing. The red light informs her the family has rung and left three messages in the time she took to have dinner with her friends. Despite her telling John that she was going out this evening before she left work. She sighs at the answering machine. She feels like poking her tongue out at it, but doesn't, feels like sticking her middle finger up at it, but she doesn't do that either. Instead, she turns her back on it to see what's in the fridge. There are only two nights left after tonight and she won't let the answering machine spoil everything. Without pressing the flashing button, she lights a cigarette under the kitchen fan. Tonight she doesn't want to think about John and the children.

Instead, she thinks about Hans. While she stands there smoking, she imagines it's Hans who rang, Hans who left all three messages, Hans who at this very moment is in a telephone box on the square in the centre telling her he misses her, that he can't stop thinking about her. In her fantasy, Hans takes the initiative, he suggests he should come over to her, he wants to come right now, he simply can't wait any longer. And she's the one saying yes, opening the door to him as he runs down the path, letting him tear off all her clothes, right there in the hall.

Afterwards they lie in silence, no need for words. They both know how complicated it all is, with families, and places in the country, and in-laws, but they don't need to speak about that tonight. It's enough that they're lying half undressed on the floor, in each other's arms. For her it would have been more than enough.

Her fantasy ends the minute she finishes the cigarette. She stubs it out in the ashtray, pours a little water into the bottom and empties the butt into the bin under the sink. She pours the wine away, doesn't want to drink any more tonight. Instead, she drinks a glass of water. Then another. She forces herself to drink one glass of water for every glass of wine she drank at the restaurant. After the third the waistband on her skirt feels tight and she looks down at her stomach, noticing how big and ugly it's become, like the belly of an old woman. She tenses her muscles and pulls in her stomach. The bulge disappears at once. She relaxes and it comes back. She gives in and pulls down the zip at the side of the skirt. Then she gives in a second time and presses the button on the answerphone.

She knew before she played them back that the three messages would be from the mountains. In the first message John files a brief report of the day on the slopes, and in the two that follow first Fredrika and then Victor says goodnight. See you on Sunday, John says. Love you, Mum, Fredrika says. Bye, Victor says.

After the last message the answering machine gives a long final beep. Then it falls silent, the red light stops flashing, and the only sound in the kitchen is the faint tick of the clock on the wall above the dresser. The clock tells her it's eighteen minutes past twelve. It's Friday already.

It's not the same having Friday night dinner with the neighbours without John and the children, but she does it anyway. She has nothing better to do, and it would seem odd to call it off just because they're not all at home. They always eat with the neighbours on Fridays, after all, and both Anki and Sören know she's been at home. Presumably they've seen her walking around inside all week. So they behave as normal. They come over just after six, nothing strange about that; except it does all feel rather strange.

It feels strange to set the round dining table in the living room and not the table in the kitchen, where the children usually sit. Mary has made a chicken casserole and rice for dinner. She serves a beer for Sören, a Fanta for Moa, and white wine for Anki and herself. Moa looks fed up with trying to follow the adults' dinner table talk, and Mary can sympathise: there isn't any decent conversation. It's stilted and slightly awkward asking Moa what she's been up to during the holiday and attempting to chat with Sören about the sorts of things he usually discusses with John, like football. Mary knows nothing about football. She doesn't find politics particularly thrilling either. However, she makes an effort and does her best to include everyone, steering the conversation unsteadily between Sören's interests and Anki's. When Moa asks if she may leave the table and put on a film in the basement, Mary practically bounces out of her seat to go and help her. When she comes back up Anki has cleared the table and Sören is out on the terrace smoking. This Friday evening is going to have an early finish. It's not even nine o'clock when the neighbours take the shortcut back home through the bushes in the corner of the garden.

Mary spends Saturday in town. The buzz of activity is as vibrant as ever. The throngs on Drottninggatan give no hint that this is the week when hundreds, possibly thousands of families have left the city to jam themselves into their mountain cabins. In the NK department store she drifts between the floors. She sniffs at a row of perfumes, tests some on her wrists, tells the shop assistants she needs to think about it, and moves on. At the make-up counter she tries a bronzer on the back of one hand and a green shimmer eyeshadow on the back of the other. She hurries past the children's department, no reason to stop there today, and finds herself in the sport and leisure section. She considers a pair of running shoes, thinking about the bulge of her stomach. But there's no salesperson around, and that's just as well, because in reality she has no desire at all to start jogging.

On the ladies' fashion floor she falls for a silk dress she can neither afford nor will ever have use for. The dress looks as though it belongs in a bygone age, a more gregarious age, an age when it would have been worn to a dance several times a week. Perhaps that's why she buys it in the end. She tries it on twice, once for fun and once rather more in earnest, and pays at the till with her credit card. As soon as she's done it, she knows she will have to ring her mother and ask for money this month as well. She could have purchased three pairs of trainers for the same sum, but that wasn't going to happen. This happened instead. On the train home she puts her hand into the bag and strokes the smooth tissue paper. She wonders what Hans would say if he saw her in the dress.

When the family returns on Sunday evening it's as though they've never been away. Mary waves from the kitchen window again, as if she hasn't stirred from the spot, and greets them in the hall in their tumult of bags and smells and noise. Fredrika tells her she was travel sick for the last bit in the car. Victor mutters about it not being fair that his sister could sit in the front and he couldn't. John carries all the luggage in, complaining he has a sore back. He always has a sore back when he drives long distances, because he's so tall. Mary gives him a pat and says, 'Poor you.' She hugs the children and tells them she's missed them. Then she carries the cases down the stairs, one after the other, along the lengthy corridor in the basement, all the way to the laundry room. She takes her time sorting the dirty clothes. Whites in one pile, coloureds in another, ski suits in a third. She can hear feet charging around upstairs, the toilet flushing, something hard being dropped on the floor. One of the children screams. John's weary voice asks them to stop fighting. Mary pours detergent into the dosing ball and tries to feel happy that they're back home, that everything's normal, that they're all in the same place at last.

After dinner, and after the children's baths, and after the first machine load has been hung up in the airing cupboard, they have sex. John takes the lead, but she doesn't protest, allows him in without objecting or wriggling free. He pushes gently, stops and turns when he's deep inside, eventually comes with one long sigh. When he rolls off he says it's so nice to be home. She doesn't answer and he doesn't ask her why.

John

It's really embarrassing, he thinks when he drops the children off outside school on Monday and continues his car journey to work, that sex has this effect on him. That he's such a predictable human being. He and Mary only need to make love for him to spend the whole of the following day filled with the sense that life is good and the future full of promise. He whistles in the traffic queues on the Essingeleden motorway; smiles like an idiot, a grateful idiot, at a motorist who pushes in from the outside lane to get into the Fredhäll tunnel. No one can ruffle his good mood today. He's looking forward to getting to work, having a chat with Kerstin in reception, joking with Uffe on the way to his office, talking to the guys about what their families did over the school holiday. Then it'll be time to get down to the day's work. The weekly start-up meetings have to be held, he has to catch up on what he's missed while he was off, he has to get up to speed. None of it seems onerous today. Quite the reverse, he's happy to be back. It's good to be in Stockholm again.

The week in the mountains wasn't quite the success he'd hoped it would be. He should have realised it would be a mistake to invite his sister and her boys. Two adults and five children sharing forty-six square metres.

Three unruly lads plus Victor, who's always rowdier than normal when he's with his older cousins. And then there was Fredrika, who was invariably excluded from the boys' games and stuck close to John and Anneli the whole time with a pained expression on her face. Seven people squashed into a poky wooden cabin with an outside toilet and nowhere for anyone to have their own space.

On the very first day he was reminded of one of his sister's most irritating habits. She literally can't stop talking. It would be one thing if what she said was remotely interesting to him, but it seldom is. Time after time he caught himself wishing, all the more keenly as the week wore on, that Mary was there. She's always had a moderating effect on Anneli. Probably because, say what you like about her background, Mary is socially skilled. She mixes with all sorts of people and manages to make every one of them believe they're telling her something fascinating, and then she contrives to end the conversation at exactly the right moment. If anything, John does the opposite, at least with his sister. He shows all too clearly that he's not interested, and that makes her carry on indefinitely, as if to prove what she's saying is actually important.

It's not like him to speed, but on the way home from the mountains he couldn't help it. He covered the six-hundred-odd kilometres in less than eight hours, with only a brief stop for a hot dog at a grill just outside Mora. Fredrika had gone green by the time they reached Tallvägen. When he pulled into the drive he saw Mary open the door and wave to them from the step. She must have been looking out for them from the kitchen window while she was preparing dinner. It made him think she'd probably missed them as much as they'd missed her. The children were so excited they raced across the lawn before he'd even parked up properly.

When he finally made it into the hall, the children had already disappeared into the house. Mary was still there and welcomed him home with a kiss on the cheek. He could smell the perfume he'd given her for Christmas, and up close he could see the eye make-up she'd carefully applied. It struck him just after the kiss that there might be traces of glittery lip gloss where her lips had touched his skin. It was a tantalising thought, and he quite fancied leaning in for another go, on the mouth this time, but he stopped in the nick of time. Mary has never been the physical sort. You have to wait for the right moment with her.

Sometimes his wife reminds him of a skittish cat, one that only approaches you when you're busy with something else or feigning indifference. They've joked about it loads of times. When he calls her a cat, her defence is to call him a dog; a harmless mutt with a wagging tail and pleading eyes, but he encourages it. It's one of their many private jokes, part of what cements their relationship.

He is just telling Kerstin in reception how radiant she's looking, when she interrupts him and tells him there's a message waiting for him in his office.

'From Maud Forsblom.' Kerstin doesn't have time to register John's compliments before launching into business-briefing mode. 'She wants you to ring no later than ten o'clock, so you'd better hurry up.' With that she shoos him out of reception.

He ambles off, disappointed that his flattery fell flat and didn't generate the delighted laughter he'd imagined in the car on the way to work. Duty comes first, he thinks as he turns down the corridor to the CEO's office on the far left; that's how it's always been with Kerstin. That was why he appointed her in the first place.

Sure enough, on his desk is a note in Kerstin's familiar handwriting.

Mtg. with Maud Forsblom cxl. d/t sick child. Pl. ring before 10 to conf. info. rec'd. K.

Why Kerstin couldn't just have told him that in reception, he doesn't really understand. But this is how Kerstin likes to work. She likes her handwritten notes, and she especially likes connecting calls between the offices' various telephone lines. And maybe, he thinks, she had a feeling that the call from Maud Forsblom was of a slightly more personal nature.

Maud Forsblom is John and Mary's relationship counsellor. They've been meeting her every Monday for a year, ever since that boozy night with the neighbours when Mary blurted out that she thought she wanted a divorce. She'd wept and said she wasn't happy, whereupon he'd comforted her, made an effort to be understanding, promised her it would all get much better if only she'd give him the chance to put things right. The next morning she'd tried to take it back, said she couldn't understand what had got into her the previous night, but it was too late. By then he'd already left a message on Maud Forsblom's answerphone.

It was partly the issue of the trip to the mountains that had triggered the emotion in Mary on that occasion, at least that was Maud's theory. During one of their earliest conversations Maud had suggested that *it might be the case* that *for too many years* Mary had gone along with *too many things that hadn't been stimulating* for her. Initially he'd thought it sounded like psychological mumbo jumbo. It also felt a little like Maud and Mary were working against him, as though they'd made a women's pact in which all the counselling sessions were designed to find fault with him, make him the villain. Still, they continued with the weekly meetings. Maud was working on something she called the *treatment programme*, which, she asserted firmly, had been successful in helping couples in crisis all over the world. There was no question of suspending the programme midway, and after a few months the pendulum swung and John began to sense a certain degree of support on Maud's side. She never said anything openly, but it seemed to him there were times when Maud too thought Mary was complaining about details that shouldn't matter. Such as the mountains, for example. Was it really such a huge sacrifice, he might think to himself, to go on a paid holiday to a winter paradise for one week a year? Obviously, it was. Before Christmas Mary had declared she had no intention of going this year, and Maud had backed her up. All John could do was nod and accept it. It was about allowing each other to be autonomous individuals with control over their own lives, he was told. Fine, he said, stay at home them. I'll go myself. No pressure. I'll take my sister and her boys instead.

Before he rings Maud, he speed-dials Kerstin in reception to tell her he's got her message. She sounds relieved, as though a weight has fallen from her shoulders, and he can't resist adding before he hangs up:
'You look so elegant today! In your Monday best!'
Kerstin's happy giggle is the last thing he hears before replacing the receiver in its cradle. No matter how professional Kerstin is, she always falls for flattery.

The next call is to Maud, and it takes less than a minute. He assures their counsellor that he understands, they don't have anything pressing to discuss today anyway, everything's OK between Mary and him for the moment. Maud sounds glad to hear it. He can't stop himself ending the call with a kindly, 'Look after your son now,' even though it's rather presumptuous to talk to Maud about her private life. She's always careful to ensure the sessions in her room are about Mary and him, not herself. That might be why Mary has been uncomfortable in their sessions recently. She doesn't like the imbalance, Maud knowing so much about their private lives and them knowing almost nothing about hers. She'll no doubt be relieved when he rings to let her know that the counsellor has cancelled. Today's just getting better and better.

Before he can start work, he needs to catch Mary. It's a long way from her office at Arlanda to Maud's clinic near Karlberg station, and it wouldn't be a good thing for any of them if Mary were to catch the bus to get to an appointment that had been cancelled. She would definitely be annoyed and that would inevitably have repercussions for him and the children that evening. He rings her direct line, but there's no reply. He tries the switchboard, is transferred by a receptionist who doesn't possess half of Kerstin's telephone professionalism, but there's still no answer. He leaves a message with the switchboard: *Maud sick. No lunchtime meeting.*

When he returns from lunch, Kerstin has that earnest expression on her face again. You can tell from several metres away that there's been a message for him or one of his colleagues in the hour they've been out. *Please tell me it's not Mary*, he thinks as he walks up to reception.

'Mary's rung,' Kerstin says in the same instant. 'You need to call her on the home number.'

He closes the office door behind him, sits at his desk and dials his home number. When he's hit the last digit he fixes his gaze on the framed photograph of Mary and the children. In the photo they're lying in the garden hammock outside Mary's parents' house in Båstad. Mary's lying head-to-toe with the children and looking straight into the camera. Her green eyes are really glinting in the sunshine. In this picture it's not just her mouth that's smiling, it's her whole face, especially her eyes. As soon as the picture was developed he knew it had framing potential. The children in the photo are several years younger than they are now: Fredrika can't have been more than seven, and so Victor must have been five. Fredrika is resting her hand on Victor's head and laughing, at what he can no longer recall, but the gap between her top front teeth never fails to cheer him up.

The first dial tone rings in his ear. He forces his eyes away from the photograph and concentrates on the conversation he's going to have with his wife. This is exactly what wasn't supposed to happen. Mary was supposed to get his message and *not* get on the bus to Maud's clinic. She was *not* supposed to arrive there to find it closed and be so angry she would take the train straight home instead of going back to work. Why couldn't that useless receptionist at the airline find her and pass on his simple message? Was that so difficult? And why isn't Mary answering? He's on the point of hanging up when he hears a deep intake of breath at the other end. She sounds croaky, as if she's been crying.

MARI

When she leaves the city, she walks the streets slowly as now. What the hell is it doing out, raining heavily? Her inner thinking is not to cry—why on earth does she behave as once, she came from someone's warm embrace when the children, the summer holidays long gone, but now, and it doesn't anymore. It's cold outside in of spring today. The paperman said he'd be here between her thighs. When she opens her legs, but into her, he senses it feels safer.

Mari flow in warm immediately later and softer still. Her father's pulse as a flower. When he is with her in a dark, white line down the ridge of his spine, more layer in front of her to see. That beat's nearer, closer, she gives a final wave to Frances, who turns off the window, then pulls out gently. He leans in back and turns up the volume on the radio softly.

There's always somebody at her door, someone with her working. In fact it's a miracle nothing untoward, with so many unknowns as it does, so it went everywhere. Between liked and sleepless on the afternoon, the room ending up in a. Maureen will need to bring the people speaking when she's been in — something that can be without there being, Erik, and the some, going in. Not since her mother took —

Mary

Before she starts the car, she winds down the two front windows. What the hell if she does get a crick in her neck, the main thing is not to get sweat marks on her blouse. Ever since she came down to her parents in Båstad with the children, the country's been in the grip of a heatwave, and it doesn't appear to have any intention of waning today. The perspiration is already forming between her thighs. When she depresses the clutch to start the engine, it feels sticky under her skirt. To her relief the car starts immediately. She reverses carefully across her father's pride and joy: the gravel drive that forms a chalk-white line down the middle of the enormous lawn in front of her parents' house. Out on the street she gives a final wave to Fredrika and Victor in the kitchen window, then pulls out onto the Ängelholm road and turns up the volume on the car radio.

There's always something in her parents' car that's not working. In fact it's a miracle it transports them as many kilometres as it does every year. Back and forth between Båstad and Stockholm, and then all Gaby's never-ending trips in it. Mary can't remember a single occasion when she's been in her parents' dark-blue Mazda without there being at least one thing wrong with it. Not since her mother took over the driving after her father's first stroke at any rate. If it's not a flashing oil light, it's a windscreen wiper that's come off. A tyre that doesn't have enough air. An indicator that doesn't indicate. There's always something, and today it seems to be the radio. However much she twists the control, the sound crackles as if it were a walkie-talkie she's trying to listen to and not a regular pop music programme. If Mary knows her mother, she will undoubtedly listen to the radio all the same. A bit of crackle would never take the edge off her good humour behind the wheel. Can you *believe* someone invented the radio, she'd probably say. And can you *believe* we have the gift of listening to it every day! *What does it matter* if there's the occasional crackle? *God is truly good!*

Mary abandons the idea of trying to cheer herself up with music. Views over the leafy Bjäre Peninsula will have to suffice instead. A cross is dangling on a string from the rearview mirror, obstructing the view ahead, and in front of the cross swings a pale-pink Little Tree, polluting the entire car. *Cherry Blossom*, it says on the front of the tree.

'Cherry Blossom, my arse,' she mutters, before tugging it down.

The smell of the chemically produced cherry blossom fades when she shoves it into the glove compartment. And the distance helps, actually. Moving further and further away from her mother really does the trick. Having time for herself, her own thoughts, not needing to grit her teeth until her temples throb and her jaws ache – there's something to be said for it. She's looking forward to the undisturbed hours stretching ahead. This vacation has felt like anything but a holiday so far.

When she asked her mother earlier that morning if she could borrow the car to deal with a few things in

Ängelholm, at first Gaby didn't want to let her go. She had been *so looking forward* to taking Fredrika for lunch at Cederström's. And wasn't it just as easy for Mary to deal with these things another day? Surely there was no urgency about *today*?

It was only when Mary discovered the planned lunch was within walking distance of her parents' house, and had also promised her mother a proper day out – with a packed lunch and everything – to Hallands Väderö the following day, that Gaby agreed to lend her the car. On condition that Mary stops at the farm shop in Sinarpsdalen on her way home and buys a capon. The fact that they'd eaten capon for dinner as recently as the day before yesterday didn't seem to bother her mother. According to Gaby you can't eat capon too often, and Mary learned long ago that it's rarely worth arguing with her mother.

Mary lights her first cigarette of the day in the car park outside the shopping centre. She has actually stopped smoking day-to-day, but since each evening at Båstad consists of apéros, wine with the main course and after-dinner drinks with dessert, her cigarettes have more or less been classed as special-occasion smoking. Besides, cigarettes offer a necessary respite from Gaby. Going out into the garden with her father and sharing the silence and a couple of cigarettes under the stars has provided a vital breathing space during her time here. Some evenings their gentle stroll across the lawn at the back of the house is the only time in the entire day that Mary doesn't feel like screaming in sheer frustration. Soon she'll have been here two weeks. As time passes the urge to smoke intrudes earlier in the day. On the way from the car park to the shopping centre she thinks that it soon won't matter if she's a smoker or not. In a few months she won't be living with John any longer and no one will have any reason to point out that *it's actually harmful* every time she lights a cigarette.

Telling John she wanted a divorce didn't go very well. The reason she'd decided to wait until the Monday after their winter holiday wasn't because she was too cowardly to say it without Maud in the room, but because she thought it would help John comprehend the seriousness of the situation if Maud was there when she told him. After all, that's the reason they'd ended up with her in the first place. In their very first session with Maud, Mary had doubts about whether she was happy in her marriage, but on that occasion she hadn't been able to express herself properly. Not when she was crying so much at the same time. She'd sat there for ninety minutes and scarcely been able to answer a single question. When she tried, John had started to cry as well. It can't have been easy for Maud to understand what it was all about, that first time, but she did her best, and since then she's worked with John and Mary every Monday between twelve and half past one. It felt as though it would be breaking the rules to tell him outside of Maud's office. That was where they were supposed to discuss this sort of thing.

But then Maud had cancelled their session on the very day Mary intended to tell him. She couldn't wait any longer. So she had to do it on the telephone instead.

It went quiet at the other end of the line after she'd said it. After what felt like an eternity she heard a businesslike, 'I understand, we'll talk about it tonight,' and then an abrupt click. In the living room, with the receiver still pressed hard to her ear, Mary wondered what had just happened. And if she should ring him back, and what she would say if she did. Failing to come up with a plausible answer to either question, she didn't ring back. Instead she collected the children from school early and started making dinner.

When John came home, the atmosphere was almost normal. They ate a completely normal dinner, covered completely normal topics of conversation at the table, and afterwards John helped Fredrika with her homework while Mary did a jigsaw puzzle with Victor. Only after the children's bedtime did they talk about it. John asked her if she'd meant what she said, and she started crying and said yes.

There was nothing out of the ordinary about Mary crying, but John didn't react in the way he usually did. For example, he hadn't hugged her this time. Nor had he tried to reason with her, or ask if there was something more he could do, or suggest possible solutions. He'd remained quite still in his place on the sofa, looking down at his hands. After a while he'd sighed and said, 'OK, that's what we'll do,' whereupon he stood up, went into the bedroom and closed the door.

She followed him, of course. She sat down on her side of the bed, asked if that was all he had to say, was he going to refuse to talk to her from now on, couldn't they be a bit more cooperative?

'For the children's sake, if nothing else.'

When he looked at her his face held no expression.

'This is your thing,' he said. 'You can work it out to your heart's content. I'm staying in the house, anyway. And now I'm going to go to sleep. Goodnight.'

Since then she has tried to work it out. She's still trying to work it out. Today she has an appointment at a bank in order to obtain documents that will demonstrate her financial viability as future owner of an apartment on Svalgången in the centre of Helenelund. In her handbag is a copy of her latest tax return, a valuation of the house on Tallvägen and a copy of the prenuptial agreement she and John signed when they got married and bought the house. The latter specifies that she owns 25 per cent of the home and has the right to the same percentage in the event of a divorce. Also in her bag is a certificate of employment, which, together with the mortgage offer letter she hopes to take away from the bank in a little while, will be sent to the property owner who at the beginning of November will have a two-roomed apartment available only ten minutes' walk from Tallvägen.

She's a few minutes early for the appointment so she sits down in one of the vacant chairs and starts going through her handbag. Her fingers feel around under the plastic sleeve holding the documents, searching for some chewing gum to hide the lingering traces of cigarette on her breath, but she doesn't find any. Coming across a pocket mirror instead, she takes it out to examine her face. It feels as though the other people in the waiting room are eying her askance. As if they can see she's not used to going into a bank on her own, and besides, maybe it's inappropriate to look at yourself in the mirror in a public waiting room? She returns the pocket mirror to her bag. Fixes her gaze on the wall and tries to appear relaxed and unconcerned about her surroundings.

Despite being well prepared for the appointment, she's nervous. In the last few years John has taken care of the family's finances and on the few occasions she's gone with him to the bank, there's been no call for any input from her. She went along when they had to sign the house papers, but she hadn't been able to make much of a contribution to the loan arrangement. She'd let John do all the talking on the family's behalf, obediently signed where the bank man indicated, and then it was done. 1B Tallvägen belonged to her and John, and since then she hasn't needed to consider money much at all. Today's meeting will be about her, and she doesn't really know the ropes. Her bank account must reasonably reflect a professional woman who's had the same employer for the last ten years, received a modest salary on the 25th of each month and one or two monetary contributions from her parents between the 10th and the 15th. Her credit card is probably maxed out, but she's seldom missed payments and at any rate she's never had the debt collectors after her. In the waiting room the minutes slowly tick by.

John doesn't want her to ring him when he's in the archipelago, where he's renovating the cabins on Långön with Anneli and his mother, Elisabeth. He told her just before they parted at Arlanda, and because the children were there she couldn't ask why. But she has her theories. After a year of trying to save their marriage, the penny has finally dropped for him too. Maybe he feels stupid for hanging on so long to the belief they had a future together. Maybe he just wants some distance. Whatever the reason, they haven't spoken to each other for over a week. She assumes, from eavesdropping on his daily calls with the children, that all is going according to plan in the archipelago. Fredrika and Victor are ready by the telephone in Gaby's kitchen every evening at six. By then, Mary has to be busy doing something else so the children don't suspect anything when she never picks up the phone. She usually fills her hands with plates and glasses and starts setting the table when he rings. From the next room she can hear the children talking about their day, and Fredrika repeating the questions she's already put to both John and Mary countless times by now.

'Why have you gone on your own with Anneli and Grandma to Långön?'

'Why do you have to be there instead of here with us?'

'Why can't you just come here?'

Mary doesn't need to hear his voice to know what he says in response. John explains, in a much more informative manner than she normally does, that Anneli will own the houses in the archipelago in future, but they'll still be welcome there whenever they want. Then he says he misses them and is excited about seeing them soon. Fredrika is satisfied with the answers, but only for the moment. She will undoubtedly ask the same questions the next day. She suspects something's wrong, but she's getting ahead of herself. This is not the way she'll discover why John is selling his share of the archipelago properties, nor the time when she learns her parents are soon going to separate and her father is buying her mother out of the house they live in. Fredrika and Victor will find out, but not yet. They have to settle all the practical details first, then tackle the emotional angle. The one that involves the children.

Mary and John have promised one another that when the time comes, they won't say which of them initially wanted the divorce. That's on Maud's advice, and for the sake of the children, because they're too young to understand that parents can stop loving each other without it being anyone's fault. The children don't need to know who's the one leaving and who's being left. It's so easy to be turned into a villain in a child's eyes; children have a kind of natural talent for seeking a culprit when their lives are buffeted and they feel threatened. Some more than others. Doubtless Fredrika more than Victor. And no, Mary would rather not be judged by her own children if she can avoid it. She wants to carry on being loved and at the same time have a life she can bear living. Is that too much to ask? She doesn't think so, but it's a moot point, as her mother and John appear to have a quite different opinion.

When they break it to the children in autumn, they're going to present a united front and keep telling them how much they love them and that none of this is their fault. They're going to say that there'll be hardly any change at all, except that Mary won't be sleeping at the house anymore, and in some ways the children will actually have more than they have today. They're going to have a new place to call their own, they'll have new beds and they'll be free to go between the flat and Tallvägen whenever they want. Most important of all, they'll still have two parents who will always be there for them, no matter what, only now in two separate places. But first she has to secure a loan and sign a contract for a two-roomer on Svalgången by the station in the centre of Helenelund.

At close quarters her banker is actually quite good-looking. He has brown eyes and dark hair drawn into a bun at the back of his head. Pointed nose, bright gaze, smooth sun-tanned skin. Somewhere between twenty and twenty-five, she guesses, as she approaches his counter and holds out her hand in greeting. The name tag attached to his white shirt spells out *Andreas*.

For a brief moment he looks taken aback by her outstretched hand, but he recovers himself at once, shakes it politely and asks her to follow him.

'We'll sit here at the back,' he says in a ringing Skåne accent, and points to a corridor running behind the counters.

The corridor is quite short. It's also quite narrow, easily allowing Mary to catch his aftershave as she walks behind him. He smells youthful, somehow, like citrus and fresh air, an invigorating walk along a cliff or beach. Mary hopes he's as nice as he smells.

'Let's see,' he says when they're sitting opposite each other at a desk and he's tapped some figures into the computer on his side of the table.

'How can I help you, Mrs...Andrén?'

She's startled. It sounds strange for him to call her Mrs Andrén. She doesn't know whether he's joking or not, but resolves to use his opening line to come straight to the point.

'Well now, here's the thing. *Mrs Andrén* will soon be going through a divorce and changing her name to *Miss Lilja*. And in that regard *Mrs Andrén* needs some paperwork she can submit for an imminent property purchase.'

Andreas' face breaks into a wide smile, revealing a straight and almost outrageously white row of teeth. They make him look rather like a film star. He definitely hasn't smoked a cigarette in his life. And he has a sense of humour, that's obvious, because he now answers in an even more formal tone than he began with.

'The bank will be delighted to help you with that, Mrs Andrén, Miss Lilja-to-be. What type of paperwork might you need?'

*

Out of her bag she takes the valuation of Tallvägen and the form with details about the property in the centre of Helenelund. She hands them to Andreas, who – still smiling – leans over the desk and examines them. It's apparent from the documents that the home Mary wishes to purchase is a conversion, that the premises were previously used by a driving school but that now it's going to be renovated and sold as housing.

'This won't be a problem,' he says, as he leafs through the papers. He looks through the Tallvägen evaluation and doesn't seem to react to the information that Mary, in accordance with the document she and John signed when they bought the house, has a right to 25 per cent of its value in the event of divorce. He continues turning the pages until he reaches the planned layout of the new apartment.

At her end of the table Mary prepares to defend her forthcoming purchase. She knows, she's going to say, that it's not a perfect apartment, it's not a perfect layout, but it's definitely the best option, at least for the moment. The flat is cheap enough for her to afford without taking on too large a loan, and because it's located on the ground floor, she'll get more square metres for her money. It's the location that swings it, more than anything else. The flat is close enough to Tallvägen for the children to be able to run between hers and John's at will, close enough for her to look in on John and the children at the house, and close enough for her and John to continue as friends who see each other often and without impediment. In addition, her future flat will be closer to the children's school, so they will easily be able to pop in on their way home, even on the weeks they're living with John. She'll just have to find a way of working around the fact that the flat isn't very well laid out, is on the ground floor and is actually one room too small. Maybe she'll be able to sleep in the walk-in wardrobe and give the bedroom to the children. It doesn't matter, the important thing is that the adjustment for the children goes smoothly. On her meagre salary she can't afford anything else, anyway, not unless she has her mother onside, and it's fair to say she doesn't.

As soon as Gaby has had a couple of glasses of wine, the fretting begins.

Gaby finds it utterly incomprehensible that her own daughter wants a divorce. Incomprehensible, irresponsible and, above all, inexcusable. It doesn't matter how much Mary tries to explain. When she says she hasn't been happy for a number of years, her mother says she must be spoiled if she believes you can be happy all the time. When she says she's been so unhappy she barely wanted to carry on living, her mother offers to pay for counselling and recommends various antidepressants. When she says she and John have been going to a therapist for the last year and she's already tried all the antidepressants on the market, her mother says with a snort, 'You haven't found the right ones.'

Nothing Mary says gets through to her mother. It never has. There's no point in even trying. For lack of any better ideas, she tiptoes around in Båstad, trying to anticipate Gaby's mood, counting her glasses of wine and keeping the children out of their grandmother's way when she has had one too many before dinner. She ducks Fredrika's mistrustful questions, tries to joke with Victor, who up to now seems blissfully unaware, strolls slowly with her father across the lawn after the sun has gone down and every night, when she goes to bed, feels as though she has run a marathon. She's counting the days until they are due to go back to Stockholm.

At least everything will be different next summer. She consoles herself with that thought when it all feels too much.

When the meeting is over and she leaves the bank, the sun is shining outside the shopping centre in Ängelholm. With a spring in her step she crosses the car park, taking pleasure in breathing in the smell of sun-baked asphalt, in a better mood than she has felt for several weeks, maybe even months. She almost floats the last few metres to the car. She actually feels like dancing before she jumps in, using the car as a prop, leaning over the bonnet and wiggling her hips seductively. She doesn't, of course, but she'd like to. She doesn't know exactly what's caused her good humour. Maybe it's because Andreas was quite obviously flirting with her in the bank, or because, without so much as batting an eye, he gave her the loan offer she requested. He pressed a few keys on his computer and it was done.

'That should be more than enough. Otherwise just send the property owner my way,' he had said with a playful wink before they parted.

She sweeps out of the car park with pop music from the radio thumping out of the speakers. She sings along as she turns onto the road that will take her to the farm shop with the capons. She doesn't even notice that the problem with the radio has righted itself, that all she had to do for it to start working was turn the engine off and start it again. She's too busy singing.

John

It's as though he and Anneli both revert to being children again during the weeks they spend on Långön. Elisabeth persists in serving them breakfast, lunch and dinner and every afternoon she shouts at them to be careful when they take a break from their renovating and go down to the beach for a dip. As the two of them descend the steep path between the cabin and the pebble beach, they laugh at their mother. They have been diving from this jetty for close on thirty years. They of all people know how to treat the sea with respect. If it had been a normal summer then it would have been John and Anneli standing on the porch shouting the same warnings to their own children, but this isn't a normal summer. This time they're here for another reason and the children couldn't come. It would have been far too complicated.

Neither of them ever imagined it would turn out like this. Not when it had been him who loved the summer house most. His sister was always too unsettled to be happy here for any length of time, but John never had that problem. He's loved this place all his life. It was here he taught himself, and then both his children, to swim. It was here as a teenager he sneaked off with the neighbours' lads to drink beer in the marina on the next island. He built the bunk beds in the little cabin with his bare hands and he'd be lying if he said it didn't feel strange now to let his share of the place go.

'You must promise you'll still come with the children as usual, afterwards,' she says, and breaks off because she knows he doesn't want to talk about 'afterwards'.

One thing at a time, he said. This is how it is now and there's no point in dwelling on it. It wasn't as if he'd had a choice anyway.

After Mary had declared she wanted a divorce, in his eyes there was only one way to resolve it. There was no question of the children being forced to leave Tallvägen. Nor was there any way Mary could afford a place to live that would be a comparable home for the children. She didn't even seem interested in trying. Appeared to be quite happy with the idea of a two-roomed flat next to the station and to assume that he would stay in the house.

To keep the house on Tallvägen he will have to pay off both Mary and the bank. But at least with him everything will carry on as normal. Selling his share of the property in the archipelago just happens to be the prerequisite.

It's not only Anneli who insists on talking about what happens afterwards. His mother can't resist bringing up the divorce. Almost every day she comes in while he and Anneli are painting. She brings a tray with coffee and biscuits and then proceeds to sit down and talk to their backs.

'Can't you try and persuade Mary to give it one last try?' she says.

'I've already done that.'

'But can't you both give it another last try?' she says.

'We've done that too.'

In Elisabeth's world last tries don't ever seem to run out. Parents should stay together forever for the children's sake, end of. Presumably that's what she herself did with their father, Gunnar. In the opinion of both John and Anneli their mother had been more of a carer to their father than a partner in the last years of his life. She dealt with both the diabetes and the insidious alcoholism, and in the autumn of his years when he flew into a temper and was mean, she always managed to calm him down and deflect him from whatever had caused his anger. She had seemed relieved more than anything else when their father finally died, but would never admit it.

John tells her that this is how it's going to be whether she likes it or not, because it will be, whether he too likes it or not.

And no, if they must know, he doesn't like it. This wasn't his idea. It's Mary who says she's been unhappy in their relationship in recent years, who dreams of a different future, who obviously doesn't think he and the children are worth fighting for. Mary, not him. Mary who thinks they've become like brother and sister rather than being lovers and has hopes of experiencing passion again. Mary who feels she can't exist as a parent, if she can't also be a woman. Whatever that means. It's not as if he's regarded her as a man during the thirteen years they've spent together.

When she started talking like this, he hadn't even grasped what she meant. After all, things were just beginning to improve. Both children were out of toddlerhood, which meant the hard part was behind them, not ahead. He doesn't know how he achieved it, because Mary can be stubborn when she wants to be, but he had managed to convince her to give it a try. And then another. For several years they kept on trying without anyone around them knowing. They had started their sessions with Maud and soon after began an intimacy and sex schedule, booked babysitters and gave one another hour-long massages. He was happy to go along with anything Maud asked them to do. As long as Mary would give them one more honest attempt.

Perhaps it was sheer exhaustion that finally made him give up when she rang him at the office that Monday after the winter break. That evening she had started weeping before she had even got her first sentence out. Usually he'd comfort her, say he was there for her, that it would get better and all she needed was to rest and take it easy. He'd ask if there was anything he could do, anything at all, to show how committed he was. But not this time. This time he just sat there looking at her and thinking that she was ugly when she cried. Then he realised what that meant: *I can't take any more. Screw this.*

If she wanted a divorce so badly, she could have it. If he wasn't the one she wanted to live with, she'd be saved the trouble. He didn't have it in him to demean himself any longer. And that's why they're where they are this summer. Mary and the children in Båstad and he, Anneli and Elisabeth on Långön. Mary is signing a lease on a flat and he is selling his share of the archipelago house to his sister, who in turn is borrowing money from their mother, who is deducting it from Anneli's future inheritance. Fredrika and Victor are having an almost-normal summer holiday, for that's what he and Mary want them to have. You should have fun on your summer holiday when you're young, on that at least they're in agreement. The bad stuff can wait until autumn.

Mary

She's standing on a stool, painting Fredrika's walls a lilac colour, when she dissolves into tears. Without warning sadness has crept into the tunes she's humming, which were cheerful at first. This isn't a violent fit of sobbing, these are silent tears. A discreet variety that would have passed completely unnoticed if she'd only been left to quietly carry on working. If Fredrika hadn't appeared at her side while she was wiping her cheeks on the sleeve of her shirt, it would've been of no concern to anyone, not even Mary herself. But that's not going to happen now. Instead Fredrika is staring at her in dismay and Mary is obliged to climb off the stool, put her rollers to one side and try to convince her daughter that everything's fine.

Everything isn't fine, of course. She doesn't even know herself why she started crying. Just before Fredrika came into the room she'd been standing there in her dungarees, singing along to herself and at the same time reflecting on how many times the family had swapped rooms in this house, how many coats there were on the walls she was painting.

When they bought the house on Tallvägen the walls in this room were an apricot colour and she and John both hated it. They swiftly repainted it pale blue and made it Victor's nursery. A while later the walls acquired dark blue wallpaper with yellow stars and four-year-old Fredrika moved in. Soon after that Mary and John painted the room white and moved in themselves. That time it needed multiple coats of paint because the yellow stars showed through the white. John had cursed while he was painting and made Mary promise never to buy such hideous wallpaper again. Six months later John became a partner at his firm and they decided to turn the room into an office. Before long it was Fredrika's turn to take ownership again, as it turned out neither Mary nor John used the office and it was actually the best bedroom on the top floor. Since then there's been wallpaper with horses, followed by creamy pink paint that was soon covered in felt-tip pen, and now a heather shade. The weeping must have surfaced out of that somehow. And Fredrika was there in an instant.

'Everything's fine, little one, I just had a splash of paint in my eye. But look how nice it's going to be!'

Mary tries to distract her with a sweeping gesture at the newly painted walls, but it doesn't work. She's hardly begun her first attempt at explaining it away before Fredrika starts chewing at her cuticles, and from there it just gets worse. She's at Mary's heels the entire afternoon, eyeing her mother's every step, twitchy with suspicion. May tries to compensate by joking more than usual, with all three of them, but none of them laugh at her wisecracks. All her efforts fall flat, and John doesn't help at all. He's attending to Victor's room and has no desire to compliment her on the end result when she's eventually finished painting.

After dinner, when the kitchen's been cleared, the dishwasher's on and the cheese puffs have been served in the large glass bowl on the living-room table, it can't be put off any longer. They've rehearsed what they're going to say for over a month now, both together and with Maud. They've even decided where they're going to sit in the living room when they should say it. John's going to be in his usual place on the sofa and she in hers, the armchair opposite. If the children start crying she'll move over to the sofa and they'll cuddle them together, as in at the same moment, so no one feels left out. They'll keep repeating that they love them and none of this is their fault.

There's a film ready and waiting in the video player. In a perfect world the children will take the news with equanimity and then they'll all watch the film together. In a perfect world the children will be sad at first, and then when they talk about it they'll see it might not be so bad after all. If they're calm enough to grasp the information about her new flat, how close it is and how cosy they'll be there, she hopes they might even be happy. It's difficult to tell what John thinks, because he hasn't been particularly keen on talking to her lately. She isn't stupid – she knows what's behind it. Deep down he's sad, but he's also proud. He doesn't want to show that he's unhappy and he'd rather punish her with his silence. In their recent sessions, Maud has underlined that all reactions are OK, as long as they don't hurt the children. They can each decide for themselves if they want to talk or not, be friends or not. It's up to the other one to respect that, Maud says. And Mary has done that. She's quelled almost every impulse to try to make him talk to her, promised herself she'll be patient with his long silences. At the beginning she made a point of repeatedly saying that she really wanted to get along with him, but as he withdrew more and more, she gradually fell silent too. So now she's waiting instead. Waiting for him, for a reaction, for a row or a reconciliation, for anything at all. For the date of the move to finally arrive, if nothing else.

She watches him while he's sitting on the sofa, his gaze directed at his knees. She used to know exactly what he was thinking, but tonight she has no idea. Is he staring at his wedding ring, or is he thinking about something else? His breathing seems even, anyway. She can't detect a pounding heart beneath his shirt. For a moment she's lulled by his calm, but when she asks if he's ready and he looks up and meets her eye, her composure evaporates.

His eyes are dark and betray traces of anger. Which he will not show this evening. He's going to say the right thing, hug the children if they cry, comfort them just like they've practised with Maud. But he still doesn't think they're doing the right thing. She can see by the way he's looking at her now. They don't agree even now and he's keeping quiet as if he wants to give her one last chance to change her mind.

In John's world all you have to do is decide. It's always worked that way for him. His life has been composed of a long series of decisions that he's made and stuck to. In his world it's perfectly natural to work your way up from the warehouse to a position as CEO in the course of seven years because that was the plan he'd mapped out. You view a suitable house and buy it, despite your wife neither liking it nor having the financial means to share it with you. You decide to stay together. In his world it's impossible to understand a wife who tries to explain that she's spent years struggling with just that. He can't grasp that everything isn't resolved by deciding.

Why doesn't he understand that this is for everyone's sake, including his own?

Tonight isn't the time to talk about this. She looks away from him, takes a deep breath and calls to the children. Her voice is too bright, almost falsetto, and she has a fixed smile on her face that Fredrika for one will see straight through.

It's clear that Fredrika is already on her guard by the sound she's creating as she makes her way through the house, slamming her heels on the floor. She stops outside Victor's room and hammers on the door, tells him to hurry up, before the thudding of her heels continues, across the parquet in the corridor and then the marble floor in the hall. By the time she reaches the living room she is glassy-eyed and even before she sits down she demands to know what this is about.

'What's happened? Say something!'

Mary's smile is still fixed to her face. She wants it to look loving, inspire a sense of calm, but one quick glance at Fredrika tells her it isn't working. John sits in silence and gestures to the children to sit on the sofa with him. They plonk themselves down, one on each side of him, Victor with a puzzled expression and Fredrika ramrod straight, as if poised to race out of the living room in a beeline for her newly painted mauve bedroom. Mary braces herself and then just tells them.

JOHN

The commotion is starting to subside but Fredrika is still shaking. It sounds as though she has hiccups, lying on the sofa with her face against his chest. For a while he thought she was going to be sick, and after that he was scared she would dislocate her shoulder, she was flailing so much to escape his grip. Now she's calmed down, with only little waves rippling through her body and ending in a hiccup. When he strokes her hair his fingers catch on the sticky skin on her neck. He whispers, 'There, there,' and 'Shhh,' and keeps patting her.

Mary is sitting in the leather armchair opposite, with Victor on her knee. He's also curled up, looks as though he's resting his cheek against her breast. She rocks him gently, kisses his hairline now and then, holds him in her arms like an overgrown baby. *Look what you've done*, he thinks, staring at her across the table separating the sofa and the armchair. *Look at the havoc you've wreaked*. He wants to annihilate her with his eyes, make her shrivel up and disappear, but he can't, because she doesn't look up. She cuddles Victor and rocks him back and forth in her arms. Neither of them sheds a single tear. It almost looks as though they're playing a game.

How can she sit there blissfully rocking, when she's done this? Can't she see how Fredrika feels? Doesn't she care? Mary, who normally bleats at the first misfortune to befall her. Now she's cradling Victor, who went over to her after Fredrika accidentally kicked him in the stomach while she was trying to break free and run out of the room. Victor started crying as well, but only from the pain. Mary called him across to her and now they're sitting there. As if the matter's closed and they're ready to move on, maybe nibble on a snack or two and watch a video. As if Fredrika's the odd one out in this situation, not them.

Perhaps he is overly brusque when he picks Fredrika up and marches out of the living room with her. Both Mary and Victor glance up quizzically as he walks past the armchair with his hiccupping daughter in his arms, but he can't bring himself to look at them any longer. Mary can carry on what she's doing with Victor, he'll have to take care of Fredrika on his own.

He catches on the door as he carries her into her room. It clicks shut behind him and everything goes quiet. Her room smells faintly of paint and is lit dimly by the bedside lamp. In the glow from the street light outside the window he sees a new poster up on her wall. Above the bedhead a black horse with a long mane is rearing up against a violet sky. Mary must have put it up as the last item of decoration this afternoon. He didn't look very closely when she invited praise from him for her efforts.

When he puts Fredrika into bed, she curls up into a little ball. She pulls the duvet around her and turns away, so she's facing the wall. After a moment's hesitation he lies down beside her. He moulds his body to hers, strokes her back gently and whispers that he loves her.

When he asks if she wants to talk, she shakes her head, but she lets him leave his hand on her back. Her skin feels warm, almost feverish to his touch, but still she draws the duvet around her more tightly. Her sobs are more intermittent than they were a little while ago, but the small shudders in her back tell him she's still crying. This is what he recognises, the old familiar kind, of a totally different character to what happened in the living room. He hopes it's a good sign.

It isn't long before she falls asleep. From the living room he can hear Mary and Victor talking to one another. It sounds like a normal conversational tone, but he can't hear what they're saying. Mary is probably going to put Victor to bed soon. It's already half past nine, there's no question of a Saturday night film night now.

In the darkness John considers whether to stay with Fredrika all night, but decides it would be a bad idea. It's better for her to wake up on her own in the morning, rather than with him beside her, reminding her of how she felt when she fell asleep. It's vital for the children that everything's normal for as long as possible, as from November there'll be nothing normal at all, and even then he's still going to make every effort to achieve it. He has no other choice. Not now that Mary wants to wreck everything. The only thing he can do is to carry on as usual and cover for the things the children are going to miss from the way things were before. That's what he's going to do, and he'll do it tonight too. He kisses his daughter gently on the shoulder and then leaves the room.

In the living room Mary and Victor have ended up on the floor in front of the fire. They're doing a jigsaw puzzle, looking as if nothing out of the ordinary has happened during the evening. John resists the impulse to say something caustic to Mary and instead he pats Victor on the head and asks in as calm a voice as he can muster:

'Hey, buddy. What are you doing?'

Victor gives him a questioning look. It's quite obvious what he's doing and both he and Victor know it. He scans John's face curiously, as if he's waiting for his father to expand upon his question, but when that doesn't happen, he shrugs his shoulders and returns to the puzzle on the floor in front of him.

'Did you know, Dad,' he says, with his eyes on the jigsaw pieces, 'we're going to Legoland next summer with Mum. There are MEGA-SIZED models there.'

John views his son's tousled hair from above. Then he looks at Mary, who doesn't raise her eyes to meet his. On his way out of the living room he summons all his self-control to say to Victor,

'Fantastic, kiddo. Legoland sounds ace.'

Mary

When she guides the neighbours from the patio door, through the living room and on into the hall, everyone pretends there's nothing special about this Friday. No one points out that if they were to knock on the door next Friday, as they've done every Friday for years, she won't be the one who opens it for them. Nor does Sören or Anki comment on the row of removal boxes that are stacked against the wall in the hall today. Moa doesn't even appear to notice they're there. Unconcerned, she uses the top tier as a place to deposit her wet raincoat before she disappears into Fredrika's room. A cursory knock followed by an equally cursory 'Come in', and the door closes behind her with a bang. The adults are left standing in the hall, Anki and Sören still wearing their dripping coats.

'Christ! It's pouring!' Sören says, taking off his spectacles.

'Ugh,' Anki says, 'proper autumn weather.'

'Come on, I'll hang your things up,' says Mary, reaching for the hangers on the coat rack.

She's been worried about this evening. She's consulted with John several times this week, asked if it wouldn't be better to call it off rather than press on as if everything's normal, and just as many times he's shrugged and said it makes no difference to him, but it's not as if they have anything better to do. He is actually right about that. Mary has almost finished her packing now. The move isn't until Monday.

John jokes with Anki when she hangs up her coat, asks her if she's bought a new perfume and sniffs at her neck and throat until she squeals with laughter and tells him to stop tickling. Sören hands a bottle of wine to Mary, says there's a heavenly smell coming from the kitchen, and Mary hugs him, tells him it's nothing special, just a lasagne. They troop from the hall into the living room, where John provides everyone in the assembled company with a glass of bubbles. An open fire is crackling away in the fireplace and when they raise their glasses, John smiles at everyone in turn. He even smiles at Mary. She gratefully raises her glass to him and smiles back, thinking it was a good idea to have the neighbours over after all.

She's going to miss going to parties with John. He makes a brilliant impression, always has done. He has a natural authority that she's envied for as long as they've known one another. She noticed it the first time they met.

He was a passenger in economy class when she was a flight attendant on the same plane. He asked for an extra beer with the meal and then another. Each time she served him she stayed at his seat a little longer than the previous time, and somehow he managed to get her talking, even though it wasn't technically allowed. It might have been that smile. One corner of his mouth twitched, but not the other, as if he was holding in a laugh, but the laugh wasn't annoying or patronising, it was just friendly. They've talked about that flight many times over the years. About what actually made them fall for each other, what he saw in her, what she saw in him. What made her pluck up the courage to ring him afterwards, what made him leave his number in the seat pocket on the plane. It was only when she was cleaning up that she discovered he'd stashed the cans of beer, undrunk, under his seat. In the pocket in front of his seat he'd also hidden a postcard to 'The prettiest attendant on the plane'. He described his manoeuvre in retrospect as a shot in the dark and since then they've recounted the story of how they met countless times, both to each other and to those around them. She still has the postcard today. Currently at the bottom of one of the packing boxes in the hall marked with the word 'Storage' in black ink.

It became apparent quite quickly that they were not only close in age and at around the same stage in life, but had a number of friends in common and their parents had moved at the edges of the same social sets for at least half their childhood. Everything fell into place – not just for them, but for their friends and family too, who coalesced as if they'd been waiting around for this very thing to happen. Her mother started to go and have coffee with Elisabeth before she and John had even moved in together. In fact, Mary's two-roomed flat on Linnégatan seemed to have been waiting for an additional resident. In their early weeks together John had repaired the radiator in the hall and after a few more months they saw no reason to delay any longer. John moved out of the rented place he shared with his friend Lasse on Lilla Essingen and in with her. From decision to implementation took about three days. That too down to John.

With John came a huge group of friends. The guys in John's circle were both entertaining and established in proper careers, and at least half of them had likeable girlfriends. The friends met regularly, singles and couples mixed without much friction and Mary was soon part of the gang. There was almost never a weekend when they weren't invited somewhere. From the start she was amazed at how much she enjoyed partying with him. He's the perfect combination of everything a man should be at a party. He clearly likes a drink, but he never gets drunk. He never makes a scene but is sufficiently amusing for people to want be in his company and laugh at his jokes. He doesn't hog the limelight but isn't a wallflower either. It's as if people seek him out. She thinks it's because he's such a good listener. And he's tall, which gives him a pretty imposing air. Even this evening, with just a few days until their separation is an irreversible fact, he behaves flawlessly with the neighbours.

The problem is that he's become boring. Not in public, but in everyday life. It's crept in, and for several years she's tried to believe it was temporary, that living with toddlers had made him like this for the time being. That all the good times with him would return once the children were older. But it didn't happen. Instead he advanced in his job and earned more, but had less desire to do what she, at least, thought was fun. In the evenings he started to go to bed early, sometimes as soon as the children had fallen asleep, and she was left alone on the sofa with her burning candles and half-drunk bottles of wine. At weekends he wanted to focus on the family and cut down on dinner parties and jollies. Friday suppers with the neighbours were more than enough social activity for John. Now it was all about family, and when John says family, he actually means the children. He wants to do what makes the children happy and nothing else. Their social life has gradually been reduced to mixing with other parents in child-friendly places at child-friendly times. Because that's the way John wants it. For him, their previous life is over. Not paused temporarily, but over for good. It took her a while to realise this.

As usual, the children eat at the kitchen table and the adults at the round table in the corner of the living room. When they've eaten their dinner, the children have crisps and sweets and watch a film in the basement. Only on one occasion, when John and Sören are smoking on the patio and Anki helps Mary to clear away the plates, is there any mention of the impending divorce. By the kitchen sink Anki gives Mary an impulsive hug and says she's sure everything will be fine, because Mary and John are such good, reasonable people.

'Much more reasonable than us,' Anki says with a laugh.

Mary thanks Anki for her encouraging words, pretends not to understand what she's referring to with 'more reasonable than us', but instead asks if she'd like a top-up. Anki would, and together they move into the living room, sit down on the sofa and sip their wine in front of the fire. Anki asks Mary if she thinks she'll miss the house when she's moved out and Mary has to reflect for a moment before she answers.

'Yes, a little, of course…' she begins and then decides to be honest. 'But to tell you the truth, this has always been more John's home than mine. I'd rather have lived in a big apartment, more central, with a bit more life round the corner, you know? You know what I'm like.'

Anki nods in recognition and confirms: Yes, she knows what Mary's like. And for that matter she's like that herself, she asserts. She can't believe how all blokes are so fixated on having gardens and patios with wood decking and outdoor furniture and lawns and gardening gear. They laugh together and raise their glasses to Mary's future in her new flat, but stop abruptly when the men come inside from the wood-decked patio.

By the end of the evening Anki is drunk. In due course she starts arguing with Sören. First come the gibes, then the open verbal attacks, until finally a full-blown row is going on with raised voices and snide mudslinging. Sören ignites Anki's rage by feigning indifference at her threat to leave him, and on they go. They've been doing it for years. This is the way their Friday nights end more often than not, especially if there's been a lot to drink. Mary tries to mediate and John starts clearing bowls and glasses off the table, knowing that the evening will soon be over.

When Anki and Sören leave, the atmosphere by the patio door is as cool as the October night outside. Sören carries his sleeping daughter in his arms and goes ahead down the steps without saying goodbye. Anki mumbles, 'Shit, sorry you guys,' before she follows him down and soon they both disappear into the darkness below the patio.

'No problem at all, don't worry about it,' John shouts at the gap in the bushes that separate their garden from Anki and Sören's.

After John's closed the door he and Mary stay where they are for a moment or two. Both have witnessed this scene so many times, they don't really have anything left to say about tonight in particular. They're not speaking, but Mary has a feeling that he too thinks it will be nice to break this Friday supper tradition.

While she's brushing her teeth she thinks how responsible she and John are to separate before they've started to loathe one another, as Anki and Sören appear to do. Their children will never have to hear what Moa presumably has to listen to most weekends. She feels like sharing her thoughts with John, but when she comes out of the bathroom he's nowhere to be found. He's not in the kitchen, nor in the living room, and the patio's deserted. Through the gap in the door from Fredrika's room to the corridor she can see a faint light. *Of course*, she thinks. Of course Fredrika's still awake. Of course she's heard Anki and Sören quarrelling and she needs the reassurance of a grown-up. And *of course* John is sitting with her. Where else would he be? Why didn't she look there first? Mary thinks about waiting for him in the kitchen, but decides she hasn't the energy. This Friday evening has been another long one.

JOHN

He hears Mary close the toilet door behind her in the corridor outside Fredrika's room, then hears her footsteps between the kitchen and the living room. They go back and forth a few times before finally approaching the bedrooms again. They stop outside Fredrika's door for a few seconds before moving away. When the door to the main bedroom closes with its distinct creak, he relaxes and resumes stroking Fredrika's back. Soon Mary's snores will reach them through the walls. It's always the same when she's been drinking.

Fredrika doesn't want to tell him why she's crying, but it's not difficult to figure out. In his head he curses Sören and Anki for their noisy argument, and Mary who insisted on turning up the music when she wanted to dance.

He ought to have known better than to let the neighbours come over this week of all weeks. Instead of giving in to the temptation of escaping yet another evening with Mary and the tension that builds every time they're alone together in the same room, he should have asked himself what would be best for *the children*. It wasn't supper with the neighbours they needed, but the presence of Mary and him. A peaceful Friday evening with plenty of breathing space for questions and speculations around the changes they're facing in their lives. Instead he gave them an adults' party with loud music and the accompaniment of a drunken quarrel and that's the reason his eleven-year-old daughter is now lying in bed in tears.

When he makes another attempt to comfort her, he keeps his face averted so she can't smell the cigarettes on his breath. He had taken refuge on the patio when Mary and Anki started dancing in the living room. It was too much, sitting there watching Mary make such a show of swaying her hips. When he rose to his feet and she shouted for him to come and dance, he had to almost sprint out into the autumn night to avoid saying something nasty. Outside in the dark the air felt easier to breathe, despite the cigarettes. He smoked three in quick succession before he could bring himself to go back inside.

'There, there, sweetheart,' he whispers into the darkness. 'Everything's going to be fine, I promise. I'm here, I'll always be here for you…'

He pauses for a few seconds, before adding '…And Mum too…'

Fredrika's abrupt snort takes him by surprise. The sudden jerk of her spine jolting against his ribcage makes him start and instantly ask himself whether he's said something wrong. When she speaks again her voice is razor-sharp.

'It was Mum, wasn't it?'

He knows where the conversation's leading, but he needs to buy time. He has to come up with an age-appropriate answer to her question, an answer that satisfies, calms and unites. But he needs a few seconds to think, and so he asks:

'Mum what? What do you mean, darling?'

Fredrika's not buying that.

'You might just as well admit it – it's Mum who doesn't want us anymore.'

A heavy silence descends on the room. He knows very well what he has to say, knows that under no circumstances should he tell either of the children who wanted what and why. Nonetheless, he's unprepared for her sudden questions. He knew they would come, but he wasn't ready for her to pose them tonight. And maybe he's had one too many beers, because his thought processes are duller than normal. He doesn't manage to think through his reply properly, and when she asks again, when she says, 'Why don't you just admit it?', the words seem to spill out by themselves.

'Well... Yes... It was Mum who wanted a divorce But it's not you two she wants to leave, you mustn't think that, it's me she doesn't want, I guess you could say... Well, not in that way, at least.'

He knows it didn't go well. He recognises at once that his answer runs counter to the way he, Mary and Maud have agreed to talk to the children about the divorce. Maud would definitely be disappointed in him if he were to relate the details of this conversation. He has to find a way to take back what he's just said and he steels himself for another attempt, at least to put forward his argument, but Fredrika gets in first.

'If she doesn't want you, I don't want her.'

Fuck's sake.

'Don't say that, little one. Mum loves you very much and you, young lady, are tired and need to sleep. It'll feel much better in the morning, I promise. Do you want me to stay and sleep next to you tonight?'

Fredrika's bed is narrow. He would definitely have to lie in an uncomfortable position and wake up with a bad back if she accepted his offer. It would be less than ideal if he already had backache before he even started moving Mary's packing boxes on Monday, yet part of him still hopes that she'll say she wants him to stay. The prospect of going to bed next to Mary, who'll be at best snoring, at worst talkative, is far from inviting.

'You can go, I'd rather be alone.'

He gives her a kiss on the neck before he climbs out of the bed. Whispers a 'Goodnight' that isn't acknowledged and hangs in the darkness as he creeps towards the door. Once outside the room he stands for a few moments to make sure that she's not crying at least. When it remains quiet on the other side of the door, he makes his way to the bedroom with heavy steps. By the clock in the hall he can see it's a quarter to one. He really ought to brush his teeth, but he can't face it. Tonight has been too much. Too much he's forgotten, too much he's done wrong, too many bad decisions. For the first time since March, when Mary announced she wanted a divorce, he admits to himself that he is genuinely looking forward to the day she moves out. Life will be simpler, at least, he thinks, as he lies down for almost the final time beside his snoring wife. Soon she'll be able to snore somewhere else, he thinks, and that's just as well, frankly.

Mary

It seemed easy enough to assemble in the instructions, and the guy in the shop promised it could be done in a jiffy, but when the bunk bed is finally delivered to Svalgången after being delayed by a week, the parts don't really seem to fit together. However hard she tries, the bed finishes up lopsided. What's more, it looks much bigger in the bedroom than it did in the shop. Even though she was so careful about the measurements before she ordered it. There's no space for the bedside table where she intended to put it, and where it was supposed to act as a divider between her bed and the children's. She'll have to buy a smaller one next time she gets paid. But that's the least of her problems right now. The main problem is that the head of the upper bunk, which will be Fredrika's, is higher than the foot, and the whole bed sways when you step on the ladder.

No matter how hard she presses on the frame, it won't go down. She has a good mind to pick up the phone and have a go at someone, but she doesn't know who. She's already tried the shop. They argue flatly that she has been sent the correct bed and if she'd wanted help with assembly, she should have ordered that at the same time as she ordered the bed itself, not two weeks afterwards.

On no account can she ring her parents. Gaby has already paid for the bed and besides, she breaks practically everything she touches. Her father is too frail after his stroke last summer, and ringing John is also out of the question. He hasn't even had time to come over with the children for a coffee since she moved in, and anyway, she doesn't want to give him the satisfaction of still being needed. She contemplates calling on one of the neighbours but doesn't know who. She's only met one person in the entrance since she's been at the new flat, and he looked the other way when she said hello. But the fact remains – she has less than a day left. Tomorrow she's going to meet the children outside school and they're going to spend their first weekend in her flat. It all has to be ready by then. It has to be nice and comfortable for them, otherwise she's blown everything.

Fredrika and Victor have always wanted a bunk bed; it'll be a surprise when they come tomorrow. It's meant to give them a sense of having their own space in her new home too. Despite the fact it's a tight squeeze in her flat. Despite the fact the patio isn't a patio, more of a square patch of concrete where the local dogs pee because there's no fence. Despite the fact she can't afford to buy her own villa or townhouse, or even a flat with a balcony and a spare room for the children. She wants them to have their own little corner in her home. And now the bed's wobbling like a rickety makeshift and she can't get it to fit together.

She'd already started to plan how she was going to decorate before she'd moved out of the house. She's been fully occupied since then. She's sewn velvet curtains, fitted curtain wire and hooks and hung them up – a burgundy one draping from the ceiling that reaches the side of Fredrika's bunk, and a cobalt-blue one that transforms Victor's lower bunk into a cosy den. The idea is that they'll be able to close the curtains whenever they want to be on their own, and if they switch on the little wall lights that she's screwed at the head of each bunk it'll almost be like having their own rooms. The new cuddly toys – which they asked for as Christmas presents but will be moving-in gifts instead – are ready and waiting on their pillows. The pillowcase with horses for Fredrika and the one with monster trucks for Victor. Under the bed there are boxes filled with new clothes and toys. Fredrika has a new diary with a key so she doesn't have to take her usual one back and forth between the house, school and the flat. Everything is almost perfect, apart from the bed.

It's only been a week and a half since she moved out of Tallvägen, but up to now the children have dropped in far less often than she'd hoped they would. Fredrika has been particularly difficult to catch in the last few days. Not sleeping over before the bunk beds were in place was part of the plan, of course, but not popping in after school wasn't. Mary has tried tempting them with ice cream, offered to help with their homework and walk with them to her flat and back home afterwards, but they've only shown up on two occasions. When she spoke to John on the telephone, he said that he thinks it's important to let them choose for themselves, at least in the beginning. At least until she's made sure they have their own space in her flat. It's better for them to come once she's had time to sort out what she needs to for them to feel at home.

When Mary has rung to say goodnight, Fredrika has sounded angry. She's said she might come by the following day, but when the next day arrives, she still hasn't appeared. Mary hasn't blamed her, but she's always been careful to invite her again the day after. And to mention casually that she misses her. She has collected Victor from school a few times. He's only eight and doesn't like walking between the house and the flat on his own yet. He doesn't say much when he's with her. Asks if he can put a film on the TV and curls up in a corner of the new sofa. He lets her spoil him, but doesn't seem to mind going home before nightfall.

Every time she feels low, she rings Mona or Irene. Her two friends have had to respond to many calls in the last few weeks. They both slept over on Saturday, Mona in Mary's bed and Irene on the new velvet sofa Mary treated herself to at the same time as the bunk beds. They raised a glass to Mary's newfound freedom and talked about all the fantastic things she was going to enjoy in her new life. They drank copious amounts of wine and danced in stockinged feet until three in the morning.

Two nights later, when John has for the second time that week refused an invitation to come for coffee and cakes with the children after dinner, she doesn't feel quite so cheerful. Mona made her take three deep breaths down the telephone to calm her sobs. 'Why does it feel as though they're all so angry with me?' Mary said, sniffling into the phone.

Her friend reminded her to breathe and take another sip of wine. It's strange for everyone, she repeated, but Mary mustn't waver. This is what she wants, and it will just get better from now on. Mona even went as far as to promise her it would. Mary, who didn't have many options other than trying to believe her friend, sighed and swallowed another mouthful of wine. Maybe Mona was right. Maybe it was only the adjustment that was painful, not just for her but for the children too. But that's the reason the bed is so important. To make everything OK again.

When the telephone rings in the kitchen Mary is convinced it's her mother. She really doesn't want to answer, doesn't have time to sit at the kitchen table listening to her mother's tales of woe, but she needs a break from the bunk beds. If she leaves the bed in peace for half an hour, maybe it will have come to its senses when she returns. Sometimes things do sort themselves out if you stop thinking about them for a while. Like the car radio in Båstad, for example. She descends the rickety steps and goes through the hall to the kitchen, stretching the cord so that she can put the telephone on the sink and lighting a cigarette as she lifts the receiver.

'Yes, Mum?'

She can afford to answer like that. It's always Gaby who rings at this time of day. At seven thirty the news comes on and Sven disappears into the TV room next to the lounge in Båstad. By this time her mother has downed a few glasses with her dinner and accordingly has even more on her mind. She needs to give vent to how worried she is for her grandchildren, how disappointed she is in Mary, how unfathomable it is that Mary's actually done what she has. Mary knows exactly what awaits her on the telephone, knows exactly how Gaby will start the conversation: *Darling, it's your mum.*

But the voice that replies to Mary's guarded opener isn't Gaby's. It's deeper than Gaby's, more attractive too. Sexy, actually. The voice on the other end of the line isn't calling to criticise Mary for her life choices, but to let her know that the meeting the next morning between finance and logistics has been cancelled and therefore she doesn't need to worry about coming into the office as early as planned. The voice on the line belongs to Hans.

Mary feels her cheeks burning as she apologises for the way she answered. At his end Hans laughs and says he knows how it is with mothers, God, how they can act up. After they've exchanged their tribulations over difficult mothers, Mary doesn't want to hang up, so she keeps chatting, saying that it was a good thing he rang, as it gave her a much-needed break. She's being driven nuts by an impossible bunk bed that she's trying to assemble in her new flat.

He seems genuinely curious, both about her new flat and about the bed project. He asks for her address and what the area's like, and after Mary has said all there is to be said about her flat, he wants to know what model of bunk bed she has. His boys have a bunk bed too, he explains, and it took him an entire Sunday to put the blessed thing together. Sometimes, he goes on, you're unlucky enough to get home and find you've bought a real Friday-afternoon job. In which case it's sometimes a good idea to leave the whole construction alone for a while, and then, when you have the energy and patience, take the thing apart and quite simply start again. Or, he suggests, and now Mary can see him smiling and scratching his constantly tousled head, you just ask a clever neighbour. And by the way, he'd love to help her himself, if it weren't for the fact he lived so far away and it was so late.

At this Mary laughs and says he's mad, of course it's not his problem she has two left hands, he mustn't even consider the thought of driving all the way from Danderyd to Helenelund to screw a stupid bunk bed together.

'Talking of the time, I'll have to start putting the kids to bed soon,' Hans says, bringing an end to their conversation. 'But it was great to have a chat. Look forward to seeing you at work tomorrow.'

After Mary has hung up, she remains sitting at the kitchen table for a while. As she tries to analyse what's just happened, she looks out at the darkness and the yellow lamps along the footpath that runs beside the nursery school at the back of her building. If you turn right along the path, after a few minutes you come to Eriksbergsvägen, which, after a few more minutes' walk, crosses Tallvägen. If you opt to go left instead, you end up in the tunnel under the railway line that leads to the square in the centre. She manages to smoke more than one cigarette in the time it takes her to sift through the conversation with Hans in her head. He's never rung her like this before. Never in the evening, either. Normally it's their boss, Liselotte, who phones to inform them if meetings are moved, but not tonight. Not this particular night, in the middle of Mary's second week of separation and living in her own flat. Is it a sign? she wonders, and lights her third cigarette of the evening. It's not certain it's a sign, she thinks. But then again: it's not certain it *isn't* a sign. The fact is, it's so far from certain that it isn't a sign, it seems more plausible that it is. And he's looking forward to seeing her at work tomorrow. He actually said that.

On that thought she returns to the bunk bed with renewed vigour. This shoddy example of Friday-afternoon workmanship will come together, whatever it takes. She can't wait to tell Hans about her triumph tomorrow. And the children will be coming for the weekend at last.

JOHN

The mountain of Christmas presents is growing higher and higher in the corner of the garage. As the children have become better at nosing around over the years, he usually locks both doors that lead to the outside and the one to the basement, but today there's no need. It's Mary's weekend with the children and there's no reason to hide anything. Instead, he wanders aimlessly between the rooms and floors, unsure what he ought to be doing. He gives himself little tasks, going up and down the stairs. Makes a cup of coffee, puts it somewhere, does a round of the children's rooms. Finds a crumpled sock under Victor's desk, takes it down to the laundry room in the basement, goes back up again. Finds the cup, takes a sip, carries on traipsing around. Finds the other screwed-up sock between two cushions on the sofa. Goes down to the laundry room again. Each time he's in the basement he opens the door to the garage, turns on the light and has a look inside. The pile in the corner is actually starting to look grotesque. He promises himself he'll stop going out shopping every lunchbreak. Then he closes the garage door and goes back upstairs.

For several weeks he's been leaving the office at lunchtime to go shopping and hasn't returned for several hours. Mary wants him to give her a figure for how much to put into his account, so that the Christmas presents come from both of them, but so far he hasn't told her how much he's spent. There doesn't seem to be any point, she couldn't afford it anyway.

Mary has never been good with her finances. No one ever taught her how to make income match expenditure, and she knows even less about how to save. Instead of thinking before she buys, she acts on impulse, arguing that it was in the sale, that she got a good buy, that she really *needed* whatever it was. Each time she made it sound like a one-off event. Her consternation at the end of the month when the bills from the credit companies arrived was as genuine as it was laughable. She would resentfully pay what she owed, only to be just as shocked at the same point the following month.

His excuse for his own high consumption is that it's temporary. He can't be certain whether he's doing it for the children's sake or his own, but some days it feels as though the only way he can assuage his bad conscience is to buy more Christmas presents during his lunchbreak, get through his work commitments at double speed and leave work early. Up to now neither Uffe nor Martin has complained, but he's afraid that it's only a matter of time before he misses something important. He's promised himself that after Christmas he'll revert to a more normal work life. He will return to eating lunch with his colleagues and spending the whole day at work, he'll stop trying to atone for his sense of guilt by purchasing gifts every other day. He'll make all of it a New Year's resolution after the holiday. Right now, this is the way it has to be. He reminds himself: it's a phase.

*

In many ways the separation from Mary feels less difficult than he thought it would. At least it does when he has the children. Being disenchanted with Mary has proved to be easier at a distance than when she's in the same room. After all the months of trying to patch things up, of sharing the blame and strain fairly, of struggling to find topics of conversation, it's a welcome change to no longer take her sensitivities or point of view into account. The feelings of guilt that she wasn't happy in their marriage and that it was indirectly his fault were already fading before she moved out.

Now he feels guilty about the children instead. His sense of failure as a husband has been replaced by a sense of failure as a parent. It upsets him that the children won't be able to grow up with both their mother and their father, upsets him that this is happening to *his* children. It's simply not fair. This feeling of injustice harbours a nagging voice that's growing louder inside him. A voice that keeps reminding him whose fault it is.

No matter how much he turns things over in his mind, it's always Mary's fault. It's her fault, but he and the children are the ones hit hardest. He's the one left on Tallvägen with all their questions, with Fredrika's constant bouts of tears and Victor's tantrums over Lego pieces that come apart and cars that won't roll across the floor fast enough. Acting as a peace broker when Fredrika says she hates her mother and the horrible flat on Svalgången. And Mary, the actual cause of it all, is sitting in her flat next to the centre of Helenelund, wondering what sum to transfer for Christmas presents. She doesn't even know the children don't want to sleep at hers. He's protected her, because that's what he's done throughout their marriage and he's obviously forgotten how to do otherwise.

After he accidentally revealed to Fredrika which one of them wanted the divorce, he has resumed the official line, which he has repeated ad infinitum: *You mustn't be angry with Mum. Remember that Mum loves you more than anything in the world. Mum is sad too. Mum's flat isn't horrible, it's terrific. And besides, she's only going to live there for a short while, just until she can find something bigger, with room for all three of you. The most important thing is that we're near each other, isn't it? And if you're there a little bit more, you'll start to feel at home there too. I promise. Believe me. Everything's going to be OK.* It's almost laughable, when he really thinks about it.

Victor and Fredrika, on the other hand, don't have much to laugh about. Prior to their first weekend at Mary's, Fredrika had cried all morning before school. At the breakfast table John had been stricter than he'd ever been with her before.

'You're going to Mum's after school and that's all there is to it,' he'd said, and added, 'it's not up for discussion.'

It had taken several days the following week before he saw his daughter smile again. A few more days before he heard her laugh with her little brother. Yet they do, now and then – they forget, and they laugh. The longer time goes on, the more frequent the moments of normality become. The children squabble and argue, bicker and fall out, play and scrap, and actually: they talk about their mother a lot less than he thought they would. Sometimes it feels as though she'd hardly been there at all.

It's not with the intention of spying on them that, late one afternoon, he passes the cube of concrete that constitutes

Mary's block of flats on Svalgången near to the centre of Helenelund. Not at all, in fact quite the reverse. If he'd had a choice, there would have been another way into the centre, where he was going to buy something to eat, but there isn't really. Not without having to take a very circuitous route, at any rate. And there's no reason to do that. That's why it turns out that he's passing her building and happens to glance into her flat. It's on the ground floor in any case and she hasn't drawn the curtains, either in the living room or the kitchen.

He can just make out Victor's back on her new sofa. The large glass bowl is on the table in front of him, the same bowl they used to serve cheese puffs when they still had their Saturday nights together at the house. He notes that the bowl is full of cheese puffs tonight as well. What he can't note though is where Mary and Fredrika are, because they're not visible in the living room or the kitchen. It looks as though Victor is sitting there all by himself.

Naturally, at the sight of Victor alone on the sofa he is forced to halt his walk. Obviously, he has to check that Victor is OK, that the girls haven't left him on his own for too long. He does it from a discreet distance, standing next to some bushes on the footpath to the tunnel under the railway line. Confronted with a sight like this, it would be unthinkable to simply walk on. Victor's only eight, after all. Too young to be left alone in a ground-floor flat, thinks John. Changing position to be able to see what Victor is watching on the TV, he moves closer to the shrubbery. It looks as though it's a cartoon. *Tom and Jerry*, maybe, but it's hard to tell. Mary's new TV is much smaller than the one on Tallvägen.

From the underpass he can hear two voices approaching. The sound of a conversation between an adult woman and a child grows louder as they near the opening of the tunnel. The child's voice is high and quite shrill, almost squeaky. And it's only too familiar.

It's too late to hide. Mary has already caught sight of him standing next to the bushes, and shouts at him with surprise, 'Well, hello there!' And a second later Fredrika's silhouette charges towards him.

He gives her a hug and explains that he was just on his way down to the shop to buy some food. Fredrika points to the carrier bag in Mary's hand and says that she and Mum have been doing exactly the same thing, buying food. They're going to make mince for dinner, she tells him cheerfully.

Mary, who has now caught up with them, nods in confirmation. Would he, she wonders, like to join them for something to eat? It would be nice to have some company, she says. If he wants to.

John doesn't want to. Absolutely not. On the other hand he does want to tell Mary that he thinks it's extremely irresponsible to leave an eight-year-old alone in front of the television on the ground floor of a building so close to the centre of Helenelund, especially when break-ins have increased significantly over the last few years. But he can't say that in Fredrika's hearing. She would immediately start to worry, and it's not worth it. He'll have to take it up with Mary another time, on the phone one evening after the children have gone to sleep. So he says that something to eat sounds great, but unfortunately it doesn't work for him. He's expecting visitors, he says, and really needs to hurry.

When Fredrika asks who's coming, he says, 'Some friends from work, no one you know.' He gives Fredrika a kiss on the cheek and finds himself hoping that his evasive answer has piqued Mary's curiosity.

'I'll collect the children after school on Monday,' he says, giving Mary a nod to check that she's still on top of the schedule.

'Of course. Have a lovely time with your friends tonight,' she replies, taking Fredrika by the hand. Her parting remark stays with him as he nears the tunnel: 'Have a lovely time with your friends tonight.' It bothers him that he can't tell whether she sounded sarcastic or genuine. It bothers him even more that he doesn't care for either option.

Mary

John is late for the family therapy session. It's the first time he's been late for one of their meetings with Maud and it feels as though he's doing it on purpose. *We're not together anymore. This isn't important to me. I have better things to do than sit in a therapist's office with you.*

Whatever it is he's trying to communicate, it's annoying. His lateness is both uncharacteristic and disrespectful, but she's determined not to let her feelings show to either him or Maud. She's spent eight minutes in polite conversation with Maud about trivial matters before the door flies open and John finally enters.

He blames the traffic. Maud smiles at him and nods, saying she has total sympathy, especially the week before Christmas. John smiles back at her and for a second they look almost as if they're in love. It's bordering on embarrassing to watch. It's even more embarrassing when Maud gestures to John to sit down and Mary makes room on the sofa, but he turns away and makes for the empty chair at the side of the table instead. They have never had this seating arrangement. She and John usually sit next to each other on the sofa opposite Maud, but now they've ended up in a more complicated triangle which forces both Maud and Mary to keep shifting their gaze to gain an overall view. For his part,

John looks only at Maud. He hasn't graced Mary with so much as a glance.

It's almost two weeks since she last saw him and, sitting straight-backed on the chair, he looks as though he's grown taller, as if he's picked today to measure more than the six foot four he's been as long as she's known him. She's imagining things, obviously. It's probably the chair. The office chair in white-stained wood is higher than either the sofa or Maud's armchair. Both she and Maud have to angle their heads to look up at him. Something tells her he's enjoying it.

After a brief silence Maud clears her throat and asks if there's anything in particular they would like to talk about before they begin. They're meeting Maud for the last time and on the agenda is a review and termination of the therapy that started almost two years ago and ends today with the cold fact of their divorce. No one can accuse them of not trying, least of all Maud, and yet Mary can't help wondering if their therapist feels she has failed. Isn't every family therapist's goal to keep families together rather than letting them go their separate ways? Is Maud therefore inwardly disappointed in her? Is that why she's smiling so lovingly at John now and not at Mary? When Maud asks if they want to discuss anything in particular, Mary shakes her head. It's time to get this over with. Maud must have an established protocol for this kind of ending.

It turns out that John does have a point he wants to discuss before they get underway. This he says too without looking in her direction.

'Well, I'd like to talk a bit about Christmas and our thoughts on the children's presents,' and at the word *presents* he turns his gaze on Mary for the first time.

Maud does the same and suddenly they are both staring at her. As if it was her turn to speak. As if she was the one wishing to speak about Christmas presents, not him. Mary is confused by the unexpected change of course. Of all the topics she thought they might talk about today, she hadn't imagined that Christmas presents would be one of them. She thought they'd thrashed this out weeks ago and were of the same mind. They've already agreed to celebrate Christmas Eve and Christmas Day together. That she'll sleep over in the guestroom on Christmas Eve and they'll host both sets of relatives in the usual way. For the sake of the children. They've agreed that John will have them on New Year's Eve, but that she'll have them the following day for a week's holiday in Båstad. They've also agreed to give the children joint presents this year. She was quite sure they'd agreed, but now it seems they're not going to. It's obvious by the way he's looking at her now. He's been keeping something bottled up.

She tries not to sound sarcastic when she says that of course they can talk about Christmas presents. Was there something in particular he was thinking about, she wonders. In the chair opposite, Maud looks pleased. She nods and her eyes follow both of them. She's presumably thinking what an excellent pair of newly divorced parents they are.

John jumps in. He's decided that he wants to give his own Christmas presents to the children this year, and from his elevated position on the chair announces that he's already done something about it and that he's booked and paid for what he has in mind. He wants to cancel their agreement about only giving joint presents and has bought a week at riding camp for Fredrika and a visit to Legoland for Victor. Just as a little extra, he says. As for the rest, he and Mary can still give joint presents. But he wants the experience gifts to be just from him and not both of them.

'It feels better like that, especially as we won't be doing it together anyway.'

Mary stares at him. She searches for a twitch at the corners of his mouth as a sign that he's teasing her, but finds nothing. With three days remaining until Christmas Eve and a virtually empty bank account, she has no chance of either asking to go shares with him or playing her own trump card. She's already taken money from her mother twice this month. She doesn't know how to answer, because his suggestion appears to be so confrontational that she'd prefer to think he was teasing her, but when she tries to meet his eye, he's already shut her out again. He gazes at a point on the bookshelf behind Maud and doesn't say a word. *He can't do this*, she thinks.

'You can't do this,' she says.

A long silence settles over the room until Maud clears her throat and speaks up. In her softest therapist voice she asks Mary to explain what 'she's feeling inside' at this moment.

At this question Mary feels a rage well up inside her. Why doesn't Maud ask what John is feeling inside, as he's the one who's suddenly changing their plans in this blatantly vindictive way? Why doesn't Maud ask what he thinks he has to gain from making his children's mother come across as miserable and mean for the children's very first Christmas with divorced parents? Why doesn't Maud back him against the wall instead of asking Mary to explain what's happening? She and Maud already know what's going on here. John has lived alone for several months and during that time he's become embittered. He wants to take revenge on her for having left him, by turning the children against her. He wants to use his financial advantage to look like the best parent, the one who cares most, the one who doesn't leave, the one whose love is boundless and who buys riding camp weeks and Legoland weekends and fulfils all their dreams, while their mother turns up with plastic toys and bubble bath and doesn't even live in the house with them anymore.

Mary doesn't know how to respond to Maud's question. And so in silence she looks at John, who keeps on staring at the bookshelf behind Maud. She doesn't actually need to see him to know how he looks right now. That pig-headed expression. Obstinacy, coolness, half-closed eyes. Hands resting loosely on his knee. He's not going to give in on this issue. Nothing she says about how she feels *inside* is going to make him change his mind. Not today and not any of the next three days. It's going to be Christmas Eve and she's going to arrive at the house as a guest and he's going to give his own presents to the children right in front of her eyes. He has decided it's his right and he has gathered the necessary ammunition to challenge every argument she could possibly come up with.

That being the case, she doesn't plan to try. Nor does she mean to describe to him or Maud how she feels *inside*. She takes a deep breath before she starts to speak.

'Well... I'm not feeling much to be honest. I was just a bit surprised. But it sounds like a good idea. They'll be really pleased. That's the most important thing.'

She smiles at him. Maud smiles at her. There might be a slightly questioning look in her eyes, but it's hard to tell because she quickly turns to John instead.

'Great. That's all I had,' he says. 'We can carry on now.'

JOHN

He's already in a bad mood by the time he opens the front door. It's not improved by her being twenty minutes early. They'd agreed that she'd come at ten on Christmas Eve morning. Not a quarter past or twenty to. It was obviously asking too much of Mary to keep to that arrangement, because she's now standing inside the gate at the bottom of the steps between two enormous packages. She's also managed to bring a suitcase and a carrier bag from the grocery shop in the centre. He stares at the packages and then at her.

'You're not exactly empty-handed,' he says in a rather more petulant voice than he'd intended.

'Merry Christmas to you too!' she says, with a little laugh.

'Mum's here!' the children shout in unison as they come charging out into the hall.

The children race past him as he stands at the door. They charge out in their stockinged feet up to Mary on the stone-paved path connecting the steps to the gate. She staggers and laughs when they jump up into her arms.

'My darlings! Merry Christmas!' she shouts, letting them climb up on her.

Still irritated, he observes their hugs from the door. He considers putting his foot down and telling them to come back in. You can't stand like that! *You might get a cold*, he wants to shout, but he doesn't. He doesn't, because the children are overjoyed. Fredrika seems particularly excited to see her mother today. She's been pestering him about Christmas Eve all week, repeatedly seeking confirmation about when exactly Mary would come, precisely how long she would stay, at what hour the other guests would arrive, in what order everything would happen during the day and evening.

She began hassling him the moment she woke up this morning. She was so fixated on Mary's arrival time, she didn't even seem to care about the contents of the Christmas stocking that he'd filled to the brim and hung on her door handle before he went to bed last night. The slime kit was clearly of no interest, and she didn't even look inside the activity book with the horses and stickers. When he asked if the packages Father Christmas had left during the night were OK, she said yes they were, but she wanted to save them until later. It wasn't very difficult to work out what 'later' signified. When Mum comes, she meant, of course. That irritated him hugely as well.

The children have stopped hugging at the bottom of the steps. They've spied the parcels at their mother's side and now they want to squeeze them, try to guess what's inside, find out who they're for. Mary laughs at their enthusiasm, saying 'Stop, stop, stop, don't touch,' to Victor, who's making his way towards them. He backs off with reluctance, takes her hand instead and pulls her up the steps.

'Hang on, sweetie, I'll just bring this bag of Christmas food,' she says and starts to drag it up.

When they reach the door she asks John if he wouldn't mind helping her to bring the rest in.

'They're quite heavy,' she explains apologetically. 'I had to come by taxi to bring it all.'

'But what on earth is it?' His hiss is discreet, because he doesn't want the children to hear.

'Oh, nothing special. Just a few bits and pieces from Mum and Dad,' she answers, before disappearing into the kitchen with both children at her feet.

She and the children start unpacking the bag of groceries together. From the hall he can hear her moving effortlessly between the pantry and the fridge, putting away all the things he hasn't asked her to buy and which he's probably already purchased. This wasn't the way they'd agreed to do it. He would pay for everything and she would transfer a sum of money afterwards, once he'd worked out what she owed. Now he learns that she's brought an extra Christmas ham as well.

'I just couldn't resist roasting one yesterday too,' she tells the children, who laugh in response.

'But *Mum*,' comes Fredrika's voice from the kitchen.

Followed by Mary's: 'But I just had to! And I knew you were doing the same thing. Come here, sweetie, so I can give you another hug. *God*, I've missed you so much this week.'

Following tradition, they eat their breakfast together at the round table in the corner of the living room. As she lights the candles and places serviettes on the plates, Mary congratulates the children on how nicely they've decorated the tree. John looks at his plate, fixing his gaze on the serviette instead of the tree, which they decorated last night, the children explain. The serviette is red with an illustration of Father Christmas on a snow-covered roof apparently on his way down the chimney. John has never seen these serviettes before. They must have arrived with Mary.

During breakfast Mary and the children go through the schedule for the day. First the children will be able to play with the things in their stockings while she and John prepare lunch. At twelve o'clock their grandparents on Mum's side will arrive, along with their grandmother and aunt on Dad's side, and their cousins, of course. At one o'clock they'll have lunch, just as they always do on Christmas Eve. At three o'clock they'll watch Donald Duck while the grown-ups clear up. At four o'clock, when Donald Duck has finished, it's time for presents. By evening all the guests will have gone back home. Everyone except for Mary.

'Because you're going to sleep over,' Fredrika says with satisfaction from her place at the table.

Mary ruffles her hair and nods.

'Absolutely, sweetie, I'm going to sleep over. And in the evening we'll just have fun together.'

'Family fun,' says Victor, with rice pudding stuck in the corner of his mouth.

'Exactly,' says Mary, wiping off the splodge with her Father Christmas serviette.

From his place at the table John watches them. Family fun. What an awful expression, he thinks, putting another piece of rye bread with Cheddar cheese into his mouth. He keeps his mouth full so that he can avoid joining in the excitement over Mary's visit and overnight stay, but there's no real need. No one asks what he thinks. They seem to be thoroughly happy just sitting there like this, having their mouths wiped and hair ruffled by their mother, the same mother who moved out and left them less than two months ago but now appears to have made them forget that particular detail.

Mary

When she goes to bed in the basement guest room, it strikes her that she's never slept there before. It's hardly conceivable, given the number of times they've changed rooms on Tallvägen over the years, but it's true. She's never stared up at this ceiling while falling asleep or waking up. She's never brushed her teeth in the cloakroom next to the sauna opposite the garage door.

The light from the streetlamp streams into the little bedroom through the narrow ceiling-height window. There are no curtains in front of it, nor a blind. The glare from the streetlamp is bright and hits the bedhead. For a moment she wonders about looking in the store cupboard for a dark sheet she could hang at the window, but realises that then it would be pitch black. Besides, she doesn't know if John still keeps bed linen in the cupboard next to the laundry room. Or whether it would be appropriate to go rummaging around now that she doesn't live here anymore.

There's no bedside lamp in the room, either. And the bed's quite hard. It's a narrow bed with a slatted base that John insisted on bringing from Långön rather than getting rid of it. To put it bluntly, it's not a very good guest room. The room, which over time has served as a playroom and sewing room, guest room and storeroom, has never been occupied by any of the immediate family. They really only had the bed there on the off chance it might be needed one day. That's probably why the room's so neglected.

She pulls the duvet over her shoulders, tries to cheer herself with the thought that at least it had been a good Christmas Eve for the children. They'd been pleased with practically all their gifts. And lunch with her parents and John's family worked out quite painlessly, given the circumstances. Victor and Fredrika had gone to sleep earlier in the evening both full and happy. Exactly as Christmas Eve should be when you're young. She tries to convince herself that that's the most important thing, no one cried and no one fell out. Apart from her and John, but that was later, when both the children were asleep in bed.

Lying in the guest room she tries to stop thinking about the nasty remarks John made before she went to bed, but it's difficult. However hard she tries to steer away from it, her thoughts keep returning to their parting in the hall. The words he used were exceptionally harsh, coming from him. He would never have spoken to her like that when they lived together. He's never called her manipulative before, or disrespectful. When he told her in a surprisingly shrill hiss that he thought the whole joint Christmas thing was a crap idea, she snapped back that she didn't want to listen to his voice any longer. Without looking back, she went downstairs to the basement and slammed the guest-room door behind her, which she instantly regretted. She really didn't want to wake the children, just show John that he'd overstepped the mark.

It seemed that most of his anger was over the two large presents. The ones Gaby had helped pay for and which Mary hadn't mentioned to John beforehand. To give Victor his own TV and music-loving Fredrika her own stereo set was clearly a violation of gigantic proportions. At least according to John, who addressed her back with a contemptuous 'Who the hell gives a nine-year-old a TV?' when he passed her in the kitchen after the present opening. She didn't have time to respond, because she hadn't noticed he was there, and she was so astounded by his comment that she couldn't utter a single word. She simply carried on washing up the ovenproof dish that had contained her Jansson's Temptation. And then Gaby had come into the kitchen and hugged John and called him 'love', just like she always had, and helped herself to an extra glass of wine from the fridge. When she eventually went back out, John went with her into the living room. Only then did Mary find the obvious answer to his question: me. She was the one who gave her nine-year-old son his own TV and her eleven-year-old daughter her own stereo. She did, with financial help from the children's grandmother and grandfather, why? She didn't give her answer, because when they picked up the thread again later, John was even angrier. There was no point in discussing Christmas presents at that point, as John clearly needed to inform her she was manipulative and disrespectful instead, and in the end she had run downstairs to the basement, and that's where she's lying now, trying to stop thinking about it.

The alarm clock by the guest bed says half past eleven. She's not tired and she has nothing to read. She considers creeping upstairs for one last glass of wine, but rejects that idea. She mustn't forget, it's not her kitchen anymore. She has to stay where she is and try to pull herself together. She needs to go to sleep and wake up fresh and when she's done that, she and John will never speak to each other like that again. When they see each other in the morning, she'll be the perfect mum, the perfect ex-wife, the perfect hostess. Her entire being will be totally perfect, the whole day, right up until the moment she closes the Tallvägen door behind her and can go back to her own home.

She'll be able to relax back at the flat. She can have a glass of wine, or two if she fancies, and eat the leftover Christmas ham in front of the telly. She can have extra mustard on her sandwich and see what's on Christmas night TV on Channel 2. She can get on the phone to Irene or Mona and make an amusing anecdote out of her Christmas Eve story. *You should have seen how mad he got*, she'll say, and her friends will laugh. She's quite sure they'll congratulate her because, in spite of everything, she and John made the children's first Christmas after the split as happy as they could.

Maybe she'll speak to Hans too, sometime between Christmas and New Year. There's a chance he might ring her one night, as he's started doing that from time to time. He usually says he's only ringing to check how she is, but then they stay on the phone for quite a long time. She hasn't even told Mona and Irene about it. So far the telephone calls are her and Hans' little secret.

The thought of Hans makes her almost feel happy again. It's exciting to think he might ring her one night soon. And what it might mean if he does. The bright light from the streetlamp outside doesn't bother her as much now. On the contrary, it feels cosy having the lamp there. It reminds her of the world outside, and that she's no longer actually imprisoned on Tallvägen. She has her own life, just a few blocks away. A life that's hers; not hers, John's and the children's. She's just here temporarily, for the children's sake. Because Christmas is for children, and because she's such a loving and responsible mum. Tomorrow her life will be her own again. That's pretty good. In fact, it's better than good, the more she thinks about it.

John

It's not especially difficult to work out what Barbro had in mind when she invited her sister for dinner the same evening that John was having a lads' night with Lasse in the basement. And that without his knowing they'd reached the conclusion together that sufficient time had elapsed since Mary left and agreed it was time for him to move on. Neither of them says it straight out, but they don't need to. It's apparent as soon as he's through the door, when Barbro casually drops into the conversation that her sister's going to pop in. It's written all over Lasse's face in the nervous look he gives first her and then John as she mentions it.

At the start of the evening it's so obvious it's embarrassing, but with every beer he drinks, the more natural Louise's presence feels. She and Barbro alternate between the basement and upstairs, and each time the girls come down, John finds Louise prettier than the time before. She possesses a natural youthfulness that's completely lacking in her sister. Her curly red hair is all over the place when she's speaking and she sounds sexily husky. Her voice is a little too deep, her laugh a little too loud, and she downs her beers at almost the same rate as the boys. They're drinking out of pint glasses that evening and when they raise them they say 'Cheers!' The London theme to the evening hasn't escaped anyone.

When John first came up with the London idea, he lied about it for the children's sake, not his own. It was to encourage Fredrika to drop her plan for a joint Saturday night watching the final of the Eurovision Song Contest; he did it for her sake, no one else's. He couldn't figure out where Fredrika had got the idea from, but she was adamant. They would definitely watch the final together. At home in the house. All four of them. She even claimed he'd promised her that on Christmas Eve.

'You promised, Dad,' she'd said at bedtime, adopting that abject expression that always heralded a flood of tears. 'You did actually promise that Mum would come and we'd watch Eurovision together. Like we've *always* done!'

It hardly mattered that he couldn't remember ever promising any such thing. Nor that he couldn't think of anything worse than inviting Mary back to sit in the living room and watch Eurovision together, *like before*. There wasn't even anything particularly wonderful about it when they were married. Besides, it had been bad enough getting through Christmas together, having to receive both his family and Mary's parents at Tallvägen and playact as joint hosts. The frosty atmosphere that had sprung up between him and Mary as soon as the children had gone to bed was something he would rather not have to experience again. Mary's mum was worse than ever that year. She had literally sprinkled the air with explicit barbs: gibes about the holy nuclear family interspersed with monologues about the greatest thing of all being marriage and love. She had practically drowned the children with expensive

Christmas presents, gifts that were obviously purchased on Mary's orders. Fredrika had received a stereo that must have been twice the price of the one John himself has in the living room, and Victor was given his own TV. Both without anyone consulting him in advance. When he and Mary had discussed it later that night, she apparently thought it was sweet of Gaby. Even though it was clear she was lying, she refused to admit she'd been in on the plan the whole time. They were still at loggerheads when they parted at the stairs down to the basement. John had half a mind to ask her to go back to her own flat instead of sleeping over in the guest room, but he refrained for the children's sake. Obviously it was important for them to wake up on Christmas morning with their mum still in the house. He'd been forced to grit his teeth and wait until the following evening to be alone with the children again. The TV still constitutes a recurring source of conflict at home at Tallvägen. Fredrika harps on about getting her own set, Victor winds her up by saying she can listen to music on her stereo instead; they go at each other hammer and tongs and Fredrika claims she wants to take her stereo back to the shop where it was bought.

They had only just managed to return to their normal daily routine – with the TV temporarily in the kitchen and Fredrika's stereo in the living room – when Fredrika started pestering about watching the Eurovision Song Contest together. Mary was hardly a help, while John tried discreetly to ward the plan off. In the car one day on the way home from Fredrika's riding lesson, at which Mary had appeared unannounced, she'd even said it sounded a 'super lovely' idea. Despite the fact that she and John hadn't discussed it between themselves.

Unsurprisingly this made Fredrika excited and her nightly nagging even worse. It was as though Fredrika's entire future depended on him and Mary watching Eurovision together at Tallvägen. It was more or less at that point that the London lie entered the picture.

Instead of trying to explain something that Fredrika was clearly too young to understand, he finally said that he had to go to London for work that day. When Fredrika had started crying, he added that he was really disappointed not to be able to watch Eurovision with her and Victor, but that was the Saturday he had to be away. It's always been this way. Ever since she and Victor were small, John's been required to travel with work now and then. That was all there was to it.

It was easier than he'd imagined to lie to his daughter's face. If Fredrika had been a couple of years older, she might have questioned the likelihood of an important business meeting on a Saturday. Instead, she just looked disappointed and went to her room, slamming the door behind her, before he had a chance to suggest he record the programme on the video so they could watch it together afterwards.

Later that evening he rang Lasse to ask if he and Björne fancied going somewhere for the weekend. Or at least letting him stay with one of them. Somehow it seemed more responsible to go away for real, rather than stay at home and hide out in the house. Especially with Mary living so close. It would not be a good situation if she and the children decided to take an evening walk and saw him sitting at home when he'd claimed he'd be in London. And it was a long time since he'd met up with the lads. In less than an hour plans for the Saturday were in place. Lasse had checked with Barbro and invited both Roffe and Björne over for a night in the basement with the old gang. Barbro invited her sister as well. To have something to do while the guys did whatever it is that guys like doing, seemingly. Billiards and poker and whatnot. In the end they don't play billiards or poker. Nor do they watch any of the old World Cup matches as planned. Instead, all they do is sit on the sofa talking. And laughing. They laugh so much that John instinctively lowers his voice so he doesn't wake any sleeping children nearby. Though there aren't any. Tonight they've all organised babysitters, so they're the only ones in Barbro and Lasse's house. All of this has been arranged for John's sake. A number of times during the evening he looks at his friends and wants to say he loves them. After a few hours he does just that.

'I fucking love you!' he blurts out into the room.

Barbro and Louise say, 'Aah!' and Björne throws himself at John in a hug that ends in a wrestling match on the floor next to the sofa. John feels happy, really happy, for the first time in ages. He can't remember the last time.

By the end of the evening Barbro and Louise have stopped alternating between upstairs and the basement. Now they're all huddled together on the corner couch, only getting up when someone needs to go to the toilet or fetch more beer from the fridge. Louise has ended up next to John in the corner of the sofa and it's such a squash he can sometimes feel her breast against his arm when he leans back. The first time it happens he pulls his arm away and apologises, but Louise smiles and in her deep voice says there's nothing to apologise for. Nothing at all. After that he just lets it happen. In the end he uses her chest as a headrest, sliding into a more horizontal position as the night progresses. In response she wraps her arm around him. Her hair tickles his neck and he can smell strawberries, perhaps even wild ones. Something sweet and red, anyway. Just like Louise herself.

It's half past two by the time they break up. Barbro goes to bed first, then Roffe and Björne leave in a taxi, whereupon Lasse goes upstairs to bed too. John had known that Louise would linger when he leaned against her chest several hours earlier. Even though it's been a long time, he remembers how this works, as if it's second nature.

They kiss each other, gently at first, then more hungrily. She tastes of beer and cigarettes and something sharp, almost bitter, a taste he doesn't recognise. She uses her tongue more than Mary used to, licking his neck and cheeks, until her saliva is everywhere and he starts to laugh. Louise laughs as well. Then she carries on kissing him, licking him, tickling him with her tongue. Obviously he can't know for sure, but judging by how eagerly her hands seek out his belt, it's been as long for her as it has for him.

His arousal when she asks if he wants her is matched by his disappointment when it becomes clear he's too drunk to live up to his eager response. They've barely started on a blow job when it becomes clear to both him and Louise that there's no chance of intercourse, at least not this time. He's ashamed of his flaccid penis in her mouth, ashamed when she looks up and tells him it doesn't matter, even more ashamed when he suddenly remembers that it was Louise Mary had been sitting next to at the midsummer party on Väddö some years ago. He hadn't suspected anything the next day when Mary had described what was lacking in Louise's marriage, nor when she expressed her sympathy for how awful it must be to be imprisoned in something so dreary and sad and utterly pointless. Not for a moment had he entertained the thought that Mary might have related to what Louise must have told her that evening as more than just an empathetic listener.

As he pulls on his underpants he apologises. Asks if he can do anything for her, but inwardly breathes a sigh of relief when she says no and that everything's fine. He suggests they sleep for a while and see how they feel in a few hours?

Now that they're lying side by side, the sofa feels narrower than it did half an hour ago. He tries to make himself as slim as he can, lying on his side with his spine to the backrest, pulling in his stomach and lifting his arm to show Louise she's welcome too. She lies in front of him with her back to his chest. Her soft bottom settles against his excuse for a dick. He puts his arm around her waist on top of the blanket and says goodnight. She responds likewise and then they lie there in the dark, silent.

It quickly gets warm under the blanket. Louise's breathing soon deepens and as she's sleeping with her back pressed against him, he finds it hard to breathe after a while. He for one can't sleep. Through strands of Louise's hair he can see the green button on the TV at the other end of the room. It moves, drifting slowly to the right every time he tries to fix his gaze on it; he has to blink hard to make it go back to the right place. Then it starts again. He lies like that for several minutes before he gives up. He's not going to go to sleep like this. Not when there's so little space, not with Louise's half-naked and in fact, he now accepts, alien body in front of him, not when he's so drunk.

He wriggles cautiously off the sofa. Louise's body falls against the backrest, she gives a small sigh but doesn't wake. As silently as he can he gathers his clothes together before creeping up the stairs and into the guest bathroom. Once there, he sticks his fingers in his throat and throws up. He feels better when he's emptied his stomach, but he still doesn't want to return to the basement. Maybe it would be just as well to take a taxi home. Sleeping in his own bed suddenly seems like the only alternative after a night like this one. He can fetch the car tomorrow. It's not as if he has any other plans. The children won't be back from Mary's until nine in the evening, arranged that way because he said the plane from London would land at half past six. He'd made sure he'd checked the timetable before presenting his lie to Mary. She of all people was an expert on the arrivals into Arlanda.

Mary

They begin their Saturday in the bakers on the square in the centre of Helenelund. After that they take the train into the city and have a lemonade in another café. In town they buy a new pair of jeans for Victor and riding gloves for Fredrika, then some brightly coloured felt pens and paper from the hobby shop in the big shopping mall. They eat hot dogs in Kungsträdgården and stroll along Hamngatan back to the station. It's already half past three by the time they're back in Helenelund.

She serves lasagne in the kitchen while they all make voting cards for the final on TV that evening. They copy the running order out of the newspaper and draw maps and flags for the various countries. Fredrika is in a better mood than she's been for a long time. Not once does she ask why they can't watch the final with John tonight. Not once does Mary have to explain it's just a matter of bad timing, nothing more.

On the stroke of eight they all move to the sofa in the living room. Victor spills Fanta over half of his top on the way, but that doesn't matter. Mary likes washing the children's clothes; it's one of the things she misses most about being at the house. To have a defined task, do something useful, be the one responsible for turning something dirty into something clean and sweet-smelling in a few hours. *Just spill it!* she almost wants to say to Victor. Make a mess!

It's half past eight when Tommy Nilsson comes out onto the stage. Three minutes later Mary awards her first five. It's a ponderous ballad that he's singing, heavy but nevertheless hopeful; she gets goosebumps all over her arms at the key change in the last chorus. She shows her arms to Fredrika, who looks sceptical and gives the song a two on her own voting card. Too boring, she says, while Victor laughs at Tommy Nilsson's hairstyle.

'He has long hair, like a *mum*,' he sniggers.

Mary laughs with him, still happy with her five.

'You can like different ones,' she explains instructively to the children. 'It's not that one's better than the others.'

They toast with Fanta and then it's the UK's turn. Fredrika asks where in England her grandmother was born and Mary answers as best she can. Victor listens as well and, greatly impressed, exclaims that Mary knows so much about the world, even more than Dad. Mary is flattered by her son's compliment but tries to disguise her pride by explaining that there's nothing special about it.

'It's just that I lived in so many different places when I was young,' she says, 'because Grandad was a pilot. Besides, you can be clever about stuff like that too – you can be good at almost anything if you put your mind to it.'

'I'm going to be a receptionist,' Fredrika says firmly.

'And I'm going to be a pilot like Grandad,' says Victor.

Mary laughs and tells them they'll both change their minds.

When the phone rings she asks the children to stay where they are on the sofa while she goes into the kitchen to take the call. But it isn't John ringing from London. It's Irene ringing from her townhouse in Täby. Irene asks if she has time for a chat and instead of telling her friend she's spending the evening watching Eurovision with the children, drinking Fanta and filling in homemade voting cards, Mary says yeah, of course, that's great.

They start discussing Tommy Nilsson, laughing over Victor's comment that he looks like someone's mother. But it soon becomes clear that Irene has actually phoned about another matter, and that Irene has had an argument with her husband that evening.

Mary treats herself to a glass of wine while she listens. It would be pretty disloyal, she thinks, to ask her friend to keep it brief when for once it's her and not Mary who needs an attentive ear. Most of the time it's the other way round.

Mary doesn't know what she would have done for the last few months without Mona and Irene. She wasn't even convinced she was any good at friendship until very recently. Quite the reverse, she felt she wasn't someone who could make friends that easily.

That was her view of herself, even as a child. Maybe it was because her family was always moving and between the ages of eight and fifteen she'd lived in eight towns in six different countries. Starting a new school became a way of life, something you did once or twice a year. If it didn't work out, it wasn't a disaster, they'd be moving on anyway as soon as her dad's job required it. It was hardly worth making an effort to find friends. The airline Sven worked for took the family to places she would never have the means to return to after her childhood, and when they did move back to Sweden, she was fluent in a number of languages.

But Gaby could never fathom why her beautiful daughter didn't have lots of friends.

'Are you nice to your schoolmates?' she would ask, without any attempt to hide what she really meant: that there was something wrong with Mary.

But now she has Mona and Irene, so she must have done something right. Over the years since finishing as flight attendants they've kept in contact. Sometimes Mary thinks that she only did it because John had so many friends: she needed to keep the only two she had so that the difference wasn't so obvious.

Mona and Irene are well aware of the way the situation with Hans has progressed over the last few months. They encourage Mary to continue sleeping with him – for the fun of it – but under no circumstance should she allow herself or him to harbour any hopes of a future together. Whenever Mary dithers about it, they remind her about his budding paunch and bad posture and they all giggle about the growling noise he makes in his throat when he gets off in the disabled toilet. Mary carries on having sex with Hans at work, but not too frequently, once a week at most. It's usually on Wednesdays. They spend Mondays and Tuesdays in a kind of flirty foreplay and on Thursdays and Fridays they pretend not to notice each other at all. After the weekend it all starts again.

The three friends have also started a book club. They began before Christmas and they've managed to meet on Thursday evenings a dozen or so times since. Up to now they haven't read a single book from cover to cover. The club functions as a front and an alibi, primarily so that Irene can get out of the house once a week and drink wine with Mary and Mona.

*

They usually refer to themselves as the on-call service when they ring. *Hi, it's the on-call agency, duty desk here. How can I be of service?* The friends often laugh at their in-joke, but occasionally Mary's laugh catches in her throat as it's obvious that it's her friends who are on the duty desk and she's the sad individual in need of assistance.

Another frequent caller is her mother. She even phones her at work. Gaby starts every call in exactly the same way and then follows a fairly established routine that involves Mary alternating between calming her mother down and asking if she can call back at another time.

'Darling, it's *your mum*,' she begins, and before Mary has a chance to explain that she's busy and doesn't have time to talk, Gaby starts asking about the children. How are the children doing, how are the children taking it, has Mary spoken to the children since last time? How is Fredrika, she's so sensitive, has Mary really thought about what she's subjecting the children to? She drones on without leaving a pause for any answers between the questions.

On the occasions when Mary does manage to get a word in edgewise, she tries to tell her mother that the children are fine. When they ring in the evening to say goodnight Mary can hear in their voices that they're all right. When she asks them about their day, they answer the same way they always have. They fight between themselves as much as they did before, no more, no less, and in between they laugh. When they sleep over and lie in the bunk bed chatting, they're actually having a good time.

John says they're behaving much as usual at home with him too. Fredrika insists on going to sleep in his bed at night and sometimes cries at bedtime, but to be frank, she did that before as well. And Mary's quite sure John doesn't mind. For two children with divorced parents, her children are doing really well. Nevertheless, her mum is still worried. And every time Mary replaces the receiver at the end of the call, she does it with a palpable sense of failure.

Mary can hear that the second half of Eurovision is under way. Voting will start soon. But she can't quite bring herself to bring the conversation with Irene to a close. They're having such a good time. It feels nice to be needed by one of her friends. Besides, no one has called out to her for the mere hour that she's been talking on the phone. If one of the children did, then naturally she'd end the call at once.

It's nearly ten o'clock by the time she slips back into the living room to find Victor asleep on the sofa. Fredrika hasn't dropped off, but she's no longer watching the TV. She's sitting on the sofa drawing and has covered her voting card with thick black lines. You can't see the flags anymore, still less what she voted for.

'Hi, darling, sorry that took such a long time,' Mary says as she approaches her daughter.

When Fredrika looks up, she gives her a dark look.

'It was no fun when you weren't here. I want to go to bed now.'

When Mary undresses to go to bed she consoles herself with the thought that at least their Saturday had got off to a good start. The day had in fact been perfect throughout, right until she took the call from Irene. Up to then both the children seemed cheerful, almost as if they were genuinely pleased to be at home with her and not with John.

That has to be worth something. She tries to tell herself as she brushes her teeth in the bathroom and turns out the lights in the living room, where crumbs from the cheese puffs are still scattered over the floor. She sweeps the worst up with her hands.

One little mistake doesn't ruin a whole weekend. She drops the crumbs into the bin under the sink. Switches off the strip light over the cooker. Blows out the tealight in the window.

You're only human. She goes into the bedroom, where Fredrika is in the same position in which she fell asleep less than half an hour earlier, with her face to the wall and the curve of her slender back to the room.

Tomorrow I'll make everything better again. She lies beside Victor on the bed, brushes some wisps of hair from his forehead. She kisses him gently on the cheek before whispering into the room, to both of her children: 'Nighty-night, my angels. Mum loves you.'

JOHN

He's in a bad mood all morning after the conversation with Mary in which she suggested they swap weekends with precisely zero warning. She was in bed with a dreadful migraine and hadn't been able to work at all that week. She conveyed this information without responding to his surprised observation that she hadn't had a migraine in all the time he'd known her, and she went on to propose that he should keep the children this weekend and let them come to her the following weekend. When he answered that it wasn't convenient because he'd made plans for himself this weekend and for the children next, she almost sounded amused. As if she assumed he was making it up. She didn't even hide the sarcasm in her voice when she asked what those plans could possibly be. He had snapped back, maybe a little too harshly, that it had nothing to do with her. Then she actually laughed. So bloody disrespectful. He told her so too. It would be one thing if it was a one-off, but this is the third time in less than six months that she's suddenly decided she has to swap. As if he doesn't have a life of his own. As if her current mood or work dictate the terms not just for herself but for them all. As if they all have to be ready to overturn their plans because she happens to have a slight headache one day.

He hoped the children were already asleep when Mary rang, because it wasn't pretty, the way they spoke to one another. He'd accused her of being selfish and irresponsible and she accused him of being anal and intransigent. He pointed out that he had played ball every time she needed to change the rota, and he couldn't help also pointing out that he took care of the children far more than she did during the week. That did it. She screamed at him that she was 'so terribly sorry' that she didn't have as well-paid a job as he did or the possibility of working part time or buying her own house or staying in the home where the children had grown up. In less than five minutes her original request to swap weekends had escalated to a row in which they flung insults at each other; and even if it had been excessively heated, in one way that was almost a relief.

She needed to hear this. She needs to consider how negligible her load is compared to his, how she's got off lightly now it's worked out that he has the children most of the week and as a result has to wrap his head around not only everything regarding their clothes, diet, school timetable, but also what the last six months have meant for them on a purely emotional level. When, on top of that, she thinks she has the right to change their weekends at a few hours' notice, he doesn't intend to let it pass without comment. She needs to learn a thing or two about consequences.

Mary was in full swing. She was screaming at him down the phone and he let her carry on for some time before he interrupted. He did so in a steady voice, to demonstrate that she was the one who was out of control and he was the one seeking a solution, not the other way around.

'Absolutely,' he had said. 'I can cancel my own activities and have the children this weekend as well. But you won't have them next weekend. It's my regular weekend for the children and I've already made plans for the *family*.'

The children react more or less as he expected to the news that they won't be going over to their mother's this evening. Victor shrugs his shoulders and says they can just see her one day after school instead. Fredrika says it makes no difference to her either, but it's obvious she's making an effort to appear unaffected. Fortunately she has something else to think about at the moment. Tomorrow morning she's going to visit a new friend, a girl she's got to know at the stables and with whom she's started exchanging several letters each week. John knows, as he's the one who helps her post them.

Tomorrow the penfriends are going to meet on their own for the first time. John is going to drive Fredrika to Jenny's address in Jakobsberg and it's clear that she's nervous. During the course of the evening she tries on various jumpers and dresses in front of the mirror in an escalating welter of curses. John pokes his head in from time to time, saying she'll look lovely whatever she wears, but she just splutters in response. Presumably this is down to Mary, he thinks. Obviously Fredrika is projecting her anger onto him, and apparently he should stop saying she looks lovely all the time. She is *not lovely* and she has the *ugliest clothes in the world*, he has to understand. Under no circumstances can he know what they write about in their letters. Once he made the mistake of asking if they were about boys and Fredrika had rolled her eyes and called him 'embarrassing'.

According to Fredrika there's a lot to be embarrassed about tonight. Her jeans are stupid, her socks are awful colours, as are her jumpers. John tries to reason with her rationally, but in the end it's impossible to talk to her. He closes her door with a sigh and goes into the hall. In the kitchen he finds Victor, who asks why his big sister is in a bad mood, and John jokes that it's a girl thing, that they can sometimes be a bit batty. Afterwards his conscience pricks over his choice of words and he wonders whether he was actually alluding to Victor's mum or his sister when he said that. Regardless, it's not a good thing to tell a nine-year-old boy that girls are batty, that much he knows. Mary's fault, that too, he thinks when he goes to bed.

Fredrika doesn't want to talk in the car between Sollentuna and Jakobsberg. At regular intervals she issues various rules for what he may or may not say or do when he drops her off in the hall at her new friend's house. He can't give her a hug or a kiss when they say goodbye, because that's not cool. He nods and says he's understood. He must absolutely not say that they're going to 'play', because people don't play anymore, they 'hang out'. That's news to him, but he nods and promises. Under no circumstances whatsoever must he stay, not even if Jenny's mum offers him a coffee; that's strictly forbidden and would be enormously embarrassing. He promises not to do that either.

What's more, she informs him, this is the last time she's wearing these 'shitty' boots. He tells her not to swear and asks what's wrong with them, but she doesn't reply.

'Maybe you and Mum can buy some new boots when you're with her,' he tentatively suggests.

Fredrika sniffs and rolls her eyes at him in the rearview mirror. He hardly dare ask what time she wants to be picked up, but when he does she says how would *she* know, she can always borrow the phone and ring when she's ready, can't she? As if it went without saying that he and Victor will be waiting at home for her to ring. As if father and son can't have anything of their own to do, just because Fredrika had other plans that day.

When he leaves the E18 at the exit for Jakobsberg it's all quiet in the car again. Behind the wheel John wonders why everyone always assumes he doesn't have plans of his own and whether the moment hasn't come for him to change that. He doesn't have time to think it through because now they've arrived in Jakobsberg and the list of rules Fredrika has given him wasn't exactly short.

Mary

It went against the grain to ring John and ask to swap weekends, but in the end there was no alternative. Not while her face looks like it does. It just wouldn't do to meet the children and freak them out by looking like some assault victim beaten black and blue, not just around her eyes, but along her cheeks too. It would have generated too much anxiety, too many questions, too many lies to keep track of in her head. One of the children would have been terrified and immediately rung home to tell John.

Despite her best endeavours she hadn't managed to come up with a single reasonable explanation for the swelling and the blueish green tinge to both her cheeks. The make-up she tried to cover it with just made matters worse. She waited until the last moment before ringing John, as the doctor had promised her it would settle down within a week, but finally she couldn't wait any longer. On the eleventh day after the operation she still looks ridiculous. It was quite simply an emergency. She had no choice but to ring John and call off her children's weekend on the grounds of her sudden, but no less dreadful, migraine.

*

She's never in fact had a migraine herself, but because Gaby had had them regularly while Mary was growing up – predominantly on the day after social engagements – she knows what's involved. It was often Mary who had to look after her mum then, since Sven would be away flying a plane somewhere. From an early age Mary could both cook for her mother and care for her for the duration of an attack. A cool towel on her brow, cold water in a glass by her bed and total silence in the rooms around her usually helped it pass in a few hours. It was best if Gaby could fall asleep at the start of an attack. She would then stay asleep for several hours and when she woke she was always especially loving.

'My beautiful angel,' she used to say, 'I'm so proud of you. Come here and you can have a penny to buy something really nice.'

When Mary was young she loved these moments. Not necessarily because she needed the money, but because on those occasions her mother's love seemed so sincere. In those days she was probably as fascinated by her mother as Fredrika appeared to be by her grandmother today, and she can still experience the feeling of being the chosen one when Gaby called her 'darling'. It could happen occasionally as part of day-to-day life, when she'd been good at something, like a test or some homework, but most often it was when she'd taken care of Gaby in a responsible manner. When she'd been a dependable daughter.

She always toed the line. She always behaved both at school and at home, diligently looked after her mother when necessary, carried out the tasks allotted to her and was seldom sick. Even if she was sick, she usually carried out her duties anyway.

*

But, be that as it may, today she has a migraine. At least if John asks. And now they've fallen out and she's lying in bed with streaming eyes and, to be frank, the headache from hell. She won't have the children for another week, maybe two if John doesn't calm down. She's had better Saturdays.

She only has herself to blame. She should never have accepted the fortieth birthday present from her mother. She should have stuck to her guns and kept insisting that she didn't want a facelift, because she liked the way she looked regardless of ageing. That's what she should have said, even if it wasn't true, even if both her mum and all the mirrors in all the bathrooms proclaimed the opposite. If nothing else, she should have stood her ground to antagonise her mum and have something to laugh about with her dad when they took their walks together in the garden in Båstad.

They did this even more than usual during the Easter holiday. Gaby was worse than ever this Easter, veering between fawning over Fredrika and Victor and bemoaning the bad choices Mary had made in her life. For four days in a row Mary was forced to listen to a litany of how tired she was starting to look, how handsome and well John had looked on Christmas Eve, how crazy it is that Mary lives in a flat and not with John and the children in the house. How basically the only thing that could save her would be to meet a new man or have John take her back. How things are going to turn out now that she's started to look old and bitter. It was at that point that the strolls with her dad had come about. He had patted her arm while they walked in the darkness and told not to take her mother's harsh words personally.

'You know what she's like,' he had said. 'She can be a bit clumsy but she means well.'

She knew that he was right. Yet some of Gaby's remarks struck hard in places where it really hurt. So a few weeks later, when Gaby caught her on the phone after a bad day at work, a day when Hans had called off their lunch date and she was feeling particularly lonely and then had a drink with her dinner, she couldn't hold out any longer.

'Book that consultation then,' she'd said, and after that it all happened very quickly.

By the following afternoon she had an appointment at a clinic on Strandvägen. And by the time the consultation was over it was impossible to back out, partly because she found it so tempting. The thought of having her eyebrows lifted to the position they'd been in before, in the days when she was young and men would sometimes turn to look at her when she passed them in the street, was harder to resist than she'd thought. In her mind she could see Hans looking at her in a different way if she was a little more bright-eyed. He would see her as a woman a man would never, under any circumstances, call off his secret lunch dates with, a woman who was both prettier and younger and also more independent than the one he lives with day to day. A woman for whom it would almost be worth leaving your marriage. Those were her thoughts then; now she's lying with a bag of frozen peas on her face, looking like a character in a horror film. She hasn't been to work for nearly two weeks and won't be able to see the children for another week. At least.

Apart from her parents, the only people who know about her surgery are Mona and Irene, and it has to stay that way. Gaby has sworn on all she holds dear, including

Jesus Christ and the Holy Spirit, never to tell Fredrika about the operation. Under no circumstances can Mary reveal to her soon-to-be twelve-year-old daughter that she's had knives and nails stuck in her face because she wanted to be prettier. Not when she lectures the same daughter that beauty comes from within and that Fredrika is fine exactly the way she is. Nor can Mary have an ex-husband smirking and asking how much it cost while he wonders where she got the money from. John has never understood and isn't going to start now. It's better that he's annoyed with her for messing up the children's timetable than that he tells her for the thousandth time how pathetic she is for still taking handouts from her mum.

Her plan is to sleep through as much of the weekend as she can, waiting for her face to stop aching and to begin looking normal again. The tablets the doctor prescribed make her tired and only ease the pain intermittently. When it's at its worst it feels as though someone has stuck knives straight into her skull, right through her cheekbones, all the way inside. Her reflection isn't just a disappointment, it's a small-scale horror scene. She avoids turning on the light when she needs to use the toilet.

If she's not better by Monday, she'll have to request a doctor's certificate in order to stay off work. The thought of both the conversation with the doctor and with work makes her shudder. Another conversation she's not looking forward to is the next one with John. If he hasn't changed his mind by the middle of the week she'll have to ring him and grovel. She'll say she's prepared to do whatever it takes to meet his requirements, as long as she can have the children next weekend. But that'll have to be next week. Definitely not today. It hurts too much and he's too angry with her at the moment.

John

After the children have gone to sleep and he returns to the living room, his eyes don't settle on the TV news, but on the gigantic fruit basket standing on the table in front of him. The reports from Estonia and the Soviet Union hover like a monotonous soundscape behind the yellow bananas, red apples, purple grapes and pale green pears. He stares encouragingly at the fruit as if they might give him an answer. That was a blatant invitation, right? A single woman doesn't enter the home of a man whom she's met only briefly with a fruit basket of this quality without any ulterior motives, does she? *Answer me, Banana! Admit I'm right, Grape!* He can't help laughing at his own thought process.

Fredrika had been as surprised by the unexpected visit as he was. Her expression when she came into the kitchen, pointed into the hall and soundlessly mouthed 'JENNY'S MUM', followed by a distinct question mark, was as bewildered as it was troubled. It was Jenny's mum, from the spectators' seats at the stables, standing there with a massive fruit basket in her arms. The same mum whose invitation to coffee at her house in Jakobsberg last weekend John had, on his daughter's orders, refused. The mum he'd noticed in the spectators' seats because she appeared to be markedly younger than all the other stable mums. Who has an unabashed laugh that reverberates between the stable walls and who sometimes talks so loudly with the other mums that she drowns out the riding instructor in the middle of the manège.

It's not something he would ever admit, but he's also noticed she appears to be in possession of a substantial bust under her slim-fit white quilted jacket. His eye may have been caught by the bust on occasion, but only for a second and when no one else was looking. And only on an evening when he'd been very distracted. Apart from that, he hasn't noticed much else. Not until tonight, when Jenny's mum was suddenly standing in his hall alleging she had a fruit basket left over. John's bafflement must have been apparent, because she swiftly introduced both herself and her reason for being there. She had a business customer for her cleaning company, she explained as she placed the basket in his arms, who hadn't been on site at the agreed time. She happened to be passing John's house now with a left-over fruit basket that she thought he and the kids might like to chomp on in front of the TV. 'The kids', not the children. 'Chomp on', not eat. Fifteen minutes later she was on her way and John returned to the kitchen, Victor and his maths homework.

On the sofa facing the fruit basket John runs through what he now knows about Jenny's mum, whose name he's learned is Netta. He knows that she runs a cleaning company, lives in a two-roomed flat in Jakobsberg, that she drives a red Ford Escort and that she's a single parent to Jenny, who is at the stables this evening. He knows that she's eleven years younger than him, and that therefore she must have had her only daughter in her late teens, and that she pronounces her vowels with a strong Stockholm accent. He also knows that her smile fills her whole face, that she has a searching look which could easily be interpreted as flirtatious, that she's at least a head shorter than Mary and that she litters every other sentence with swearwords when she speaks. What he doesn't know, on the other hand, is what she sees in him, if she sees anything at all.

He has to be too long in the tooth for her, almost an old man in comparison. His hair has already gone grey at the temples and he is a single father to two children for whom he basically has responsibility all week. He has a routine office job and for the present no social life outside it, if you don't count intermittent beer nights with Lasse and Björne. He has never, as far as he's aware, been viewed as the handsome type, and however much he exercises at the gym, he has no bulging muscles. When he buys suit trousers a tailor has to both take them in and lengthen them.

And yet he was the one Netta came to visit tonight. She drove to him with her fruit basket and not anywhere else. But why? Several hours in the spectators' seats at the stables or a few minutes in the hall in Jakobsberg? Can it be something Fredrika has said that's aroused her interest? Or had she really only been in the neighbourhood and happened to know his address?

This conundrum occupies him for the rest of the evening. It's a welcome distraction from the news and what he normally deals with at this time of night. Only occasionally does he tell himself to stop being such a pathetic newly divorced forty-two-year-old. His warnings don't help much and he's soon at it again.

Perhaps a fruit basket is just a fruit basket. Whatever the case, both the visit and the fruit basket were a welcome break in the day-to-day. On reflection, they were actually the most exciting thing to have happened since Mary moved out, and whether or not Netta had ideas he decides that it's OK for him to at least fantasise that she did. It's been so long since anyone had designs on him, surely he can afford to dream a little? He can, for example, dream about what might have happened if the children hadn't been at home that evening. A tantalising scenario unfolds in his head. So tantalising that for a moment he debates whether to go down to the basement and dig out a porn film from the hidey-hole in the garage, but somewhere he draws the line. There has to be a limit.

Mary

She recognises him from a few metres away. Standing in front of the deposit-returns machine at the entrance to the grocery store is none other than John. There's no mistaking the long back, whose vertebrae curve out through his sweatshirt each time he bends over his carrier bag of empties. Not for someone who has seen it every day for over ten years. She's on her way out of the shop when she catches sight of him. She has a heavy shopping bag in each hand and as she approaches the returns machine she briefly wonders whether to carry on walking and look the other way. Pretend to study the notice board in the entrance, where offers of dog-sitting hang alongside notices of missing cats and cheap cleaning services. She could turn to look at the notices and inch past him, back to back, with just a few centimetres between them, and then walk on home. But for some reason that doesn't happen. For some reason she hears her own voice exclaim, 'Wow! Hello! What are you doing here?' in an overly surprised tone.

John turns, looking embarrassed.

'Oh, hi. Yeah, right. I'm just…doing some recycling.'

He nods towards the bag between his feet. Somehow it makes her happy that they both seem so nonplussed at bumping into one another on a regular Thursday afternoon in the centre of Helenelund. Actually what's more remarkable than the situation is that they've never run into each other like this before, rather than it happening now. After all, they use the same pharmacy, the same off-licence, the same post office and the same grocery shop. They both recycle their empties in the same returns machine, which is always gungy and gets stuck every time you try to use it.

It must have been weeks, if not months, since they last saw each other without the children. That must be what's disconcerting, thinks Mary, when she stops in front of him in the stale odour of beer emanating from the returns machine. Must be why neither of them appears to know what to say after the initial *Wow – Hello – What are you doing here*?

'Nice sunglasses,' John says after a few moments.

'Oh, thank you. Spring at last. Isn't it lovely?' she says, trying to smile to see if the ground between them will withstand a little friendliness.

It does. John smiles back at her and says he agrees, finally some spring warmth in the air. Not to mention the light! What a pleasure when the evenings start to draw out. A real pleasure, they both agree.

She would really prefer to go out into the square and continue the conversation there. It feels strange to stand around indoors in her sunglasses. It seems over the top to walk around the grocery store like a film star, especially now that the bruises have almost completely disappeared. She's not even certain that he would notice the marks if she took her sunglasses off now. But she doesn't want to chance it. Not being sure how bright the strip lights above the returns machine are, she definitely doesn't want to give him an excuse to ask what's happened to her face. And she doesn't want to spoil the light-hearted, almost chummy atmosphere the encounter has presented so far. She takes a tentative step towards the door to see if he follows her, but he stays where he is, with the bag of empties between his feet.

'I'll just finish this and then go in…and…' he says, looking towards the interior of the shop.

'Yes, of course,' she's quick to reply, 'and I'm off home with these.'

She nods at the bags she's carrying.

'I took the opportunity to do a big shop today, with the children coming tomorrow,' she explains, even though he hasn't asked and might reasonably be expected to know that her week with the children starts tomorrow.

'I get it. But… So you'll pick them up after school tomorrow? Then we'll be in touch in the week about when they're coming back? Shall we aim for Tuesday, as usual?'

John gives a little wave with an empty Coke can before turning to feed it into the machine. Mary would have liked to wave too, but it's impossible. The grocery bags are heavy, and it would definitely be odd if she put them down on the ground just to wave one last time. Instead, she calls out to his back, a tad too loudly given the distance between them: 'By the way, how about we have a coffee together on Sunday with the children, so we can talk about Victor's birthday? The children and I can make a chocolate cake and bring it round?'

John turns towards her and for a moment he appears to be considering her words. He looks at her intently, perhaps suspiciously, as if trying to determine whether there is some other motive behind the suggestion she's just made. She smiles at him to demonstrate that's not the case. *Just a bit of chocolate cake*, her smile tries to say. *Nothing else. Just spending some time with the children together.* After what seems like an eternity he replies.

'Of course, let's do that. Come at three on Sunday and we'll have a coffee.'

JOHN

He's just in the middle of saying goodnight to Fredrika when the phone rings in the kitchen. They have reached the point in the bedtime routine that always, no matter how hard he tries to avert it, reduces his daughter to tears, and he has just begun to tie himself in knots over the fact that he can't *swear on his life* that he and Mary will never get together again, but that he genuinely believes it's not going to happen, when the ringing from the kitchen interrupts his line of reasoning and he's obliged to leave his daughter and go to answer it.

Netta's bright voice greets him on the phone. She sounds as free and easy as she did in the hall last night, maybe her voice slightly younger, when she asks if the fruit was good. He stammers something courteous about fruit being both nutritious and tasty and immediately wants to slap himself in the face for once again sounding such a strait-laced old buffer. Fortunately Netta doesn't feel the same, since she carries on unperturbed to ask him if he thinks it would be fun, no, 'cool', to find something they can do with 'the kids' together this weekend. Go to the cinema, maybe, or to a swimming pool? Or a museum? What do John's kids like doing at the weekend, Netta wants to know.

Lowering his voice, John replies that his children like most things. He doesn't speak softly because he's telling her a secret, or because it's a lie – in fact Victor and Fredrika do like most things, just so long as something happens – but because he suspects that Fredrika is standing at the door to her room listening. If she is, then she won't necessarily like what she hears. Besides, it's Mary's turn for the children this weekend.

Netta says it sounds very useful to have children who like most things. Jenny, she says, would prefer to spend every waking hour at the stables. Then she starts to laugh, the same ringing laughter as yesterday in the hall, and John can't help smiling into the receiver. Not so much because what Netta said was particularly funny, but because her laugh is infectious. And it feels nice that a woman rings him at half past eight on a Thursday evening and laughs and asks him out.

By the end of the conversation he has promised to call Netta back the following day and tell her what the children would most like to do next weekend. He has written Netta's number down on a Post-it note, which is now in his trouser pocket. Back in the bedroom he's faced with an indignant Fredrika. She has indeed listened to the telephone conversation from her bedroom door.

During what's left of the bedtime routine she interrogates him, at times in tears, about what he thinks Netta's purpose was with the conversation. He states that he definitely isn't itching to find something cool to do with Jenny and Jenny's mum next weekend and the very best thing, in fact the only acceptable thing, would be for him and Netta to break off all contact right away.

'What do you mean? Is Jenny's mum supposed to be *in love* with you now?'

He can't help laughing as he gives her a hug.

'Obviously she's not in love with me, silly billy. We're grown-ups, believe it or not, and grown-ups don't just fall in love like that.'

Fredrika doesn't laugh with him.

'Maybe she's on her own, like us,' he ventures.

Fredrika says she doesn't give a damn if she is, and then she cries for a while longer. When she's calmed down, she returns resolutely to the point in the conversation at which he had been forced to leave her earlier, and now she wants him to give her a figure. What were the chances in a million that he and Mary will get together again? In ten million then? A hundred?

He tries to comfort her by saying that, whatever happens, he and Mary will still be good friends. He reminds her that they're going to have coffee and cake together on Sunday; won't that be lovely, he says in a desperate attempt to cheer his daughter up. It doesn't work particularly well. When Fredrika finally falls asleep there are wet patches on the pillow next to her face. He gently raises her head, turns the pillow over so the dry side is uppermost and brushes the stray hairs from her brow. 'Little sweetheart,' he whispers into the darkness, 'how you suffer.'

In the kitchen the telephone is in its normal place. The room is quiet and nothing about it gives any hint of the conversation that took place here just now. He looks at the phone, suddenly at a loss. What he's going to say to Netta when he calls her tomorrow he has no idea. Perhaps it would be best to meet up on their own, without the children, this weekend. Perhaps it would be better if he didn't ring at all, to avoid the risk of setting something off. Better for the children, at any rate, and they're the most important now. The children are always the most important for John.

Mary

Hans has been avoiding her at work for almost three weeks. Irene and Mona are convinced something has happened in his marriage. Perhaps his wife has become suspicious, they speculate, or his conscience has pricked. Mary suspects that in the end the operation made her uglier, not prettier. After the swelling and the bruises had finally subsided, the result had been a disappointment. Her eyes still don't look bright, not the way she remembers them from her younger days at any rate. The whites are still bloodshot and the bags underneath are almost more obvious than they were before.

She receives no clues from Hans, because he disappears every lunchtime and when he returns he doesn't pass her desk the way he used to. He doesn't join her when she's standing by the coffee machine in the lobby, no longer makes use of the double throat-clearing technique outside the disabled toilet that has become their shared signal that the coast is clear and she can let him in. Maybe it's just as well, she tries to tell herself. The thing they had together was never intended to develop into anything more than what it was.

Nevertheless, life at work feels drearier now. She goes in without the feeling of excitement that has marked the last six months; the sense that the day might well hold surprises and unexpected twists has almost completely gone. She misses that feeling. Misses having something to look forward to, misses the thrill that her trysts with Hans added to life, misses his sidelong glances when she passes his desk. She misses it, and she can't stop puzzling over why it ended so abruptly. Even Irene and Mona seem to be fed up with talking about him. 'Forget him,' they say, and tell her to move on, tell her that she can easily find another lover, that they'll be just as happy talking about something else when they meet up. Though Mary can certainly imagine it, she doesn't really know what that something else might be. Apart from her job and the children she has no real subject matter to fill their conversations.

Perhaps that's why she's started to miss John a little. And why after book club this week she's struck by an impulse to phone him when she comes home. Maybe it's not missing him as such that triggers it, more a need to hear a familiar voice. She wants to listen to him relate an anecdote from his day at work, or to ask how his sister is, or his mum, maybe make plans for Victor's birthday party next week.

Of course, she could go to bed. That would be the most sensible thing to do, given that the number of glasses drunk at the restaurant exceeded four, and she has to get up early for work tomorrow. But that's not going to happen. Tonight it feels perfectly natural to ring John, even though it's after eleven when she taps the numbers into the telephone by the bed.

When she hears the engaged signal she's surprised at first. After trying again, to make sure she put the right number in the first time, she starts to worry that something has happened. Is there something wrong with John's mum for him to be on the phone so late at night?

Or with one of the children? It has to be something out of the ordinary. If there's one thing she learned during her years with John, it's that he's not a telephone person. The fact is, that was one of the things she found most boring about him. Telephone conversations with him were always brief and involved calculating, coordinating or confirming. If he's on the phone in the middle of the night, something must have happened, that's the only logical conclusion.

She wanders into the bathroom, brushes her teeth and rubs the expensive cream from the clinic around her eyes. She fetches a glass of water from the kitchen, turns off the living-room lights and returns to her bed. Tries to ring again. It's still engaged. She lies down under the duvet and tries one more time. Still engaged. The children must have left the receiver off the hook. There's no other explanation. But it still bothers her that she can't get through.

What if she'd needed to get hold of him urgently? What if something had happened to her, the children's mother, something he needed to help her with? What if she'd actually been taken into hospital and needed to contact the children in the moments before she died? She becomes more annoyed with every further attempt. With the telephone clamped between the pillow and her ear she makes one last try. She's only going to ring one more time and then she'll assume that one of the children has been playing near the phone that evening and it has accidentally been left off the hook.

She must have fallen asleep during the final attempt, because when she wakes she finds the telephone receiver in the bed next to her pillow. At first she can't understand what it's doing there, then her memory clears and she feels a wave of intense shame, swiftly followed by equally intense nausea. Crouching over the toilet she thanks her lucky stars that the line was engaged at Tallvägen when she tried to ring during the night. It really would not have been a good idea to speak to John yesterday. It would have been a very bad idea, quite frankly. Even if he hadn't spelled it out, she knows he would have felt total contempt for her, both for ringing so late and for drinking on a weeknight.

She knows that silent condemnation better than anyone by now. She knows what his eyes mean when she takes a sip from a wine glass or lights a cigarette. *Ugh*, they say, *ugh, what a bad person you are.* Just as he's thought every time she's needed to borrow money from her mum to scrape enough together for the bills or when she's been obliged to change their plans for the children's weekend. He thinks she's bad, disgusting, worse than him. If they'd spoken yesterday his moral high ground would have soared even higher.

Instead everything is more or less as usual. She takes the seven minutes past seven train from Helenelund to T-Centralen and the quarter to eight bus from Central Station to Arlanda. When she arrives at the office it feels like a long time since she tried to phone John. It feels even longer since the last time she sought an approving glance from Hans as she passes his desk on the way to her own.

Perhaps that's why he acknowledges her today of all days. Maybe it was because she didn't look at him when she came in that he now comes to stand behind her by the coffee machine at precisely ten past ten. When his familiar breath warms her ear and his deep voice asks if she'd like to have lunch with him the following day, it's as if the last few weeks haven't happened. The telephone call to John didn't happen, nor the operation and the sick leave; the weeks without Hans in the disabled toilet definitely didn't happen. On the contrary, it's business as usual. She knows exactly how this works.

Tomorrow she'll put extra care into her make-up before she goes to work. At lunchtime she'll wait until all her colleagues have gone for their break and then go into the toilet on the right, the one with the wheelchair symbol, nearest the front entrance. She'll wait there until she hears Hans clear his throat twice outside the door. When she hears him, she'll open the door, just enough for him to slip in.

Once he's inside it will all happen quickly. Within seconds he'll have ripped off all her clothes. He'll leave her bra, but he'll pull it up so it's above her breasts and pushes them down, towards her stomach. He'll squeeze them hard, pinching her nipples, while he turns her around. He'll keep his trousers on; pulling them down will suffice to achieve the objective for this rendezvous. She'll lean over the toilet and hear him moan when he enters her and then groan far too loudly when he comes. When it's over she'll giggle and he'll ask her to make less noise while he pulls his trousers up. Only after they've both listened carefully with their ears to the door do they sneak out, first Hans and then Mary. After that they'll eat lunch together at Bistro II. They'll do this as colleagues, not lovers, and from then on everything will be normal again. It already feels as though everything is normal, even though it hasn't happened yet.

John

A bouquet of flowers is delivered to work. When Kerstin steps into his office with the bouquet she looks excited, as if she seriously intends to stay in the room while he unwraps the paper around the flowers.

'Someone has an admirer,' she says with an expectant smile that he doesn't reciprocate.

Instead she is given his haughtiest look, a look that's intended to indicate distance and say, 'If there's nothing else you can go now.' And it clearly works, because she disappears from the room as quickly as she entered it.

After he's made sure the door is shut and the clicking of Kerstin's heels has receded down the corridor, he feels bad. Was he unnecessarily harsh? Kerstin is a good colleague, an efficient receptionist. She's very well organised, loyal and almost always in a good mood. Of course she didn't mean any offence with her remark. She was probably simply happy for him. *He's had such a hard time over the last year*, he can hear her think.

Be that as it may, he reasons, he can't allow her into what's happening in his private life. How would that look? He and Kerstin are absolutely not on the level of sharing personal details with one another. Be it his divorce, his children or a bouquet of flowers from his daughter's friend's mum. He doesn't even know whether Kerstin is still living with Sven-Åke, still less if her grown-up children have moved out or not. He knows she's good at her job, she has a friendly face and well-pressed clothes and a telephone voice that inspires a feeling of security and trust. Besides, it would be entirely unsuitable for him to entrust her with something no one else knows about, not even his own children.

The small card in the middle of the bouquet bears the same handwriting as the postcard he received through the letterbox last week. It's a sweeping script, with round letters and soft curves. A smiley face at the end. Four little words: *Thanks for having me.*

He can't help but smile. Why does she persist with all these cards and flowers? Doesn't she understand that it's embarrassing in front of his colleagues, not to mention the children? The thought of ticking her off next time they meet makes him ridiculously elated. He knows in advance how she's going to take it.

She'll laugh and say it's his turn to be courted now. Then she'll argue that it does everybody good to receive a few cards or flowers now and again. He'll say it's not necessary, she really doesn't need to, she shouldn't spend her money on flowers for him, to which she'll reply that she can't think of a single thing she'd rather spend her money on. Then she'll tell him to stop being such a curmudgeonly old sod. At the word 'sod' he'll pretend to be affronted and so she'll say it again. Then they'll grin at each other until one of the children, probably Fredrika, will interrupt and ask them what's so funny. He's only known Netta for a month and already he understands exactly how it will go.

It's so easy to date Netta. All he needs to do is to lie back and things both unexpected and enjoyable happen almost daily. Flowers arrive at work, notes drop through the letterbox, his favourite licorice appears under his pillow, and she literally erupts with ideas for activities he would never have thought of himself. In their nightly telephone conversations they've already shared their general life stories. She has told him about Jenny's biological father – a British bartender she ended up in bed with on a charter holiday to Cyprus – and he has shared the story about Mary. From time to time they've touched on deeper topics, but above all they've laughed. They've laughed so much that some nights he's had to cover his mouth with his hand so as not to wake the children.

The roses in the bouquet are pink, purple and red. Four of each, twelve in total. A significant number, and a colour combination Mary would never have chosen. She would definitely have said they didn't match, were a childish mixture, but not Netta. She doesn't care about that sort of thing; she does as she pleases. That's what he likes so much about her.

He lays the flowers on an empty corner of his desk. He can't help wondering if this was how Mary felt when they first starting dating. That she could simply lie back and everything just kind of happened. In many ways he was Netta in those days; it was he who took the first step and left the card in the seat pocket on the flight to New York. The postcard had been his version of Netta's fruit basket.

When he disembarked at JFK he wasn't even sure it was the flight stewardess who cleaned out the seat pockets. Still less did he think she would call him even if the card did reach her, but he couldn't bear to let the opportunity pass. He had to give it a shot; Mary was by far the most beautiful woman he had ever seen and the very first time he spoke to her, he could see she had a dreamy look in her eye, something enigmatic he wanted to unravel. It was as if she didn't belong on the plane but was just visiting. Her dark blue blazer and the knee-length skirt seemed to have been created for a different kind of body to hers. She was a head taller than all her colleagues, looked as though she needed to bow unnaturally low to serve the passengers; and when she did, she smiled inwardly, as it were, instead of outwardly. Rather as if she worked in a nursery and was serving a group of children their snack, while she was dreaming about being in other places, other surroundings, where she didn't need to fold over to fit in.

When she served him she had seemed both cool and on her guard, as well as clumsy and absent-minded, and he had started to joke compulsively to lighten the mood when she managed to spill coffee on his hand. Then she broke into a smile that was warm and seemed genuine; he thought she looked as though she wanted to laugh but wasn't allowed. So he continued to joke and order drinks and she continued to smile and stifle her laughter and in the end he left that card. It took almost three weeks before she rang him, and from that moment on he was the one who did the courting, and she was the one who could lie back.

It took quite a long time for him to grasp that the expression she wore on the New York flight was not the expression of someone who was temporarily deployed in the wrong place at the wrong time; it was one of her fundamental characteristics. It wasn't until they had had two children, moved from flats to houses, travelled to numerous cities and she had changed her airline job three times in the course of seven years, that he realised she was quite simply made that way. She was always longing to get away. Always wanted something other than the thing she had.

Netta, on the other hand, wants to be there. She makes that crystal clear. She wants to be there so much that she doesn't give a damn when he asks her to stop buying flowers and she doesn't particularly care about his doubts and his lectures on caution. It's still not clear exactly where this liaison might lead, but even that doesn't seem to pose a problem for her. She shrugs her shoulders, how can anyone know, life is short, she says, they might just as well give it a go and see what happens. He has to confess, he likes the way she thinks.

Mary

The fact that they've landed themselves in trouble is clear the next morning, when Liselotte summons them both to a meeting after work. Their boss doesn't give a reason in her terse request, which incidentally isn't an invitation, more of a demand that they report to her office at five o'clock, but both Mary and Hans instantly know what it's about. You don't have a meeting with the boss at five o'clock on a Friday unless there's a problem. Somebody has evidently given the game away and their 'thing' – they've called it a 'thing' for want of a better word – is going to have consequences. They haven't yet worked out exactly what form the consequences will take, but it seems quite obvious it will involve some kind of sanction.

Hans panics more than Mary. Presumably because he thinks he has more to lose than she does. A wife, for example, a marriage he still claims to be well functioning, a house in Danderyd and two little boys for whom he has no intention of becoming an every-other-week parent.

Over lunch at Bistro II Mary tries to calm him down. They usually go here after their assignations in the disabled toilet, partly on account of the restaurant's very nice Caesar salad, but primarily because none of their colleagues can be bothered to walk all the way to Terminal 2 in their lunchbreak. At the restaurant she tries to comfort him, make him think logically, not let his thoughts race ahead.

'Whatever it's about,' she said, 'your marriage isn't at risk.'

When he doesn't answer but just shakes his head at the salad on his plate, she tries again.

'Listen... Whatever she knows, she has no right to ring your wife.'

But Hans is inconsolable. He keeps repeating that he's been an idiot for letting it go on for so long. He finds it difficult to concentrate on the food, rocking and writhing on his chair, wearing a haunted expression. He scratches his head, takes his spectacles off and puts them back on, until finally he places them next to his plate and blinks tears right into the Caesar salad. He mumbles, more to himself than to her, that he should have ended it straight after that first time at the conference. Or even better: *before* the first time. His eyes still on the salad and not on Mary, he goes on to say that it hasn't been worth it; she has to agree.

'No, you're right,' she interrupts his mumbling.

Her sharp tone seems to surprise him and his eyes switch from the salad to her, as if he suddenly remembers that she's sitting there opposite him. She carries on: 'It really wasn't worth it, it was never important and to be honest wasn't much fun, but can we stop this now? Can we just try to grit our teeth and wait until we know what the meeting's about before we do anything rash?'

He doesn't understand her gibe. Nor, it seems, does he feel like gritting his teeth. On the contrary, he wants to seize the opportunity to end their relationship this instant. Speaking incoherently, he tells her that he's been thinking about this for a long time, how wrong it is, what they're doing, how he's constantly plagued by a bad conscience. That was why, he says, he'd kept himself to himself after she was off sick in spring, because it had gone too far, lasted far too long, he can't look at himself in the mirror without feeling disgust.

He's being assertive for nothing, because Mary doesn't offer any resistance. She doesn't protest. How would that have looked? Humiliate herself in front of a married man who doesn't want her anyway? Besides, he's not important; she and her friends have repeated that ad infinitum. Hans isn't important. Hans is just a bridge between what went before and what's going to come. He's a bridge, which has, admittedly, spanned the gap for quite a long time, but a bridge nevertheless. Not a future.

When they part in the walkway between terminals, Hans looks relieved, as if a heavy burden has fallen from his shoulders. When he tries to give her a friendly pat on the shoulder she backs away and gives him a brief wave instead. Then she turns on her heels and walks away. Her steps don't take in the direction of their shared office, but towards Terminal 5. Not once does she turn to see if he's following her. Instead, she enters the tax-free shop, where she purchases a new lipstick and a bronzer with a gold shimmer. She applies the new lipstick while she's still in the shop, being extra careful about the outline.

Back in the office she takes a detour to avoid passing Hans' desk. She doesn't grace him with so much as a glance when she sits down at her own. She turns on her computer, concentrates on the text that pops up and immerses herself in crew scheduling for next week's flights between Sweden and southern Europe.

She doesn't look in his direction for the rest of the day. Not until three hours later, when they're both sitting opposite Liselotte, does she acknowledge his existence.

Clearly Liselotte has no intention of informing Hans' wife. She begins the meeting with the facts: she knows that Mary and Hans have had a relationship that goes beyond 'professional boundaries with colleagues' and which is 'strictly contrary to company policy'. It has been drawn to Liselotte's attention by not just one, but several of their colleagues, who have spoken to her about it in confidence. Although neither Hans nor Mary ask her to, she emphasises more than once that she can't 'divulge her sources'. On the other hand, she repeats a number of times that their colleagues feel 'very uncomfortable' on account of the current situation. One of them could even hear their groaning in reception when they had external guests visiting.

When Liselotte says that, Mary has to stifle a laugh. Hans and all his noises. He can never keep quiet when he comes, not even with his mistress in the office toilet. The thought of reproducing this passage from the conversation for Mona and Irene obliges Mary to stare down at Liselotte's desk and tighten her lips. She fixes her eyes on the grain in the mahogany wood, clamps her mouth shut and tries to neutralise her expression before she can look up again.

When she does finally break into a smile, neither of the others joins her. Hans stares down at his clenched hands, looking not unlike a shamefaced schoolchild. Liselotte is more reminiscent of a strict headteacher, sitting on the other side of the desk and eyeing them over the top of her spectacles.

'Normally,' Liselotte continues, 'I would have restricted myself to a warning, but since this matter coincides with another issue which affects the whole team, I will take this opportunity and tell you about it first. Because it also provides a solution of sorts to the problem we have here.'

Liselotte informs them, in confidence, that the airline they work for has been acquired by a Danish company, which means that after the summer parts of their operations will be centralised and henceforth carried out from Copenhagen.

'More specifically, logistics and...well, crew scheduling,' she says, now looking directly at Mary.

John

The look on the children's faces when Netta tells them to take off their blindfolds in the back seat of the car is priceless. At the same moment as they rip off their handkerchiefs, he switches off the loud music coming from the car radio and looks at their baffled expressions from the front seat. One by one they blink and try to take in what they can hear and see. What can it mean, they seem to be wondering, with all these cars parked in tight rows around theirs? Where is the loud racket in the garage coming from? Is it the sound of an engine? A fan? And why are all the cars nose-to-tail?

Fredrika puts two and two together first.

'THE FINLAND FERRY?' she screams in a high voice.

Jenny and Victor turn first to her, and then to each other.

'Are we on a…boat?' Jenny asks, rather more cautiously.

'What d'you mean, Finland?' Victor asks. 'What are we going to do there?'

All the children's eyes are now firmly on the front seat. Both John and Netta sit in silence, straining to maintain a straight face to keep the children guessing for a few more seconds. When Fredrika shouts, 'Well say something then!' Netta finally starts laughing. She nods and confirms: Yes, they certainly are going to Finland. On a boat. They're going to sleep on the ferry for two nights and spend the whole of Saturday in Helsinki. There's a disco on the ferry, she tells them, and a play area and a cinema and a pool and spa. They're going to have lovely things to eat and drink and have a little mini break together in Helsinki.

'Cool, isn't it?' she asks, clearly pleased that this came as such a complete surprise.

'Ye-e-e-es!' the children reply as one from the back seat.

Today even Fredrika is beaming. Fredrika, who hasn't beamed very much at all recently. When John sees it, his gratitude to Netta almost makes him weep. He hasn't seen the children this happy for months. The idea Netta came up with was brilliant; he had been worried for no good reason at all.

'They're going to be thrilled, I promise you,' she'd said when he had wondered whether they weren't taking things a little too fast.

They make their way up the narrow staircase, fetch the key cards from the information desk and take the lift up to the eighth deck. There they separate into families and divide themselves between the two cabins: John will sleep with Fredrika and Victor, Netta and Jenny in the next-door cabin. Netta has arranged for the cabins to be adjoining, just as she's organised everything else for this trip. She even double-checked with the ferry company's booking service to make sure it would work out like that.

Inside the cabin Fredrika and Victor lay claim to the bunks. Both want to sleep on the top, both climb up and down the small ladder to check which bed is best. Miraculously, both are happy with their eventual choices. Fredrika's top bunk is next to the wall between their cabin and Netta and Jenny's. She empties the contents of her rucksack, which John had packed and smuggled into the car last night, over her entire bed. Arranges her diary and clean changes of clothes, the little soft toy in the form of a dog that's been almost cuddled to bits, and her toilet bag. Then she knocks on the wall. There's no sound for a few seconds, then the same knocking comes back. Jenny clearly chose the top bunk too.

They have dinner in the largest of the boat's restaurants. There's a buffet and the children go up several times, filling plate after plate that they just pick at before going up for the next. Only after they discover the dessert counter do they eat with any great appetite.

'Watch your stomachs,' John warns them as they approach the counter with soft ice cream and chocolate sauce and meringues for a second time.

'Let them have it,' Netta says, smiling at him across the table.

She's taken her high heels off under the table, and her foot is now stroking the back of his calf. His body reacts instantly to her touch, his diaphragm begins to tighten in a way that means he has to focus all his attention on the food on his plate in front of him. When the children return with their bowls of fudge sauce, raspberry coulis, ice cream and meringues, he gently pushes her away under the table. He gives her a warning look, to which she responds with a teasing smile.

You know the deal, he tries to convey, without saying it out loud.

Come on, behave, he tells her with his eyes.

Who, me? I'm not doing anything, she replies, following suit.

Her raised eyebrows and playful smile are incredibly irritating. It's irritating because it's infectious, and here he is again, flashing his ridiculous grin at her. The children, who are now full, declare they want to move on. They want to explore the rest of the boat, test the slot machines, inspect the sweets in the tax-free shop, check out the youth club. Victor wants to go to the cinema so he can copy down the screening times. They rise to their feet and start moving towards the restaurant entrance.

John and Netta lag behind. She has to put on her shoes before she can stand up and leave. Like a true gentleman, John helps her by pulling out her chair when she's ready. As they walk towards the exit, Netta rubs her hand over his jacket at the small of his back. His hand meets hers behind his back and squeezes it for a few seconds. He has to muster all his self-control not to pull her towards him and kiss her on the mouth in the middle of the restaurant, for all to see.

'Thanks for making this happen,' he whispers in her ear instead.

'I love you,' she whispers back.

She says it as if it were the most natural thing in the world. She looks straight into his eyes after she's said the words, her expression no longer irritating, nor provocative. She looks serious, as if she's said something that she means and really wants him to take in. He gazes at her and tries to do precisely that. Netta says she loves him. She's known him for six weeks and three days and she already loves him. He is loved by someone again.

Mary

On a normal Friday at this time she would be sitting on the train home. If it's not her weekend with the children, she usually takes her time in the grocery shop in the centre before walking back through the tunnel under the railway to Svalgången. She chooses her weekend food with care, testing a number of cheeses at the delicatessen counter, chatting with the cute guy at the till who's always so pleasant. Then she takes a short detour to the off-licence. And maybe another to the florist on the corner of the square, if she can afford it. She's usually home by about seven, at any rate. Then she'll prepare something fancy in the kitchen, put some music on in the living room, treat herself to a glass of wine while she stands at the cooker and potters about with the food and the table. By dinner time she'll be on the phone with either Irene or Mona for company.

Today she's not doing any of that. When she arrives at Stockholm Central Station on the airport bus, she doesn't catch the Bålsta train. Instead, in the corner of the bus terminal, she sits down in a bar with leather booths and subdued lighting. She's walked past the pub with the Irish-sounding name hundreds of times, but today is the first time she's stepped inside. The place appeals to her for one reason only: it's anonymous. And almost completely empty of people. In one corner a couple of businessmen in suits are sitting with their wheeled suitcases, at the bar a woman with her hair piled on top of head is sipping a cocktail, but apart from that the place is empty. Except for the bartender, who is young and has a shaved head, a snake tattoo on his neck and rings in his ears and who looks extremely bored when she goes up to the bar. No sane person would want to be a regular at a pub in the corner of a bus station, she thinks when she places her order. Especially when it costs almost seventy kronor for a measly glass of red wine, she thinks, after she's paid and is on her way to her booth.

She chooses a table by the window with a view of the bus terminal. The sharp contrast between the fluorescent lighting outside and the tealight glow at the table gives her a good vantage point without the risk of being seen herself. She needs to give herself time to think; under no circumstances can she go home to the flat just yet. It's not her weekend with the children and the hours between Friday evening and Monday morning will feel unbearably long if she goes straight home today. Instead, she'll sit here for a time. She might even come up with a solution tonight.

She considers her options. If she chooses to move, her salary will remain the same and the company would assist with a flat in Copenhagen and two weekend trips to Stockholm each month. If she chooses to quit, she has to hand in her resignation as soon as possible, preferably Monday morning. She'll keep a full salary for two months but will then be obliged to find a new job in an industry where there are almost no jobs available. She is expected to give her answer in writing and both she and Hans are placed under a gagging order because the rest of the company don't know about the Danish buyout yet.

The first glass runs out fast. She waves to the tattooed man at the bar, holds up her index finger and mimes 'another' when she gets his attention. She still doesn't feel ready to go home. Still hasn't figured out an answer to her dilemma.

Outside the window the after-work rush has been replaced by a sluggish Friday-night shuffle. She tries to count how many hours are left until Monday morning, when she needs to give her decision to Liselotte, but her brain is addled and she can't work it out.

She can't stop her thoughts wandering to Hans. Hans, who was her lover until just a few hours ago. Hans, who should have been the bridge between what went before and what would come next. What does it mean if the bridge didn't quite reach? she wonders, taking a sip. What do you do when you find yourself at the end of a bridge? Jump into the water, presumably. You jump in and start swimming. But where to? In which direction? She doesn't know. She takes another sip. The wine has a noticeable taste of vanilla.

Hans is likely to be back home in Danderyd by now. He got in his car straight after the meeting and is no doubt already sitting at the dining table. His wife has probably made something special, as you do at the weekend. Then they'll have a cosy night in front of the TV with the children. Crisps or popcorn, maybe a film. And they'll have sex tonight. That's what men with a bad conscience do, according to the books she's read and the films she's seen. They have sex with their wives to assuage their guilty conscience. Maybe it doesn't just apply to men. She remembers what it was like with John after the conference when Hans laid his hand on her leg under the table for the first time.

Best of all would be to find a new job. Then she wouldn't need to move. But how is she going to find a job before summer? She can only do one thing. Crew scheduling is the only ground job she's had, and one by one ground staff are being replaced by computerised systems. She's just not going back to being an air stewardess. She's far too old for it; she was too old eight years ago when she was offered a ground job in the first place, and would probably not even be called for interview if she applied today.

When the third glass of wine arrives at her table, she's pondering whether she should change career. She ought to be able to get a job in a hotel, or why not a haberdashery? She's always liked sewing and knitting and over the years she's sewed several items of clothing for herself and the children. Imagine working with yarn and fabrics every day. When all's said and done, perhaps that's exactly what she should do: have a trip into town, take a look in the craft shops around Hötorget and Gamla Stan, ask if anyone needs additional staff. Someone might say yes if she offered her services cheaply?

On the other hand, maybe Denmark wouldn't be such a bad idea. Only for a year, definitely not any longer. If she rents out her flat on Svalgången while she's away, she could almost get rich in the process. Rich enough to buy something larger for herself and the children, at least. She's sure she'll be able to borrow her parents' overnight flat in Gärdet for weekends with the children, and didn't Liselotte say she'll get the trips home to Stockholm paid for? Victor and Fredrika would surely think it was more fun to spend their weekends in Gärdet than on Svalgången. How great to be so close to everything. The museums and cinemas, restaurants, all the hustle and bustle of the city. It might be precisely the new start she needs.

While she finishes off the third glass of wine she wavers back and forth between one course of action and the other. She musters all her willpower to refuse the bartender with the snake tattoo when he asks if it's time for another. He's become nicer as the evening's worn on. When she goes up to pay her tab at the bar, he even smiles. He has a fine row of teeth, shiny and even, especially his sexily pointed eye teeth, not unlike Tom Cruise's. A wilder version. Probably younger too. She wonders how old he is. How many years younger than her he might be. He seems to like older women, anyway, because the gaze that follows her as she turns her back to walk out of the pub looks quite lustful. She feels herself rising in his estimation and she adds an extra wiggle to her hips as she goes out into the bus station. She keeps it up until she reaches the escalator down to the train. She stops there when she notices that she's swaying. She has to hold on to the handrail to regain her balance.

JOHN

When Mary told him about the move, his first impulse was to demand sole custody and never let her see the children again. The second was to offer all his savings for her to stay in Sweden and not take the job in Copenhagen. The third was to charge over to Svalgången and strangle her with his bare hands. Netta helped him come up with the fourth alternative, which was to let Mary go, maintain a united front for the children, and at the same time be prepared to be around for them even more himself.

'Believe me, she's only going to lose out in all of this,' Netta tells him when they're having lunch a few days after the news.

As if that were any consolation. As if he's only interested in whether Mary wins or loses, and not in what's best for the children. He's offended to begin with, but he understands after Netta has explained what she means. Her reasoning is that he's not going to be able to influence Mary's decision anyway, that she's going to go regardless of what he does, and the best thing he can do, therefore, is continue to be a dependable parent for the children, a parent who doesn't make a scene and doesn't show any anger towards their mother. And that it doesn't help the children to know that he and Mary go around being furious with each other, and of course she's right. Netta is wise beyond her years, he'll give her that.

They've met at their regular place, the run-down pizzeria in Norrtull that's easy to reach by car from both his and Netta's direction, but even so is sufficiently far away for him to avoid the risk of bumping into any of his colleagues, who would presumably wonder what he was up to with a perky thirty-year-old every day.

They've been doing this for a while now. They've even established a routine for their lunches. Whoever arrives first orders for both of them; Netta alternates between a ham salad and a shrimp salad, and John between a capricciosa pizza and a calzone. After they've finished eating they take a walk in Haga Park, where they might stop on one of the footpaths for a canoodle if there's no one around. They press against one another until Netta starts to moan and John has to stop what he's doing to prevent her drawing unnecessary attention their way. Finally they leave each other in the car park outside the pizzeria, and the next time they meet will usually be in the evening with the children. Then they pretend they're good friends, though Netta calls them 'mates'. They're mates who see each other and eat together. Good mates, who sometimes stay over at the weekend. Nothing strange about that. It might be nice to have a glass of wine with dinner, and then you can't drive, of course. Obviously they wait until all the children have fallen asleep before they descend on the guest bed in the Tallvägen basement.

In many ways the relationship he and Netta have is the kind of thing he experienced as a teenager. They sneak around, furtive and tentative, they hide and giggle at their own pretence when no one else can hear. None of the children know that they're more than just friends, at least that's what he hopes. It's chiefly he who insists on it being like this. It mustn't go too fast at such a sensitive stage of the children's lives, and therefore it's best if they put on an act. Even if it's starting to feel difficult to keep his hands away from her when other people can see them, he's decided this is the best way. You can't rush into things. Especially when there are children involved.

Now that Mary has decided to move and leave her children in the lurch, he's even more sure it's the right decision. There are limits to how much change two children should be expected to cope with in a given year. On that point at least he is adamant. More adamant than he was on the question of whether he and Netta should sleep together on the first overnight stay. He was quite quick to bend his own principle that you should know each other for a few months as a minimum before hitting the sack together, to Netta's great delight. And his own, for that matter, but it didn't affect the children. It happened on the Finland ferry when Jenny and Fredrika were at the youth disco and Victor was at the cinema with the children's club, so that was different.

At the end of lunch, when he's had the chance to complain about Mary and Netta's had the opportunity to express how odd she thinks it is that Mary doesn't just find another job, one in Sweden, anything really, instead of moving abroad, Netta suggests that they should give the children something special to look forward to this summer, now things are going to be so difficult with their mum.

'It's exactly what they need,' she says, 'something cool to think about instead of lying in bed moping and fretting half the night.'

It turns out she has several suggestions for what that might be. The truth is it's all been planned out before she tells him about her ideas at the pizzeria. This summer, she says, they should let the girls each hire a horse and spend the holiday in her aunt's cabin outside Leksand. She's already had time to speak to a riding school in the area and check with her aunt about which weeks the cabin is available. The plans are in place, now all that's needed is John's approval and for him and Mary to agree about the summer weeks. That's how she presents it. As simple as ever.

Despite his bad mood when he first arrived at the pizzeria, she manages to make him laugh again today. There are many things you can say about Netta, but she doesn't waste much time on the passage from idea to execution. But he puts the brake on. Of course he does. He does it very amicably but firmly, almost sternly, because he knows she loves it when he does that.

On the footpath alongside Brunnsviken lake, where their conversation has taken them again this lunchtime, Netta starts gently punching his arm.

'What d'you mean?' she says. 'Friends can't go on holiday together now all of a sudden? What kind of boring old fart have I actually found, huh?'

She punches him harder and harder until in the end he's forced to defend himself. They wrestle with each other for a while, before ending up on a park bench. It's not particularly difficult for him to win against her; she's not very tall, and not very strong either. When they start to kiss, he slips his hand inside her red hoodie and gently squeezes her breast. She gives a little squeal to begin with – his hands are cold against her warm skin – but she soon leans in against him, exactly as she usually does. He carries on, still marvelling that anyone can want him as much as she does. He marvels at her breasts too. She really has round breasts. They point forward, and not downward. What's more, she likes it when he touches them, unlike Mary, who would always pull away when his hands approached. Netta clearly doesn't feel the same, because on the park bench she presses against him, breathes deeply into his ear and between the breaths whispers, 'Christ, I want to have sex with you.'

He doesn't respond with words, but it's obvious he feels the same. They stay on the bench for quite a long time. It's calm on Brunnsviken today. It's half past one and they have to half-jog back to the car park outside the pizzeria so that he doesn't miss his meeting in the office. While they run, Netta teases him about poor fitness.

'We ought to go out running in the evenings. Come on, it'll be cool,' she says, and laughs at him as he breathlessly shakes his head.

By the time they part he's given her permission to go ahead with the plans for a few weeks' holiday at her aunt's summer house outside Leksand. He's also made her agree to wait a while longer before they tell the children that they're more than just two single parents who happen to like finding things to do together. Netta looks like a happy schoolgirl as she bounces off towards her car. He watches her go, holding back a laugh that's once again bubbling up in his throat, and gives a final wave before he settles himself into the front seat of his white Volvo.

As he drives back to work, the smile won't leave his face. He hates being someone who compares women in this way, but the fact remains: Netta has made him laugh more during the few months they've known each other than he's laughed in the last ten years with Mary. That says something, he thinks, even if he's not quite sure what.

MARY

He's lying to protect her. She knows he's lying to protect her. She knows he's well-intentioned, but he doesn't understand what he's doing. He doesn't realise that what he thinks is protecting Fredrika is in fact resulting in her drifting further away from her mum, even more than she already has. By enabling this he's causing her damage, instead of providing protection. A child needs their mother. Fredrika needs Mary. And John needs to stop helping their daughter create this distance.

When she rings and tells John this, he denies it. He lies, claims that Fredrika has gone to bed early again tonight, that they'll have to discuss the matter another day.

'It's a lot for her to take in,' he says. 'We'll have to let her digest this at her own pace.'

When Mary screams at him to – *for fuck's sake!* – give the phone to Fredrika so that she can talk to her, her own daughter, whom she gave birth to and raised and has as much right to speak to as him, he lowers his voice to a hiss and says the conversation is over, they'll be in touch tomorrow. He ends by saying that Mary can use the opportunity to sober up in the meantime. Then he hangs up on her.

She stares at the receiver for a few seconds before flinging it onto the floor. The cord drags a bowl of peanuts from the coffee table; they fly across the rug, bounce onto the floor and roll under the sofa. She stares at them too. Bloody nuts. Bloody flat. Bloody John. He has no right to do this. He has no right to speak like that. No one keeps her own children away from her like this. Not even their oh-so-perfect dad.

She decides she'll go to Tallvägen and ring the doorbell. If he wants war, he can have war. She just needs to simmer down first. Clear up the nuts, breathe, settle her nerves. She can't go to see her children when she's as angry as this with their father. She has to cool down, and then she has to sort this out.

She goes into the kitchen. Her hand is shaking when she opens the fridge. She contemplates whether to have a glass of the wine she opened at the weekend, just one, to calm down, but decides that would be a bad idea. John's not going to have any evidence to corroborate his condescending comment about her needing to sober up. He ought to be ashamed when he opens the door. She obviously doesn't need to sober up, because she's sober already. He'll be aware of that when they see each other and it's only right for him to feel stupid when he goes to fetch Fredrika.

Fredrika's going to be intractable at first, but when they've had a chance to speak, she'll start listening to her mum. Mary will emphasise that it's only for six months and how much fun they'll have when they meet at the weekends. Not to mention how much fun it'll be when they come to see her in Copenhagen. You can come whenever you like, Mary will say, every weekend and every holiday. You and Victor are always welcome, you're the most important thing in my life. You know that, right? Fredrika will understand; Mary just has to explain it the right way.

When she leaves the flat, she can picture them soon having a hug in the hall at the house. Victor will be there too. They'll be laughing when they end up in a heap on top of one another, Mary at the bottom and the children on top of her. Fredrika will be laughing too, through the tears that will soon stop falling. Maybe Mary will tickle them to make them laugh even more. In that case she'll have to be careful, keep an eye on their heads, make sure they don't hurt themselves on the hard stone floor.

John will be standing at the side, watching them. He'll be annoyed to begin with, because he thinks it's too late and she's messing with the children's bedtimes, but when he sees them lying on the hall floor, he'll relent. The children's feelings are more important than an extra half hour asleep. This is something of a crisis. Everyone's going to sleep well afterwards. Mary needs this atonement to be able to sleep at all. She increases her pace in order to arrive all the sooner.

She stops at the gate on Tallvägen. She's out of breath and needs to recover after the fast walk; her fitness is definitely not what it was. It's drizzling and the darkness pools on the lawn behind the cedar hedge. The kitchen light is on, and the yellow one in the hall, and probably the lights in the living room too. But Fredrika's room looks dark. Mary looks at her watch. Quarter past eight. Fredrika can't be expected to be asleep at this hour.

For the last time she repeats to herself what she's going to say when John opens the door. Attempts to recreate the scene with herself and the children hugging in a heap on the hall floor, their warm bodies climbing over hers, the relief afterwards, the sense of being forgiven, being understood. For some reason it doesn't work. She can't conjure it up in her head.

Instead she can see John in front of her. He's standing like a wall in the doorway, his feet wide apart, his silhouette spreading out to the four corners of the door. He won't let her in to see the children. Instead he says she's made her choice, she's made the choice to let them down yet again, and enough is enough, now she has to face the music. The children don't want to talk to you, he says. Go home and carry on with planning the rest of your life. You're not welcome here with us. Neither I nor the children want anything to do with you. Don't look so pathetic. No one else feels sorry for you. You only have yourself to blame. Now, go.

By the gate Mary shudders, because fantasy John is so real, standing there. It makes no difference whether she tries to explain to him that she had no choice, that she has to move to keep her job, that she's dying of loneliness in her flat, and what she said about moving because she wanted to was just a stupid lie to save her stupid face. She asks him to forgive her, but fantasy John tells her he doesn't care about her lies anymore. He doesn't care what she says at all, because it's not her words but her actions that count. That's the last thing he says before he shuts the door and leaves her standing on the steps outside. In her imagination it's raining more than it is in reality, but otherwise the scene feels so authentic, she loses heart and goes home.

John

In the playground he sees her before she sees him. She's walking through the throng of parents with a wary expression on her face, as if her eye is seeking something out. In her arms she's carrying two bunches of flowers, which she tries to shield as she weaves her way between the people in the square concrete yard. It will be a matter of seconds before she spots him. He's always been easy to find in a crowd because he's so tall.

Mary is also quite tall. Even without heels she's taller than most of the mums she passes in her zigzagging progress across the playground. Compared to the others, she's actually still stylish, he's thinking. Her natural grace hasn't changed appreciably since the divorce, she still has elegance and poise. Her expression is alert, observant and at the same time considerate. When she knocks into an elderly man with a rucksack, she immediately stops and turns to him. She lays a hand on his arm and appears to ask him if he's all right. The elderly man, presumably a proud grandad, smiles at her, then says something that makes both of them laugh. She gives him a friendly wave as she moves on. The smile is still on her lips when she catches sight of him standing in the shade of the birch trees. He smiles back, waving to show he's seen her too. She starts heading in his direction, faster now, with more purpose.

As she approaches he finds himself wondering if she's sleeping with anyone. The thought flashes through his head in a split second. It comes, it goes, and there he remains, still holding his hand at shoulder-height after waving to her.

Not that it would matter, he thinks, if she were. It would be a good thing. It would take the edge off what he's intending to tell her tonight, if he knew that she was also dating someone. Now that both of the children, his mother and Anneli are aware of the situation with Netta, there's really only the mother of his children left. And it's better that she hears it straight from him than through the grapevine. Both he and Netta are agreed on this. And that's partly why he's invited Mary to dinner at Tallvägen tonight.

When she reaches him there's a slightly awkward atmosphere. He doesn't know whether he should lean forward to hug her or just say a quick, relaxed hello. She doesn't seem to know either, so there's a kind of halfway house where they air hug, with her flowers like a crinkly wall between them. He hears something that might be the sound of a kiss on the cheek next to his left ear.

'That's nice of you to buy flowers for the children,' he says, when they've finished air hugging, mostly for something to say.

'What?' she asks, appearing not to understand what he's talking about.

He nods towards the bouquets in her arms to give her a hint.

'Ah, these, they're for the teachers,' she says, laughing.

Only now does he see the names on the wrapping paper. In her neat handwriting she's written *Margareta* on one and *Ingegerd* on the other. Margareta and Ingegerd are Fredrika's and Victor's form teachers. He feels silly for not having realised at once. The next moment he's angry with himself for not having thought of buying his own flowers for the teachers. As if she could read his mind, she says she's written both their names on the cards.

'Hope that's OK?'

'That was nice of you, thank you,' he says, adding, 'and of course, I'll happily share the cost.'

'God, no, that's not necessary,' she says, and with that they fall silent.

He'd like to say something else, but doesn't really know what. The natural topic of conversation, work, seems like a minefield. He'd rather not ask how preparations for the move are going either, after the row they had when she first told him about moving to Copenhagen.

He knows he was unduly harsh on her on that occasion, but she'd also blurted out things she shouldn't have said. She'd called him self-righteous and a male chauvinist pig and accused him of deliberately damaging her relationship with the children, to which he had replied that she didn't need his help with that, she'd made a good job of it by herself. Today it just feels simplest not to touch on anything related to her move. Nor does he want to talk about the children too much, especially not when there's an imminent risk of her wanting to discuss what they've planned for the summer holiday. It's not the right time to tell her about Netta's aunt's cabin, and it's absolutely not the right place. Not here in the school playground.

He turns his gaze to the temporary stage the school has erected in front of the middle school building. She follows his lead and stretches up on her toes to be able to see the entrance to the canteen. They both wonder aloud where the children are. Why aren't they ever coming out? It's already five past ten.

When the children do finally emerge from the canteen block, they move along slowly in pairs and up onto the stage like a Lucia procession. Fredrika is hand in hand with her best friend Cecilia, Victor beside a red-haired boy John doesn't recognise. He's not from the football team, that much he knows. He asks Mary, who says it's Tor, the Ljunggren family's youngest lad, he must remember him? From scout camp in year two?

John doesn't. He has no recollection whatsoever of Victor either talking about or taking part in a scout camp with a sandy-haired boy in the same class called Tor. It bothers him that she could supply his forename and surname without any effort at all. He should be the one who knows most about Victor's friends at school, not Mary, who barely sees them at all during the school week. He vows to himself that he'll be better at memorising what the children are talking about in future. He doesn't ever want to be the kind of dad who won't listen, who hasn't a clue. Other dads might be like that, but not John. He's a good dad. Present and available.

Up on the stage the children have sorted out their places. The tallest are at the back, Fredrika is in the middle row, and in the front row Victor is tugging at the white shirt that John helped him iron that morning. Piano music begins and the children start singing. The summer hymn 'Blossom Time is Coming' is accompanied by the same music teacher both children have had throughout their time at school. Siwert Svedberg was already beginning to look his age when Fredrika was in year one. Today it's nothing short of impressive that he can remain upright without help.

'Christ, he's old,' John whispers in a sudden flash of intimacy that he fails to curb.

'Shhhh, don't say that,' Mary whispers back. He pretends to be affronted, but he can hear in her voice that she's close to giggling too. He forces himself to focus on the children so that he doesn't draw attention to himself with a gratuitous howl of laughter. He looks at Fredrika, in her rainbow-coloured skirt and pink tie-neck blouse. Then at Victor, in his white shirt with three-quarter sleeves and his slicked-down parting. They're beautiful, he thinks to himself as they sing. We did well after all.

He glances at Mary from the corner of his eye. She's moved too, he notes. She wipes away the tears with the back of her hand. She has pale pink nails today. Summer hands, she would say, if he made a comment on them. Something tells him she's thinking exactly the same thing as him at the moment. They did well, actually.

Mary

When John gives her his news he's cautious, almost ashamed, it would seem. Or maybe he's scared. As if he's been waiting for the right moment all evening, and when the children are finally in their rooms busy with something else, he serves up his big news with a last glass of wine in the kitchen. Just as she's on the point of calling it a day, giving the children a cuddle and saying it's time to go home.

She should have been suspicious when she was invited to have dinner with him and the children after the last day at school, but she wasn't. On the contrary, she'd interpreted it as a signal, a kind of symbol that it was time to bury the hatchet, that finally he was prepared to start cooperating more and wanted the holidays to begin *on good terms*. That was what she'd believed. How wrong she'd been. How naïve she was. She should have realised that he was up to something when he topped up her glass during dinner, if not before. He was never usually that generous, not with wine, not when the children were present.

When he spills his news, both of them are equally surprised. She by his news, he by her reaction to his news. Bursting into tears as suddenly as she does – the sobbing seems to well up between breaths – comes as a shock to them both. She's been prepared for a moment like this, has known that the day would come sooner or later, she'd reckoned on this before even she'd moved out. This is what men do. They move on sooner than women, that's all there is to it. She's smart enough to have noticed how these things usually work.

In her fantasies she's always been happy for John when he tells her he's met someone. She's wished him luck, given him a friendly hug and never in her wildest imagination has she needed to remind him to tread carefully with the children at first, because he would already be aware of that. In the same dream John has been relieved that she takes it so well. He thanks her for her magnanimity, then they carry on being a modern divorced couple who always put their children first. That was how she's imagined it would be, but it's not quite how it turns out.

Instead she puts on a show that's as unworthy as it is embarrassing. Her lips say the right things, that she understands and she's happy for him, *really happy*, but the tears keep flowing, and when she attempts to smile across the kitchen table, all she can manage is a twisted grimace. When John reaches out to pat her arm, she pulls away so abruptly she knocks over the glass of wine on the table in front of her. The wine spills over the edge of the table and they both leap up, but she's the one to reach the sink first for the dishcloth. She bends down under the table to wipe it up and he sits down again.

Under the table she reiterates everything she wants to say, all that she imagined she would say when this day came. She says that it's not a problem for her, she's just happy for him, that everything really, *really* is OK. But it's as though she only cries more with every sentence she utters. When he tells her what his new friend's name is and how old she is, she starts to laugh through the tears.

'What sort of name is Netta for a grown woman?' she asks. 'And excuse me, but eleven years younger, isn't she practically a child herself?'

John doesn't laugh with her. She doesn't know what he's doing above the table, as she can't see his face, but he's not laughing at any rate. Under the table all she can do is register his silence and it makes her feel intensely ashamed. Her comments about age and nicknames make her a nasty, bitter person, her tears make her a lonely, jealous one. John's feet don't move on the floor. He doesn't sound very happy when he starts speaking again.

'Listen... I'm sorry... I didn't know you'd feel like this, maybe I should have waited for a better moment...'

When he says this she's filled with the urge to overturn the chair he's sitting on. She wants to see him crash to the floor and when he lands she wants to press the wine-soaked dishcloth over his face, right over his mouth so it can never utter its condescending remarks again. She wants to suffocate him – yes, suffocate him – with her bare hands and a smelly dishcloth, and if it wasn't for the children being just a few rooms away, she might have done. Or at least given it a jolly good try.

Of course she doesn't. She finishes wiping up under the table instead of smothering him, and when that's done, she stands up. She turns her back on him while she rinses out the dishcloth in the sink, remains facing away as she takes a serviette out of the holder on the worktop and blows her nose. With her eyes directed to the tiles behind the worktop she says she's tired and needs to go home to bed. When he replies that he thinks he'll stay up for a while in case she changes her mind and wants to talk about it some more, she's already out in the hall putting on her jacket.

She doesn't close the gate behind her when she leaves. She leaves it open, couldn't give a damn if it gets dented by a car driving into it in the dark on the narrow street, couldn't give a damn if that happens to her too. She walks down the middle of the road, striding along, hears John shouting after her from the steps. Couldn't give a damn about that either.

'Mary? Can't we talk about this? Are you just going to leave now?'

She keeps walking. She has no intention of turning around. No intention of answering. There's nothing left for them to talk about. She has no time for him now, has other things to do, a whole life to pack up. A whole future to work out. When she turns left at the corner of Tallvägen and Eriksbergsvägen the sound of his voice melts away behind her. Not until she reaches Svalgången, enters her hall and locks the door behind her, does she bang the wall with her fists and let out a scream. This wasn't how it was supposed to be.

Part Two

FIVE YEARS LATER

Mary

She usually takes the opportunity to ring while Rolf is watching the news in the living room after dinner. Somewhere between the sport and the weather she makes sure he has all he needs, then leaves him on the sofa. She goes upstairs to the kitchen area in the open-plan house, passes the dining room and walks into the hall. Here she closes the office door behind her, sits down at Rolf's desk and dials the number for the farm outside Eskilstuna. Usually she's back in the living room before he has time to notice she's gone. She doesn't often get hold of the children these days when she tries to speak to them.

It's always Jeanette who answers now when Mary rings the children. Never John, never one of the children, only Jeanette. Even on the answerphone it's Jeanette's voice announcing that 'the Andrén family' are unfortunately not at home. The message ends with a jaunty invitation to the person ringing to seize the day because you never know how many you have left. The valediction puts Mary in such a bad mood she often hangs up before the recorded voice gets that far. She regrets it afterwards, wishes she'd hung on and said something, if for no other reason than to pass the ball to the children, but by then it's too late. She has to wait for a few more nights to pass before she tries again. It would all be much easier if it wasn't Jeanette who answered all the time. If it could just be Fredrika sometimes, like it was before.

In Kolarvik, Mary misses the way things were before. She misses ringing Tallvägen from Copenhagen, misses hearing Fredrika's breathless voice at the other end, misses the knowledge that her daughter has just torn through the house to get to the telephone first. She can hear Victor's croaky voice in the background, indignant and cross because yet again he's lost the race against his big sister to reach the phone mounted on the wall in the kitchen first. Most of all she misses the way Fredrika used to answer. Fredrika's imitation of Kerstin, the receptionist at John's office, was touching on a number of levels. Both in the way she used her deepest voice to sound like an adult, and the way she was so convinced that she would be a switchboard operator when she grew up.

When she was little, Fredrika's favourite pastime on school Inset days was to go to work with John. His office outside Farsta trumped Mary's at Arlanda, despite her impressive view of the runway and the fact that John had scarcely any time to look after Fredrika while she was there. She used to sit next to Kerstin in reception with a stack of paper and some coloured pencils and could stay that way for hours, without a single word of complaint. Wide-eyed, she would watch Kerstin answer the telephone, direct visitors and press the switches on the panel to connect incoming calls; every so often Fredrika would be allowed to have a go at answering calls herself. On those occasions, she'd come home in the evening to give a euphoric reprise of the events, even more convinced than the last time that she would be a receptionist when she grew up. There were no other options up for consideration. It didn't matter how many times John endeavoured to encourage their daughter to aim a little higher – didn't she want to be the boss, like her dad, he used to say – but Fredrika didn't.

In the beginning, when Mary rang the children – this was before Jeanette moved into Tallvägen and long before she and John married and took it into their heads to buy an equestrian centre outside Eskilstuna – she and Fredrika used to play a little game. Fredrika would answer in her receptionist voice, whereupon Mary would play tricks on her. She would alter her voice, pretend she was a stranger who was ringing on important business and needed to be put through to someone, and quickly. It might be a dissatisfied client who demanded to speak to the chief executive, or an obstinate lorry driver speaking with a broad Värmland or thick Skåne accent who needed to be put through to someone in charge at once. That game always worked. But they didn't play it all the time. Often it was enough for Mary just to play herself.

'Hello, my name is Mary Lilja,' she would say, 'and I would like to be put through to the sweetest girl in the whole world.'

At that Fredrika would start to giggle and say, unfortunately, that girl didn't live there. She must have the wrong number. Then Mary would revise her request, and wonder if she could possibly speak to the coolest girl in the whole of Sollentuna instead. That would make Fredrika laugh even more, at which point Mary would also start to laugh, and after that the phone calls seemed to evolve of their own accord.

Of course, it's not Jeanette's fault, not entirely, but since she came into the picture and took over the role of switchboard operator in the children's lives, communication between Mary and them has suffered. It's definitely become more sporadic. She's aware that it's in some part down to her, but it doesn't help that every time she calls she's forced to give lengthy status reports to Jeanette on her life with Rolf and the cats. What's more, for the last few months Jeanette has sometimes refused to get the children when Mary has phoned. It's been dinnertime, or some homework had to be finished, Fredrika's been about to go down to the stable and couldn't stop, or Victor's been in the middle of a match on the TV with one of his friends up in his room. Or the children have been busy doing their weekly household chores and could therefore under no circumstances come to the phone. As Mary understands it, Fredrika has to vacuum the enormous first floor of the house once a week in order to get her pocket money, and Victor has to do the dishes after dinner every second day.

Mary doesn't share her thoughts about this with Jeanette. Her opinion – that it sounds practically despotic to force children to do housework in return for pocket money – isn't something she can bring up in their conversations. Especially not when Jeanette's the one holding the power and her own behaviour has to be impeccable for her to be allowed to speak to the children in question at all. It's better to keep quiet and show where she stands when they meet, she and the children. She usually slips a few hundred-krona notes into their coat pockets when they come to visit. Since Victor comes more frequently than Fredrika, she gives him a little extra, which he in turn sneaks into his sister's pocket when he gets home. Between her and the children it's a system that is as formulated as it is unremarked. At least when they're with her, they don't have to do domestic chores in order to feel valued. Mary just thinks it's fun to look after them.

Sometimes when she rings, neither of them is at home. But Jeanette doesn't tell her that until they've spoken for several minutes. Only when Mary has provided details on how it's going with her job hunting, or her attempts to stop smoking, or what food she gives Rolf's cats, does Jeanette announce that neither of the children is at home. She promises to tell them that their mum has called, but it's doubtful whether she keeps her promise, since the children return her calls less and less often. Mary waits, puts off ringing again for as long as possible, but when sufficient time has elapsed, she does anyway.

Today is one of those days. Fredrika will be seventeen in just over a month and Mary needs to know what she'd like as a birthday present and when the best time will be for her to come for her traditional birthday-celebration visit. Typically, both she and Victor come at some point around their birthdays and usually stay for the weekend. They both check into their guest rooms in the basement on the Friday afternoon, ready to celebrate for three consecutive days. This year they've not had the chance to discuss when that's going to happen, so it's particularly important for her to speak to Fredrika. But, of course, it's not Fredrika who answers today either.

'Mary! I'm so glad you called! It feels as though we haven't heard from you for ages. Is everything OK? The children and I were wondering where you'd got to.'

Mary bites her tongue to stop herself stating the obvious: that she's been here all the time, on the same telephone number she's had for years, ever since she came back from Denmark, to be exact. Instead she hears herself apologising, explaining how much she's had on recently, tying herself in knots accounting for Rolf's variable schedule and losing the thread a few times before finally returning to the point of the call. She finishes by saying she's tried to ring and no one's answered, because it's true she has, and she wants that to be noted, at least.

'Oh my goodness, how strange!' Jeanette says. 'We didn't notice. We have caller display now, you know. Do you remember what day you rang?'

It goes against the grain to admit that she doesn't know what day it was when she last rang. She thinks it was less than a week ago, but she's not quite sure. The days with Rolf have a tendency to merge into one, and although nothing much happens, sometimes they seem to fly past. It's been like that ever since she moved in with him. After six months in Denmark, when she was first signed off on sick leave with exhaustion and then spent every working day trying to stop herself from fainting every five minutes, Rolf and his life in Sweden looked like utter paradise. His proposition entailed a quiet life in a quiet village with a handsome man, in a house with an enormous garden and a view across one of Lake Mälaren's northern fjords, twenty kilometres south of Enköping. Each month is identical to the month before, and yes, she likes it. She likes the fact that sometimes he's flying and sometimes he's at home. Likes the fact that he fiddles about with his motorbikes in the garage when he has time off, and that he rings to say goodnight every evening when he's away. As for her, she doesn't do much with her days. She potters about in the garden or sits down to knit or sew. Takes her small car for a trip into town now and then. When she's not shopping or cooking, of course, which takes up a significant number of hours in the week.

On the phone Jeanette continues to tell her about the Andrén family's new caller display. She seems inordinately proud of it. Mary doesn't want to be rude, so she tries to sound interested, even though she knows exactly how it works since she and Rolf have an identical one. After Jeanette has had her say about the family's new device, which apparently didn't show that Mary has rung during the last week, there's a pause after which Mary hurriedly asks if Fredrika or Victor might possibly be at home.

Jeanette says she's very sorry but Victor has a maths test tomorrow and for that reason he's upstairs studying with John. It's terribly important, she says, that he finishes this particular piece of work.

'He has a bit of a hard time with maths, poor thing.'

Once again Mary says nothing. She doesn't point out to Jeanette that she's talking about Victor as if Mary didn't know him, as if it would be news to her that Victor finds maths difficult, and to cap it all, as if his problems with numbers weren't a trait directly inherited from her. And, incidentally, as if it wasn't Mary who'd helped him with his first maths homework, who'd carried him in her womb, who's loved him all his life and actually, being his mother, knows him inside out. She doesn't say any of that, because she knows it's futile. Besides, it wasn't Victor she wanted to speak to this time, it was Fredrika.

'Well, Mary...' Jeanette begins, and now it sounds as though she's bracing herself.

After they've hung up and Mary has stressed that Fredrika or Victor should only ring if they have time and feel up to it, Mary finds that she has a telephone number noted down on a slip of paper next to Rolf's keyboard. She doesn't remember when she did it, but she's written OLA??? In large letters above the phone number. The three question marks in a row are perplexing; it's not like her to use question marks like this, and three in a row look vulgar, bordering on aggressive, so she hastily jots down the number on another piece of paper. She doesn't add any question marks to it, not even a name, just a telephone number, in her normal, neat handwriting. Then she throws the first note into the wastepaper basket beneath Rolf's desk and goes back into the kitchen.

Rolf is watching the news when she comes out of the office. When he hears her clattering with the dishwasher in the kitchen, he asks her if everything's OK with the children. His eyes don't leave the television as he does so, and consequently he doesn't see her as she answers cheerily that they're fine and they say hello. Normally his obvious lack of interest in her children would bother her, but not today. She has more important things to think about, her own maths to work out, so she carries on with the dishwasher and starts to do the calculations in her head.

Today there are five weeks and six days left before Fredrika's birthday. According to Jeanette, she's been with Ola for... Did she say six months? During those six months Fredrika has visited her and Rolf at least three times, could it be four? Last time Victor came on his own, but the time before Fredrika was there too, wasn't she? And on one of the occasions they both stayed the whole weekend, from Friday evening to Sunday afternoon; she knows that because they had roast lamb for Sunday dinner that time. She and Fredrika must have spoken on the phone at least...ten, maybe twenty times in the last six months. At least. At the very least?

But Fredrika hasn't said a word about anyone called Ola. She might have mentioned his name as one of her friends, it's possible, but it doesn't ring any bells. Fredrika hardly ever mentions any of her friends by name, and when she does it's with such strange nicknames that it's easy to forget them. It's Tusse this and Linde that, and Mallan and Joppe and Svalis, but, all the same, she hasn't spoken about an Ola, has she? Wouldn't Mary have reacted if her daughter had talked about an Ola who was, more to the point, her new boyfriend?

Under those circumstances it would be odd if Mary were now suddenly to ring this Ola and introduce herself as Fredrika's mum. For that reason, she decides to wait. She'll give Fredrika a week to ring back of her own accord, and if she doesn't – but she definitely will – then she'll have to ring Ola after all. They have to plan how they're going to celebrate her birthday.

In the living room the news has finished on the television. Rolf has started to flick between channels but can't seem to find anything that sparks his interest. Besides, he has to get up early tomorrow. He has to be in his car by a quarter past four to be in time for his flight to Athens. In the meantime, it would help if Mary could make up a sandwich box for him. If she does it this evening, she won't have to get up with him at the crack of dawn. She opens the fridge and shouts down to the living room:

'Do you want ham or salami tomorrow?'

Rolf's reply is as expected. She doesn't really know why she asks.

'Ham, please. I always think salami leaves such a funny taste in my mouth.'

He treads heavily as he mounts the three steps up to the kitchen. Soon he's standing beside her, looking over her shoulder into the fridge, as if to see whether there's anything he fancies. Mary takes out the ham and the butter and closes the door in front of his nose. He gives her a gentle pat on the back as she passes him on her way to the island unit.

'You're an angel, Mary, a bloody angel. I've always thought so.'

JOHN

The alarm clock goes off at a quarter past four. Half an hour later they assemble up at the hunting cabin in Bergvallen. This year there's Åke and Hasse, Helena and Ulf, and then Lennart and him. The same gang as last year minus Benke, who couldn't join them this year on account of his hip operation. His elkhound is going to go with Ulf, who is acting hunt leader this time. As the team's newest member, John has to share a turn with Hasse again this year. Their first stint of the day is by the marsh, right behind the cleared area at the end of Norra Byvägen. John is pleased when Ulf allocates this place to him, because the marsh is a good position. Historically it's one of the best. Good visibility and not too difficult to get to. Last year Åke shot a bull there, and since then Fredrika and Jenny have sworn they've seen elk in the area on several different occasions when they've been out riding. It's a good place to start the first day, that's all he can say. And in excellent company. The elk hunt couldn't have got off to a better start.

John likes Hasse. Hasse is what he would call a decent chap. Easy to deal with, possessing invaluable knowledge of both farming and hunting, always helpful, always generous, never jokes that John's a bloody Stockholmer, as some of the others still persist in doing.

In contrast to John, who's only had his hunter's licence for two years, Hasse has had his for almost forty. He began hunting with his father when he was a lad, and then took his own boys out into the forest before they grew up and, regrettably as far as Hasse's concerned, lost interest in game hunting. Now he has to put up with John instead, but he doesn't seem to mind that. In recent years they've even become friends outside the hunting team. Hasse might occasionally pop over to the farm for a coffee. Or to lend John and Netta something they need for their work. Wire for the henhouse was the latest thing. John and Netta try to do the same for Hasse. Favours for favours, that's the kind of way it works out here in the countryside. Helping each other with essentials, sharing responsibility for the rural neighbourhood, flashing their headlights if they meet cars on the narrow forest roads. They chat together at village meetings, have a couple of beers at the community centre's monthly pub evenings, and, at the end of October every year, spend several consecutive days together for the elk hunt.

They take the track north from the hunting cabin. It's still dark outside and they need torches to light up the path as they walk along in silence. They slow down for the last stretch, as the ground becomes more uneven. Hasse is breathing more heavily than John on their way uphill, but there's nothing strange about that, he's several decades older, after all. It's genuinely impressive that he's still up to all of this.

They don't talk until they've reached the mound where they're going to spend the first shift of the day. Hasse asks how things are going with the family, and John is so startled at the sound of his voice that he misses his step as he's about to sit down on a rock.

'All fine,' he says, pretending he hasn't just fallen on his backside. 'Netta's busy with the animals and the children... And yeah, they have their own lives at school. Lots of homework and whatnot. Both the girls have boyfriends now and Victor hangs out mostly with the Ekströms' lad down by the motocross tracks in Ångbacken. And then they need a lift to their mum's sometimes at the weekends. You know how it is, a lot of logistics. How about yours?'

'Pretty good,' Hasse says, and with that the formalities are out of the way and silence settles over their shared lookout.

They help each other build a fire and this year Hasse doesn't need to explain why they're doing it. This year John knows that the smoke indicates the wind direction, and wind direction is vital for strategy. While the fire burns, Hasse lights his pipe and a few minutes later John follows his example. In fact he stopped smoking several years ago, but the elk hunt grants a kind of exemption. Netta's OK with it as long as he stops as soon as the hunt is over.

They puff on their pipes and stare out across the clearing. The biting cold nips at their cheeks and John scratches his moustache. It's damp and smooth, more fluff than whiskers. His facial hair has never been impressive. It's sparse, soft and sandy-coloured. Not especially manly. Nevertheless, he grows his moustache before every elk hunt. He thinks it's part of it, somehow. This year his underwear is of better quality than last year. It has to be wool, not synthetic. Hasse taught him that too.

They sit for quite a long time without anything happening. It's become lighter between the trees at the other end of the clearing and something might appear at any second: a roe deer, a hawk, a stag, a fox. Best of all would be an elk. Calf, cow or bull, it doesn't matter today because it's the first day of the hunt and everything's allowed. They also know that there's just as likely to be absolutely nothing, that's much more common, but it doesn't matter. That's not actually why they're sitting here, at least not in John's case. It's for the atmosphere. The calm, the silence, the wordless connection between the guys in the team. The comradeship here is of a different quality to the camaraderie he had felt in Stockholm, and even if it took time for him to get used to it, he has to admit, he likes it. He likes living in the country.

It came as a huge surprise, both to himself and to his friends still left in the city, that he liked it so much. He can still burst out laughing when he thinks of his sister's immediate reaction the day he announced that he was thinking of selling his share in the company and devoting himself one hundred per cent to country life after six months of commuting between Stockholm and Eskilstuna.

'No way!' she'd shrieked down the telephone. 'I won't allow it!'

As if it was her future they were discussing, not his.

He and Netta had laughed about it later that evening. Little sister Anneli. A city rat through to her marrow, she'd need some time to get used to the idea. Indeed, so would his mum. It had taken a few return trips when he'd both fetched her and dropped her off at the door on Lidingö before she finally adjusted to the new distance. But it was fine in the end. His mum has shared the last few summers between Anneli on Långön and his family on the farm outside Eskilstuna. She's even started calling it 'Tuna', like the rest of the family. Anneli usually joins them with her boys in time for the haymaking, and last year she actually said that doing some physical work was a nice change. John and Netta could scarcely believe their ears.

Since then, haymaking has become the high point of the summer, at least for John. There's something about the team spirit, everyone helping everyone else across both farming and generational divides. His mum has responsibility for food and coffee, while the rest of the gang beaver away outside. Netta and Hasse are in charge of the work in the fields while John, his sister and the youngsters drag hay bales from the yard into the loft, until the last load is stowed away and they all have blistered hands, aching backs and clothes drenched in sweat and covered in earth and oil. Even the kids seem to enjoy it, despite the hard work, and despite being woken up early in the morning on some of the sunniest days of the summer.

It didn't come as a surprise to anyone that Netta liked living in the country. It was her idea they should move there in the first place. What had started as an entertaining activity to occupy themselves at the weekends had developed within six months into a serious project and, before they knew it, they'd put in an offer on an equestrian centre in Södermanland.

Mary's protests from Copenhagen had subsided the moment John pointed out the obvious: that she actually had no say in the matter. Not when she herself had left not just Stockholm, but Sweden, six months earlier. Of course she made some half-hearted attempts over the phone to emphasise that her move was only temporary, but she soon gave up and there was silence from her side. She sent some encouraging letters to the children, but there was no attempt from her to make them want to live with her when she returned from Copenhagen. Just as well. He was prepared for Mary's complaints; it's part of her character, so to speak.

On the other hand, he took the children's protests more seriously. It had been a shaky spring preceding the move. Fredrika had resumed her nightly weeping, which didn't improve when he and Netta took her to the new school to meet her prospective classmates.

'Shitty clothes,' she had sniffed in the car on the way home, 'and *no one* to be friends with.'

Jenny and Victor had an easier time of it, partly because their nearest neighbours have a daughter and a son of similar ages, who quickly took them under their wing. But poor Fredrika struggled. For the whole of the first year in high school she traipsed around looking miserable. It had been difficult to witness and tried the patience of them all, not least John. That's probably why, when the time came, he laid out almost twice as much money on her pony compared to Jenny's. He and Netta had quarrelled about the purchase of that horse for several weeks.

Happily, today that is all just a memory. Now the phone doesn't stop ringing in the evenings and if it's not her friends Fredrika is talking to, it's her new boyfriend, with his long hair and all his allergies.

As for Netta, basically the broad smile hasn't left her face since the day they received the keys to the farm. She says she's never been as happy as she is now and she's plainly telling the truth. By the end of the first week she'd made friends with half of the inhabitants in the village, she mixed effortlessly with the farm neighbours and had soon joined both the dog training club and the village association. She signed up as a volunteer at the local riding school and before the end of the first month she'd thrown both herself and John into the village hunting team. She said it felt like coming home.

At this time of the morning she's probably already gone down to the stable. The children might sleep for another hour, but not Netta; she has chores to do at first light. In all likelihood she's racing around between the stalls; he can picture her rosy cheeks. She feeds the horses before changing their blankets from the thin ones to the slightly thicker ones, and finally she'll let them out into their respective paddocks. The geldings in one and the mares in the other. After that it's time for the hens. The droppings have to be cleaned out of the coops, eggs have to be carried up to the kitchen, and then she'll go back to the stable. She mucks out all the horses' stalls, apart from Fredrika's and Jenny's, because she thinks it's important the girls fully appreciate the responsibility of looking after your own horse. You can't just do the enjoyable bits, in her opinion, and let someone else deal with the crappy stuff. She's right about that, of course. Even if there has been a fair amount of fuss about the horses recently. Between him and Netta, but above all between Netta and Fredrika, who has shown less and less interest in helping out at home over the last few months. Sometimes he can hear them shouting at each other down in the yard. They yell so loudly, they can be heard all the way up at the house. It will usually make him leave the room and find something to mess about with at the other end of the house, or down in the boiler room, so that he doesn't have to listen to them. It sounds so horrible when his girls argue with each other.

Netta's right that his kids were more spoiled than Jenny when they first met. He and Mary had demanded too little of their children while they were still married, and that didn't really improve after the divorce. When he started dating Netta he was still buttering their bread in the mornings and driving them to and from school, even though they were nine and twelve. When Jenny was the same age, she took care of the cooking once a week, knew perfectly well how a washing machine operated and could get herself to both the stables on the train, and to school on the bus.

Netta has taunted him about it over the years. She's called him overprotective and his children spoiled, but he's always humoured her. In a way she's right. Yet on occasions he'll still secretly muck out Fredrika's stall when he has a reason to go down to the stable. Fredrika has to concentrate now that she's right in the middle of upper school. It's not surprising that she doesn't have as much spare time, when she's commuting almost two hours every day to school in Västerås. She has to have some time for relaxation as well, he reasons, and that's when Netta's anger with him reaches its peak.

Netta thinks that John is working against the family strategy by taking Fredrika's side in any conflicts that arise between her and Fredrika. He doesn't think so, but it's difficult to win Netta over when she's made up her mind about something. He learned when they first started dating that most things go Netta's way in the end. And it usually turns out pretty well. There's no point in making a fuss about it. The fact is that was one of the reasons he fell for her in the first place.

It's still quiet over the marsh. John leans forwards on the rock, tries to reach his boots with his hands, but it hurts. It's his bloody back again. It annoys him that he suffers from backache after barely an hour into the stint; it's a curse being as tall as he is. Forever this troublesome back.

Forever the need to stretch and twist, visit the physiotherapist, knock back painkillers. All the stretching exercises he does at night and still he wakes up as stiff as a board in the morning. You might have thought it would be better living in the country, that his back would feel good with some proper work and not just sitting on an office chair all day, but no. It's rather the reverse. Now it takes nearly an hour before he's loosened up fully in the mornings. It's probably because it's still so early that he's in such infernal pain sitting on the rock next to Hasse.

He tops up on coffee from the flask and rises to his feet. He takes a couple of turns around Hasse and the rock. The sound of damp twigs snapping beneath his boots disturbs the silence and Hasse looks up, wondering what he's doing. John explains apologetically that it's his back. 'Bloody back,' he says, sitting back down to wait again. Isn't it unusually still in the forest today?

When they've finally sat through their hours by the marsh, Hasse's hunting radio starts crackling. Ulf's message that it's time to meet up in the cabin for the morning's coffee break and changeover is more than welcome. The thought of the sandwiches waiting makes John's mouth water. He stands up and asks Hasse if he needs a helping hand, but Hasse just stares at him and shakes his head.

'You save your back,' he says, and bounces up in an infuriatingly spry manner.

Together they start walking back down the slope they'd clambered up in the dark a few hours before. John keeps his eyes on the ground so that he doesn't trip over a root or slip on the moss. In front of him Hasse is taking easy strides in his classic Graninge boots. Funny really, John thinks. The guy's sixty-five and yet he's so much more agile than him. It's almost enough to make him ashamed.

Mary

Rolf isn't as pleased with his new timetable as she is. He's scheduled for the flight to Bangkok the first Monday and the third Wednesday of every month, and each time he goes, he'll be away for the following three or four nights respectively. He's always in a bad mood the morning before he goes on a long haul, makes extra noise as he huffs and puffs to put on his uniform and complains that he's far too old for this. Then she'll usually give him a pat and say he isn't at all.

'Fifty-seven is no age for a pilot,' she says, without any clear idea of what would be too old.

If his collar is askew, she straightens it; if his shoes are dusty, she polishes them, and she slips a lunch pack into his bag before following his heavy footsteps across the gravel driveway to the garage. There she kisses him on the cheek and wishes him a pleasant journey. Then she stands by the gate, where she remains, her arm in the air, until his car disappears down the forest road that will eventually take him first to the E18, then the E4 and finally to Arlanda. When the sound of the engine has faded away and the only noise is of the wind in the trees surrounding her, she walks across the lawn to the red-painted wooden cabin in the corner of the garden. There she turns on the radio, pours herself a glass of wine from the cabinet under the antique kitchen sofa and sits down. She stretches out her legs, lights the first cigarette of the day and lets the best days of the month begin. May they never change his schedule again.

It took some time to persuade Rolf that the cabin in the corner of the garden – where, when she met him, he kept his lawnmower and all the tools and spare parts he seems to need for his motorbikes – was actually destined to be something other than a storage space. She worked on it quietly and methodically, approached the subject gradually and paused her attempts the moment he showed the slightest sign of irritation.

He was sceptical to begin with, but at the same time he had problems making his case. Deep down he must also have felt that it was a waste to have a fully operational guest cottage that was only used to house oily tools and clunky machines. Besides, it was a long way for him to haul the things up to the garage each time he needed to use them. His garage in Kolarvik is quite large. All told, he had to drag the stuff nearly a hundred metres every time he wanted to mend something in the garage.

At first she thought he might initially have put the things in there out of sheer obstinacy. Perhaps it acted as some kind of low-intensity revenge on his former wife, Gunnel, who'd been the one to use the cabin during their marriage, by contaminating it with all the dirty machinery. He doesn't have much good to say about Gunnel today, and quite rightly. She left him without any warning after a yoga trip to Asia the year before Rolf and Mary met. His children are a different matter though: he worships them in a way that's almost unhealthy.

When he talks about them you would think they were small children, despite the fact they're both well over twenty. If they're not around physically, he makes sure they're in your head by speaking about them all the time. It's Jenina this, Bill that. Bill has pulled this off at work, Jenina has been awarded this research grant, have you seen this image from Jenina's ultrasound? And so he goes on.

'Yes, darling, it's absolutely fantastic,' she usually says in response.

From time to time she tells him about something Victor or Fredrika has achieved, mostly to redress the balance. She might show him a photo of Fredrika soaring over an obstacle on her horse, or Victor standing astride his motocross bike and grinning under his huge helmet, but for the most part she listens and goes along with it. Rolf quietens down sooner if she does. When his children ring in the evening and he puts on his tender dad voice, she usually withdraws, to the laundry room in the basement or the flowerbeds in the garden, so that she doesn't have to hear him. There's something about dads and the way they speak to their children that bothers her, it always has done. It's better if she walks away and does something else.

It soon became evident that her initial argument for fixing up the house in the garden didn't go down very well with Rolf. He couldn't see any point in doing it purely so that the children didn't have to sleep in the basement when they came to stay.

'But isn't it just cosier having them close?' he had said.

By 'them' he meant Bill and Jenina, but she didn't comment on that. It was only when she changed strategy and included her mother in the equation with regard to the cabin that her campaign of persuasion began to yield results. Ever since Sven died from complications following his third stroke, Gaby has kept inviting herself to Kolarvik, and there isn't much either Mary or Rolf can do about it. She just turns up, more or less unannounced, and sometimes she stays for nearly a week on one of her visits. It was probably the thought that he wouldn't have to watch her pacing around the house like a cat on hot bricks that finally made Rolf back down over the cabin. After two months of consolidated attempts to persuade him, in the end Mary got what she wanted: a free hand in the cabin, which would now officially be a guest cottage to accommodate her mother in particular.

She launched into the plan immediately. She purchased the paint the following day and set Rolf to work on extending the garage the day after that. It had taken three weeks of their second summer together, and then it was all done. The machines and tools went into the garage and Mary had appropriated the right of free access to the house she had longed for ever since her first visit to Rolf in Kolarvik.

That time she came as a spur-of-the-moment guest, after a dinner in Stockholm that didn't quite get finished and which had resulted in Rolf sleeping over at her parents' flat in Gärdet. The intention was to go their separate ways on the Saturday, but when he asked if she would like to come with him, see where he lived and meet his cats, she couldn't really find a reason to say no. It was Saturday, after all. And she had nothing in particular to do. Her flight back to Copenhagen wouldn't depart until Monday morning and neither Fredrika or Victor had been able to meet her that weekend. Fredrika had some show-jumping event and Victor had turned her down for some vague reason that was never explained to her. A spontaneous trip to Enköping with a handsome pilot sounded as attractive a proposition for her Saturday morning as anything else.

Once installed in the house, Rolf made sure she felt at home. After a guided tour, during which she walked wide-eyed through the rooms of the large timber-built house and congratulated him on how beautiful he'd made it, he seated her on one of the sun loungers on the terrace and served her a glass of wine. It was August and the afternoon sun streamed between the birch trees onto the south-facing terrace. Below the garden Lake Mälaren glistened, and they lay on the loungers together for several hours. At some point Rolf told her about his interest in birds and he pointed in the direction of the nature reserve that evidently lay a few hundred metres southwest of the garden. It was when Mary was following the line of his arm that she discovered the cabin for the first time.

'What's that gorgeous little house?' she remembers asking.

'Oh, nothing much. Just where I keep my tools,' she recalls him saying, which gave him the excuse to tell her about another of his great interests: restoring old motorbikes.

Today she thinks of the house as her sewing workshop, and not the guest cottage. Partly because neither her children nor her mum have slept there yet, but primarily because that's what she uses it for. She has finally found a place for some of her favourite activities in life: sewing and knitting.

In the sewing workshop she makes plans for her future as the proprietor of her own textile business. That's where she thinks up ideas for company names and logo designs, where she's made up numerous pairs of curtains and baby blankets, and where she's taken photographs of all her creations. It's also where she's read various books on business studies and one on advertising design. It all happens in the workshop, more or less in secret, because she wants it to be a surprise when she presents her plans to Rolf. If she knows him as well as she thinks she does, this matter is going to require a strategic campaign of persuasion too. For the time being it's simply better if he thinks she's pottering about in the garden or doing a crossword under the pergola when she's not with him in the house.

When she moved in with Rolf it was never with the idea that she would be his housewife. On his worst days Rolf reminds her of this.

'But sweetheart, shouldn't you look for some work?' he'll say, a worry line etched between his bushy eyebrows. 'You can't sit around here all day. Isn't it boring for you out here when I'm away on a flight?'

When he says that sort of thing, she nods and pretends to agree that she needs a job. If she's feeling particularly obliging, she'll even go into the office and write an application letter. She puts the letter on the passenger seat in Rolf's car, with the address uppermost, so that he'll remember to put it in the postbox next time he drives into town. *Look how good I've been*, that means.

After a few days he's usually forgotten whatever it was that troubled him, and then a few more weeks will pass. For her part, she's not in a hurry. She doesn't actually require a job, not when she has everything she needs here, in Rolf's house and beautiful garden. She has food in the cupboards, flowers in the borders, and now the sewing workshop as well. The money from the sale of the flat is certainly beginning to run out, but there's really nothing to worry about yet. It isn't as if Rolf charges her rent.

The red-painted cabin has two separate rooms that are connected by a long, narrow hall. Both rooms have pastel walls, pale pink in the west room and mint green in the east. Both have a view over the lake below the garden, though in the west room it's slightly better than the east, as the lilac bush in the corner of the garden blocks part of the view on that side. In each room there's a place to sleep: in one it's in the form of an antique kitchen sofa, which she's restored herself, and in the other a single bed on which she's piled so many burgundy velvet cushions that it now more closely resembles a sofa. Along one of the walls there's a shelf that boasts hundreds of beautifully patterned fabrics instead of displaying the spines of books. Along another wall is her sewing bench, and on top of that her two sewing machines. A rectangular chest, which can also be used as an extra bench, houses some of her yarns, and the ones that don't fit in the chest are in the large wicker basket in the west room. In the same room are her coffeemaker, a water jug and a little fridge she picked up in a flea market for a mere fifty kronor. It was so cheap even Rolf couldn't complain. He just looked at her suspiciously when she arrived at the car with it.

What on earth will you do with a fridge? he appeared to be thinking.

Never you mind, she thought back. But they never discussed the matter.

Rolf is good like that. He's a nice man, good-hearted by nature, and he doesn't feel the need to question everything in detail all the time. As long as she prepares his dinner, does his washing and helps him follow his flight rota, he lets her spend her days doing pretty much whatever she wants to do. All the same, it's of the utmost importance that she makes sure she doesn't spend too many hours in the workshop when he's at home. It's obvious he finds it problematic if she's there when she should really be with him. At one point he asked her, half in jest, if the only reason she was with him was to have her own cottage, and at another he actually tried to forbid her from keeping her bottles of wine in there, but she drew the line at that. It was clear he was doing it to control her and when she accused him of that, all he managed to say was that he cared about her and he didn't want her to overdo it. She had thanked him for his concern on that occasion, ruffled his hair, kissed him on the cheek and promised that she definitely wasn't overdoing it. With that, the subject fizzled out.

The creation of sofa cushions is scheduled for today. In a craft shop in the city centre last week she'd come across fabric with a pretty brick-wall pattern. She couldn't help but buy it, despite the price per metre being outrageous. There had to be an immediate phone call to Gaby, by the end of which she had received a generous contribution into her bank account and was able to afford almost eight metres of the beautiful fabric. It was quite late when she left the workshop that night. When she got back up to the house Rolf had already gone to bed, so for the sake of domestic harmony she hasn't been down there once all weekend. She's been saving herself for today, longing to hear the crunch of the gravel under his tyres, to see him drive away.

When the phone rings she knows before she picks it up that it's her mum. Gaby is the only one who rings her regularly, and she rings even more frequently when she knows Rolf is away on a long-haul flight. How she's managed to memorise his rota is beyond Mary's comprehension. It's hard enough for her to keep tabs on it herself, yet Gaby almost never misses. Sometimes he's barely steered the car out of the drive before the cordless phone starts to ring in Mary's pocket.

The duration and content of the phone calls are, on the other hand, harder to predict. It depends on the day, and as usual with her mum, that fluctuates. One day Gaby can be laconic, complain bitterly about how lonely it is to grow old and describe the bottomless grief of being widowed, only for her to relate anecdotes from first one social event and then another that she's favoured with her presence in Båstad the next. From time to time, she rings solely because she wants to express her deepest concerns. Her favourite subjects are the craziness of Fredrika and Victor living with John and not with Mary, together with the risk of Rolf finding another woman when he's away travelling with his job. Today looks as though it's going to be one of those days.

'*Mary Anne*, you have to listen carefully to me.'

Mary stifles a sigh and rolls her eyes. It sounds excessively formal when Gaby calls her Mary Anne. She clamps the telephone receiver between her shoulder and her ear, while she simultaneously starts pinning the fabric and confirming with a 'hmmm' that she's still there.

'He looks good for his age and you know what men are like, especially pilots. Are you looking after him properly? Make sure you're nice and trim and be there for him in every respect. You know what respects I mean, don't you? I don't have to spell it out?'

'No, Mum, you don't need to. I look after him. There's no need to worry.'

'I mean the *intimate respect*, darling. Are you there for him so he doesn't have to look for someone else?'

'I look after Rolf in the intimate respect, Mum. Can we stop talking about this now?'

'You must listen to your mother! These things don't come for free, especially when you start getting old, I'm telling you. You've always been pretty, I've always said that, but nature is what it is. Above all for us women. We have to work on our outward appearance, that's how we get them to stay. Just think how it was for me and your father! If I hadn't put up a fight, he would have gone sidling off to someone younger, believe you me, I know what I'm talking about. I lived with a pilot for over fifty years.'

Mary stifles another yawn. She knows only too well how long her mother and father lived together. She knows equally well what her mother is alluding to with the words 'good for his age'. Rolf has a good head of hair and nothing amiss with his eyes either. Light blue and almond-shaped, with dark eyelashes like nature's own mascara. During his talk she'd been impressed as she studied his fringe of eyelashes from her seat towards the back of the hotel conference room. He had come as a representative for the group of pilots whose working hours she and her colleagues spent days scheduling, but it had been difficult for her to focus on what he was saying. It was partly due to the eyelashes, but also because she'd never really given a damn about how he and his pilot friends fared at work. Well aware of the approximate size of his pay cheque, she still found it practically impossible to feel sorry for him, as he stood there insisting upon the importance of pilots receiving their statutory rest period between flight duties. By the end of his address she was almost asleep, but that wasn't Rolf's fault. She was incredibly tired back then.

After she'd been in Denmark for a while she'd become utterly exhausted. Most of the time she would fall asleep with her clothes still on in front of the television in her flat in Nørrebro. She didn't have the energy to get herself up and out, couldn't face making any new friends, could scarcely even find the strength to be angry with John, who had announced that he was moving with the children to a farm outside Eskilstuna. The only thing she lived for was her weekends with the children and she saved all her energy for the Fridays when she took the flight home to meet them in her parents' overnight flat in Stockholm's Gärdet. The most she wished for in those days was to sleep. As was the case on that particular day. Right up until the moment outside the conference room when Rolf asked her if she'd like to have a coffee with him, peering down so that his lashes cast a shadow halfway over his cheeks.

The rest is history now. It feels like a long time ago, but above all it's fifteen kilos ago. Rolf says his new stomach is the result of her cooking, but she's not sure. She thinks it's more to do with his age. He is twelve years older than her, after all.

When she thinks back to the day she met Rolf, it feels as though they've been together for thirty years and not three and a half. A lot has happened since then. He has concluded his drawn-out divorce from Gunnel, Mary has left both her job and the rest of the aviation world. Rolf's children have had children of their own and hers are well on their way to being adults too. He has become a grandfather; she has become both fatherless and jobless. They cohabit in Rolf's enormous timber-built house, and this is where they are now: she with her passion project in the sewing workshop and Rolf, with his expanding stomach, in an Airbus A330 on the way to Bangkok.

All in all, she would contend that everything has more or less ended up in the right place. And were it the case that Rolf wanted to sleep with a younger air stewardess from time to time, it really doesn't matter to her. It's not as if she's in the mood for it very often anyway. But she can hardly say that to her mum, who would be consumed with her perennial anxiety about Mary being alone and sad again. So Mary promises her, in as few words as she can muster, that she takes care of her partner in every conceivable respect that a woman can take care of her husband. And when she has promised it multiple times, in more words than she would have liked, they end the call and Mary can finally return to the pattern.

When she has finished the first sofa cushion she'll take it up to the house and photograph it against the off-white bedspread in the bedroom. Then she'll treat herself to one glass on the terrace. As the afternoon sun is setting, she'll put one of the patio chairs against the wall of the house and use the other one as a footrest. She'll take a blanket from the living room to lay over her legs and there she'll sit, comfortable in the chair and the sun, and browse through a magazine. She might do a crossword too. She'll enjoy the music on the radio in the kitchen, but most of all she'll enjoy the effortlessness of life when Rolf is on a long-haul flight. She doesn't even have to think about dinner, because yesterday's chicken stew is still in the fridge. When afternoon becomes evening and the sun disappears behind the birch trees along the forest road, she'll eat her stew on the sofa. Then she'll try to ring the children at the farm. Maybe this time one of them will answer. Maybe today will be the day when Jeanette is out running errands and it will be Fredrika or Victor who picks up. Maybe one of them will answer and also be in the mood for a long conversation with their mother. It really feels as though that might happen. This day has been filled with potential. And on Sunday Fredrika's coming to celebrate her birthday.

JOHN

That he's ringing Mary on a Thursday evening has nothing to do with the fact that Netta is at the dog training club between seven and nine on Thursdays. He could just as easily have done it when she was at home, but it worked out this way instead. Besides, he's already spoken to Netta about the matter several times and it just ends up with him feeling as though she's ridiculing him. She dismisses his concerns in a way that makes him feel stupid. Last time she laughed in his face.

'But, please, don't tell me you don't know what's going on? You're not still kidding yourself they're lying there doing their homework whenever Fredrika stays the night?' she had said when he'd tried to discuss his unease.

'Besides, she's already on the pill, so you don't need to worry about becoming a grandad just yet,' she'd said, with a laugh that sounded like contempt. As if she couldn't care less that her own bonus daughter appeared to be practically on the point of moving out.

Since Fredrika will be going to Mary's to celebrate her birthday, it felt like a good time for a bit of reconciliation. Stranger things have happened than a dad ringing his children's biological mum to talk about how their offspring are getting on. Nevertheless, to be on the safe side he shuts the office door behind him before he sits down by the telephone.

He thumbs through the address book until he finds the page for Mary. It's become quite messy over the years. Under the crossed-out phone number for the flat on Svalgången is another crossed-out address in Denmark. Under that is the telephone number for Gaby's overnight flat in Gärdet and at the bottom Rolf's number followed by an address outside Enköping. The last lines are in green felt-tip pen and in Fredrika's dense handwriting. She can't have been more than fourteen when she wrote it. She was probably relieved when she did, as Mary's move to Rolf's also meant the end of her stay in Denmark.

When Mary mentioned in passing that she'd started dating a pilot from work, John could have mocked her by saying she was so predictable, but he bit his tongue. One of the things he and Mary used to joke about when they still lived together was that sooner or later air stewardesses and other female staff would go out with pilots, or at least engage in extramarital affairs with them. He used to tease her about there being a real risk that she would leave him for a pilot, and she used to shudder, 'Over my dead body,' she'd say in response to his jokey comments. 'It's not going to happen. I'd rather take a boring economist.'

But after six months in Denmark, the situation had clearly changed. Suddenly it was fine for Mary to meet a pilot and move in with him only months after his divorce. The move was just temporary – that's what was said at the time. The plan was that she would find somewhere to live as soon as she had a new job. But the months passed, a new job didn't materialise and there was no more talk of a move. Today she has lived with Rolf for more than three years. Might it even be nearer four? By now the children have started describing their visits to his flashy house outside Enköping as 'going home to Mum's'. At this point they have both got to know the moustachioed man who now pays for their board and lodging when they meet their mum on holidays and weekends. Victor says he's cool and Fredrika doesn't seem to have anything against him either, even though she goes to Enköping less often than her brother.

'Hello?'

Mary answers after only one ring. He's surprised by how quickly she picks up, and isn't there something about her voice that's different? It's kind of wheezy. It cracks when she speaks, as if she's been drinking whisky or smoking hundreds of cigarettes or been silent for so long she needs to clear her throat to get her vocal chords going. Maybe she just has a cold. Or, this is the way she sounds nowadays. Perhaps it's as simple as the fact that she's growing old and ageing has taken its toll on her voice. Whatever the reason, it makes him lose his thread. He introduces himself with exaggerated formality, using both his first name and his surname, as if they didn't know each other at all. Mary interrupts him halfway through his surname.

'For heaven's sake, John, tell me what it is. Has something happened?'

He reassures her and apologises for not saying what it was straightaway. All is well with the children, no worries, he's ringing for a different reason. Mary clears her throat again and then gives a deep sigh at her end.

'Bloody hell, you gave me a scare. You can't do that!'

He recognises her voice at last. It's a while since they last had a chat. Can it have been as long ago as Victor's birthday, when he brought the children over to her and Rolf? In that case it's been nearly three months since they last spoke. Whenever it was, he really wants to know how she is, now he's got her on the line.

Mary sounds suspicious initially, but she starts to tell him nevertheless. She describes the business she's set up, which sells fabric and yarn by mail order and through advertising in various craft magazines. And takes orders for all manner of handicrafts, both by telephone and by email. She says that business is slow, but she hopes it will improve when she's attended a few more trade fairs and started to make a name for herself in handicraft circles.

He commends her for taking the plunge. Mary has been talking about this for as long as he's known her, and he wants to encourage her now, so he says he knows things will definitely improve. It's just a question of persevering.

He does have some experience. He made that same journey once, and it turned out well. Mary was with him at the time, she must remember how many years it took him to work his way up to the position of CEO in the firm where he worked. It took even longer before he was invited to be a partner.

'I of all people know how it is to work your way up from nothing. But look at me today,' he says proudly.

It sounds boastful when he talks like this, but his intentions are good, the idea is to be encouraging, because he has done well, it has to be said. Not everyone at his age can sell off their share of a company and start living the good life in the country overnight. If Mary fights on and doesn't give up, then one fine day she might do the same.

It seems she's taken it the right way, because she sounds genuinely happy when she tells him it was nice of him to say so, really kind. He explains that he's not being kind, he does actually mean what he said. He really thinks it's courageous of her to strive for her dreams, and he wants her to know that.

And he's curious. What did she do to get her own email address? Wasn't it terribly difficult? He and the family haven't even managed to bring internet to the farm, even though he knows it's the new craze. He's not a complete dinosaur, though, he's seen how it works on the neighbours' computer, and for months Victor has been pestering him about getting a modem and some kind of separate telephone line to the farm. Mary clearly has both of those things and not only that, she can put together her own adverts pointing people to her own email address. Even though she insists her adverts are poor and she had to pay for help to build the templates, he's impressed, properly impressed. With Mary. It's been a while since that was the case.

When he hears someone moving in the hall outside the office, it reminds him that he had a reason for calling. Here he is sitting and chatting about adverts and emails when there was an important matter he wanted to discuss. But he doesn't want Fredrika or Victor to hear what it is, so he has to wait.

If he holds the receiver slightly away from his ear he can listen for steps in the hall at the same time. They move from the stairs, past the office and into the kitchen. It must be Victor going to get an evening snack. He usually does at about this time, at least when Netta's out. She thinks it does him no good to consume so many sandwiches in the evening and tries to make him eat a proper dinner instead. John can rarely face the effort of making a fuss over this. Let the lad have a sandwich if he wants one, is more his attitude.

He lowers his voice as he continues.

'Well,' he whispers into the phone, 'the reason I rang was that I wanted to talk a bit about Fredrika, if you have time—'

'I'd love to,' Mary says. 'What's wrong with her? I'm so looking forward to Sunday, you know. It's been far too long since the last time we saw each other. It's easier to get hold of Victor, but Fredrika... Oh, how I miss her! Did you hear that she's going to bring her boyfriend this time? I feel a bit nervous. Jeanette says he's nice?'

'Ola, yes... It was him I wanted to talk about. Or rather, Fredrika and him, I mean. He's nice, a good guy, you can tell he's in love—'

Mary interrupts him again.

'Aah, how sweet! Doesn't time fly! Our little girl, with her own boyfriend. I feel quite emotional when I think about it.'

Suddenly her voice has that same croaky sound again. He stops short. Was that what she was doing when he rang, sitting there crying? And if it was, does she intend to start again now, on the phone, before he's even had a chance to say what he wanted?

John twists round in the office chair. He wonders where Rolf is at the moment. It can hardly be John's job to comfort her. He's only met Rolf briefly when he dropped the children off, but his impression of Mary's boyfriend is that he's the quiet type. Calm, the sort that does everything slowly and methodically, who moves slowly and speaks slowly. He speaks softly too, under his moustache.

He needs to get to the point quickly so that Mary doesn't get more emotional than she may already be.

He wants to bring the call to an end and get back to his own affairs. He actually does have important jobs to do. Apart from having to feed the horses, he also needs to fire up the boiler so that it doesn't get too cold in the bedrooms tonight. He doesn't really have time for this conversation.

'Well, anyway, as I was saying: Ola. I thought you might like to, I don't know, have a good look at them, see if you think everything seems to be OK. So yeah, I *believe* it's OK, but, after all, he's quite a lot older than her... And, well, I don't know, you are a girl and all that—'

'But, John,' Mary interrupts him for the third time that day, 'of course I'm going to check on her! I'm not going to do anything else on Sunday *except* keep an eye on her. Do you want me to ring you afterwards and tell you what I thought?'

Now she suddenly sounds upbeat instead of croaky, and when she puts it like that, it sounds absolutely preposterous. Obviously he doesn't want Mary to spy on their daughter and ring him to give him a report afterwards. What is she thinking?

His idea to call Mary in order to discuss Fredrika's behaviour feels idiotic now. Clearly Mary can't contribute anything to this after only having coffee with them for a few hours. It isn't her job to monitor how Fredrika's feeling. It *could* have been, definitely, but she basically resigned from that job, unbidden, several years ago. Besides, didn't she sound a bit patronising, as though she were thinking deep down that he's silly, touchy, exaggerating, an overprotective dad who is having difficulty letting go? Exactly like Netta, in that case, who also seemed to think it quite acceptable for a sixteen-year-old to move in with an unemployed twenty-two-year-old.

He decides to end the call and do what he can to erase it from both his and Mary's memory.

'No, you know what?' he says. 'I just thought you should keep your eyes open. Not ring me to report back afterwards. I thought you might want to be a little more involved in her life, might be interested in hearing what's going on and stuff. But there's absolutely no obligation. It was more of a thought; you can do with it what you like.'

That was a trifle harsh, he can hear it himself, but it's too late now. He's already presented his case, and she has interrupted him a number of times so it serves her right.

'Of course I want to be involved! I said, I'm really looking forward to—'

He interrupts her. It's his turn.

'Listen, I've got to get going and sort out a few things here, so have a great time. Good luck with the adverts and the business and all that. Have a lovely time with Fredrika and Ola on Sunday. Bye!'

The receiver is halfway towards the cradle before Mary's voice stops him.

'Wait!' shouts the strangled voice. 'John? What just happened?'

'As I said, have to run. Have a good time. Talk soon. Bye!'

The receiver goes down with rather too heavy a crash.

Mary

When she puts on the dark green silk dress with the paisley pattern, it feels rather grand. It's been hanging in her wardrobe for months without being put to use. She considered wearing it for the crayfish party with the neighbours in August, but at the last moment chickened out. Not so much because of Rolf's comments that she looked 'a bit excessive', but because it would have been a nuisance if she'd spilled any of the crayfish sauce on the beautiful creation's delicate material. Since then she's really just been waiting. Since July, when she bought it in the summer sales, she's been waiting for the right occasion. That occasion is today, for today there's going to be a celebration. Fredrika and Ola are arriving on the twelve o'clock train and Mary has spent all morning on the decorations. She's decorated both herself and the living room.

    She couldn't resist picking balloons that matched her dress. Dark green, orange and pale pink, they're now all hanging in the corner of the large room. She's laid the table with the best china and on the kitchen island, next to the coffee things and a dazzling bouquet of white germini and orange roses, the pile of presents stands ready.

'Isn't it lovely?' she asked Rolf, when he popped in from the garage for a glass of water.

'Beautiful. You're so clever,' he said, before immediately disappearing again.

She contemplated telling him to change into something more festive too, but decided to let it go. Fredrika isn't coming for his sake, and besides he always gets so grumpy when he has to squeeze himself into anything other than jeans and a T-shirt on his weekends off. It's better for him to be in a good mood rather than dressed up today.

It's almost empty in the car park behind the station. Mary shivers next to the car while she smokes and bitterly regrets not wearing a jacket over her dress. She also regrets leaving her handbag in the hall, because now she can't have a chewing gum after the cigarette. Nor can she touch up her lipstick. She throws the cigarette onto the ground, squashes it under the tip of her sole and climbs into the car to warm up. She turns the radio on and off a few times. Turns the heater on and then off again. Checks that the back seat is clean, brushes some crumbs off the passenger seat. Why aren't they here?

At last she sees them coming out of the station building. They walk towards the car park hand in hand and Mary starts waving from the front seat. As they approach, her waving becomes frenetic, with both hands, so that she can be seen through the condensation on the inside of the window. Fredrika spots her first, says something to Ola and then begins waving with her free hand. Ola follows his girlfriend's example and does the same.

They look quite funny as they near the car, each with their arm in the air; funny because they're so similar. Almost the same height, almost the same clothes – both in torn jeans and black boots – and almost the same hairstyles. Fredrika's hair is dyed black, Ola's is dark brown. Hers is straight and loose, his is wavy and tied back in a ponytail, but still. They are visibly alike. Despite the age difference, they look about as old as each other. Mary can't decide if it's because Fredrika appears older than her seventeen years, or Ola younger than his twenty-two. They seem well-matched as they come closer to the car. And Ola, as she can see through the condensation on the windscreen, has a friendly smile. Kind eyes, warm and inclusive.

Now that there are only a few metres left between the youngsters and the car, it feels odd to remain inside, waving. Mary opens the door, jumps out of the driver's seat, saying 'Hello!' and 'Welcome!' and 'Isn't this super!' as she opens her arms. The kids say 'Hi!' and 'Thank you!' and 'Yeah, it's really great!' and give her a hug. Ola hugs Mary too, even though she's never met him before.

'Great to meet you at last,' he says after the hug, and appears to be on the point of saying something else, maybe that he's heard so many good things about Mary, but he doesn't have time, because Fredrika interrupts:

'Bloody hell, it's cold. Can't we get into the car?'

On the journey back they talk about Fredrika's school. From the driver's seat Mary converses politely with the kids, who chose the back seat when they jumped into the car. She asks if Fredrika still likes school now she's in the second year, if it's annoying having to commute between Eskilstuna and Västerås. Fredrika replies that it's so-so, that there's an insane amount of homework, that 'it's tough getting up early' in the mornings, but she manages. Especially now she has Ola, who lives near the station. When it's clear that she doesn't intend to elaborate further, Mary switches focus and asks Ola what work he does. Ola explains that he's a jobseeker but sometimes he does temporary work at a retirement home in the outskirts of Eskilstuna.

'How exciting,' says Mary, trying to sound as though she really does think it's exciting to work with old people.

'Well, yeah… Maybe not that super-exciting, but I do actually like it,' Ola says from the back seat.

'He's, like, the favourite of all the senile old biddies, at least half of them are in love with him,' Fredrika says, which makes Ola laugh and say she's exaggerating.

'That's wonderful,' Mary says, and she laughs too.

In the rearview mirror Mary sees Fredrika lean her head on Ola's shoulder. A second later Ola starts stroking her hair. It strikes her that his display of affection comes naturally and Fredrika barely seems to notice that he's touching her. Mary averts her gaze and tries to concentrate on the road. In the absence of any inspiration about how to continue the conversation about the retirement home, she gives them the news from Kolarvik instead. She begins with the guest cottage, tells them how nicely she's decorated it, that Ola and Fredrika are welcome to stay there as often as they like. They nod from the back seat and Ola says, of course, that sounds nice. Mary moves on to the wealthy Stockholm family who have bought the house nearest the beach and never say hello when they walk past with their dogs, despite the fact that she and Rolf have shouted hello several times. When Ola says that sounds like a typical Stockholmer, Fredrika digs him in the side and reminds him that actually she comes from Stockholm. The kids begin a kind of seated boxing match in the back seat, Mary loses the thread and can't think what else she intended to say, and so she drives on in silence.

When they've arrived and settled down at the dining-room table for coffee, the conversation starts to flow a little easier. Very much thanks to Rolf, who has come in from the garage exclaiming that something in the oven smells good, introduced himself to Ola and hugged Fredrika.

'Isn't it cold in those trousers?' he asks after hugging her, gesticulating towards Fredrika's torn jeans. She laughs at him and said that could well be the case, which seems to break the ice.

Mary serves her homemade almond cake and the orange princess cake with seventeen dark green candles arranged in a circle on the top, as well as caramel cookies, vanilla buns, coffee and Coca-Cola.

'There's wine, if anyone wants some?' she says, but no one does, so she puts the unopened bottle back in the fridge.

While they eat, Ola interrogates Rolf about his job.

'It sounds dead cool to be a pilot,' he says, and draws reference from *Top Gun*.

Rolf clicks his tongue and says it's not in the least cool, if Ola only knew how boring it can be sometimes.

'You do know that, like, all my family are pilots or air stewardesses, don't you?' Fredrika says, looking at Ola.

She tells him about her grandmother who was an air stewardess and her grandfather who was a pilot and also about Mary having worked most of her life in aviation.

'It's kind of like a family curse,' she says.

'Talking of Grandma, I have something for you,' says Mary, holding out an envelope containing the notes and card that Gaby left the last time she visited.

Fredrika reads the card, which finishes with several lines about how much Gaby loves her granddaughter and how they've always been kindred spirits, the two of them. When she's finished, she thumbs the little bundle of notes and sighs.

'Oh, Grandma,' she says dreamily.

'You can buy a whole pair of jeans for that,' Rolf says, as he helps himself to a second slice of princess cake.

Fredrika, who chooses to ignore Rolf's joke about her trousers, starts telling Ola what an extraordinary grandmother she has. She relates more than one story – the one from Tenerife when Gaby dragged six-year-old Fredrika with her into very deep waves and nearly killed her in the process, and the one about how her grandmother stops to talk to homeless people in town and calls them darling. Ola laughs at her tales and says that he must meet her soon. Fredrika promises that he shall; as soon as her grandmother returns from Spain, maybe they can go to her house in Båstad and spend the weekend there? She describes Gaby's home in Båstad with feeling, sets out in detail what her summer holidays have been like ever since she was a young child, how every day contains one surprise or another because Gaby is so restless and inventive and up to all kinds of crazy antics.

'She's kind of like me, even though she's seventy-five,' she tells Ola, who once again says he really must meet her soon. When Fredrika launches into an account of the time her grandmother took over a piano in a restaurant without asking for permission first, Mary excuses herself and starts clearing the table. The kids stopped eating ages ago and if she doesn't take the cakes away from Rolf, she jokes, she's frightened he's going to burst.

When Rolf has disappeared back to the garage, Fredrika and Ola lie down on the sofa in the living room and ask if they can switch the TV on. Mary, who is still dealing with the dishes in the kitchen, looks in on them from time to time, asks if they'd like their cups refilling, or maybe some cakes or buns in front of the TV, but they refuse everything. Still stuffed, they say.

They have arranged themselves on top of one another on the sofa, in a way that feels intimate, almost sexual. Fredrika uses Ola's crotch as a sort of headrest, which makes Mary feel embarrassed every time she comes anywhere near them.

They're watching a documentary about South Africa. From the kitchen island Mary tells them that South Africa is one of the most beautiful countries in the world, and ever since she visited Kruger National Park when she was young, she has never stopped dreaming of going back. Immersed in her memories, she describes the light, the smells, the nature, but when neither of them replies with more than a brief remark, she stops talking and tries to give her full attention to the dishwasher instead.

At half past four it's time to give the kids a lift back to the station. Mary hadn't been able to work out quite why it had to be the five o'clock train, but it was something to do with a Sunday tradition at Klarre's and some programme on MTV that Mary had never heard of. By this stage she has given up hope of them staying for dinner, and neither of them has accepted her suggestion of going down to the cottage to see how prettily she's decorated it, either.

'Maybe in a minute,' says Fredrika, but that minute never seems to come and suddenly it's half past four.

In the station car park they embrace again. Mary thanks them for coming and Fredrika thanks her for all the presents. Ola thanks her for the coffee and cakes and Mary says it's just a pleasure to have the excuse for baking and making things nice. When they've finished thanking one another and Fredrika has promised to give Mary's love to her little brother, she and Ola walk towards the station building. Mary remains standing beside the car. She keeps waving until she sees their backs disappear through the automatic doors, and only then does she permit herself a cigarette from her handbag.

When she's home again and about to hang her new dress back in the wardrobe, she notices that there's a dark stain on the front of it. It's rust-coloured, the size of a five-kronor piece and right in the middle of the bust. She suspects it's blood at first, but when she sniffs at it she finds it's coffee. She can't decide whether it's worth an attempt to rescue it with some stain remover, or whether she should just throw it in the bin right now. No one appeared to think she looked particularly good in it. Rolf's only reaction when she'd shown it off was to ask if she thought the youngsters would dress up, and Fredrika's sole comment was on her new hairstyle, which she had called 'different'. Mary nearly froze in the car and had to hold her stomach in all day so that she didn't split the thin fabric at the waist. She decides to put off any decision about what she ought to do with the dress and puts it back in the wardrobe. Rolf would definitely be annoyed if he saw that she'd stuffed it into the bin after only one day's use.

*

She will at least keep on the elegant underwear. Just because the dress turned out to be useless, the lacy bra and the thong don't have to suffer the same fate. It would be a waste not to make use of them, especially now that she's made an effort to wear them all day. And it's actually been a long time since she and Rolf had sex, so long she can't remember exactly when it was. Rolf has never been the passionate type, but he seldom says no when she offers herself. And he has a certain predilection for lace and bras where the nipples show through the fabric, she's known that for a long time.

It was once a sure way to get him going. It was just a case of putting on the right sort of underwear, pretending she had something to attend to which required walking through the house in said underwear, and she could count on him ambushing her en route. It's been a while since she's used that trick, and, standing in the bedroom, she wonders whether it isn't about time she revived it. She can hear Rolf moving about between the kitchen and the sofa in the living room. It sounds as though he's opening and closing the fridge. He's probably having a third helping of the leftover princess cake. She hears his heavy tread as he descends the two steps that link the living room and the kitchen area in the open-plan arrangement, the grunt as he sinks onto the sofa, the sound of the TV channels changing as he wonders what he'll watch tonight.

Soon, she decides, she'll go out to him in her underwear. She'll just let him finish eating what's on his plate first. Then she'll sit next to him on the sofa, say 'Hi' in a slightly deeper voice than usual, upon which he'll turn his gaze towards her. He'll be caught by surprise at first, but he'll quickly recover, and when he does he'll respond with a 'Hi' that sounds very much like her own, but deeper still, and he'll reach out a hand towards her. He'll stroke her shoulder but his hand will soon find its way to her breast. Maybe he'll articulate what's in his thoughts, that she's incredibly sexy in her underwear. But they will definitely have sex, and he will definitely be attentive to her enjoyment too, because Rolf is that sort of person. And when they've had sex on the sofa in front of the television, she'll feel in a much better mood than she does at the moment, she knows.

She stands by the door, opens it a fraction, listens for sounds from the sofa below. When she's made sure it's all quiet on the sofa where Rolf is sitting, she opens the door, takes a few cautious steps across the dining room floor, and has almost reached the stairs to make her entrance, when the telephone rings.

'Dammit,' says Rolf, fumbling for the portable phone next to him on the sofa. 'That gave me a fright,' he mutters to himself, before answering, 'Yes, Roffe here?'

Mary freezes at the top of the steps down to the living room, unsure whether it's the right time to carry on down to the sofa, or whether she ought to go back to the bedroom. Before she can make up her mind, she needs to know who's ringing. If it's John wanting to discuss Fredrika's visit, she'd like to take the call. In that case she'll have to fetch her dressing gown from the bathroom before she can sit in the office and talk. There's no way she'll be able to concentrate on a conversation with her ex-husband about their daughter, if she's sitting shivering in her bra and pants in Rolf's office. If it's Bill or Jenina, she decides she'll go back into the bedroom. It could take some time, he could be sitting there for half an hour or more and she can't face listening to that conversation. She'd rather wait in the bedroom.

It's neither Bill nor Jenina on the phone. It's Susanne from the house further up the forest road, who's just about to take an evening walk with her dogs and wonders if Rolf and Mary would like to join her. Mary grasps this when Rolf laughs and says he really *ought* to join her, having eaten a hell of a lot of cake this evening.

'Mary's eldest was here celebrating her birthday,' he explains, whereupon Susanne clearly says something funny, because he laughs again, louder this time, and says, 'Yeah, exactly.'

He's still not detected Mary standing there half-naked. Nor does he see her go back into the bedroom, where she sits down on the edge of the bed. He's too busy arranging a time and place with Susanne to think about where in the house Mary might be just now. When he calls up from the hall a few moments later, she's already put on leggings and a T-shirt over her underclothes.

'Did you want to come too, by the way?' he shouts before he leaves.

'Thanks, but I'm a bit too tired this evening,' she answers from the edge of the bed. 'But say hello to Susanne from me.'

JOHN

Ulla Eriksson is well over seventy and runs a clinic in her own home. She's a licensed psychologist who lives in a bungalow with white stone cladding about half an hour's drive from the farm on the E20, towards Kungsör. He and Netta drove there after the morning session in the stable. On the journey he took the opportunity to question Netta about Ulla's credentials. He admitted he thought it was a bit weird to receive patients in one's own home. In the car Netta swore that everything was in order on that score. Many psychologists work like that, she said, and Ulla Eriksson, moreover, is both qualified and experienced. Retired but still active, with good references. Both Charlotte at the dog club and Maj-Li in the choir have been there with their other halves.

'She's absolutely not into any hocus-pocus, she's a proper psychologist,' Netta said, 'worked for decades for the local authority before she retired.'

When Netta first announced that she wanted them both to visit a psychologist, he couldn't for the life of him understand why the two of them, of all couples, would want to go into therapy. They're good together, aren't they? They have a wide social circle and a regular sex life. They hardly ever argue, apart from niceties like cleaning and facets of parenting.

But Netta stood her ground. Her contention was that there wasn't any danger, they were just going to give the relationship 'a health check', as a kind of precautionary measure, nothing more serious than that. So here they now sit. On a dark green sofa visibly sagging in the middle. He and Netta both slide inwards towards each other repeatedly, but it doesn't bother him. It's not as if he has anything against sitting close to his own wife. In the corner of the room there's a fireplace and the pictures hanging on the walls indicate that Ulla once married a younger version of the man who let them in through the patio door at the back of the house just over a quarter of an hour ago. The walls also tell him that Ulla has at least two children, three or four grandchildren and a fondness for vast landscapes painted in oils.

On the sofa beside him Netta is halfway through an account of how their relationship began. She has covered both the glances between the spectators' seats at the stables and the fruit basket and she's now reached the period when they kept it secret from the children and the outside world. He could tell she enjoyed describing their first fumbling lovemaking on the Finland ferry as the moment when she knew she really 'had him hooked'.

Up to now no one has asked him to speak, and he's fine with that, he doesn't know if he'd have much to add anyway. Besides, it's Netta who has need for this, not him. He's here mostly as company for her, like the good husband he tries to be. A good husband, who is without question interested in nurturing the relationship but who maybe didn't of his own accord think there was cause to bring a third party into the process. But absolutely. As far as he's concerned Netta is welcome to share, if it makes her feel better. He's not someone to object to his partner's needs, quite the reverse. And in any case the tale about the ferry is quite an amusing story.

Sitting opposite them, Ulla Eriksson doesn't look like a psychologist, at any rate not like the psychologist he and Mary had met before the divorce. Where Maud Forsblom wore silk blouses and knee-length skirts, Ulla wears a dark green fleece and baggy trousers tucked into pair of thick socks that look too big for her. Her hairstyle, just like her thick spectacle frames, looks as though it belongs in the seventies. The thin plait is probably greyer now than it was then, but something tells him it's been her signature feature throughout the greater part of her professional life.

Ulla leans back in her chair and listens intently to what Netta is saying. There's a notebook on her knee, but up to now she hasn't picked it up once. He can't help wondering if deep down Ulla Eriksson isn't also asking herself why they're there. Presumably she views them as a useful addition to her pension rather than a couple in true crisis. At least that's what he would have thought, if he were Ulla Eriksson.

Besides, isn't that usually the first thing you talk about? Why you've come to the clinic? Don't you usually start with the actual reason, and then move on to the account of the relationship and how it began? At least it was the last time he did this. Netta seems so affected by her own romantic tale that there's no doubt whatsoever about whether or not she loves him deeply. Ulla also seems touched, smiling at the part about the hotel in Trosa where Netta proposed on the floor beside the bed. Sometimes she turns her gaze to him and he smiles too and gives a nod in agreement. It was a great night in Trosa, he wants her to know that he thinks so as well. And the fact that she actually proposed in a place called Trosa without her trousers is also pretty funny. He smiles and strokes Netta's back as she speaks.

Her mood changes when she reaches the move from Stockholm. He tries to listen carefully so he doesn't miss any details, paying particular attention when she describes how the arguments between herself, John and the children, above all Fredrika, have escalated over the years since they moved to the farm. She speaks of tense silences between them lasting days and of his inability to address the problem and take a side. She calls him evasive and afraid of conflict, says she never really knows where she stands with him nowadays. She sounds more and more upset as she goes on, and when she reaches her conclusion that it feels as though their family now consists of two camps waging a silent war against each other, her voice cracks and she starts crying.

'The worst thing is I feel so bloody lonely all the time,' she weeps.

What's she talking about? What war does she mean? Who's at war with whom? This doesn't feel like the right time to ask, because Netta's doing the talking at the moment, and if there's one thing he learned with Mary about taking turns at speaking, it's that you can't interrupt your partner in the therapy room. That's rule number one when you go to marriage guidance. You have to wait your turn, even if you don't understand or agree with what your partner's saying.

When Netta leans forward to take a handkerchief from Ulla's coffee table, he seizes the chance to move his hand from her back, which he's been patting, to her shoulder, like a light massage, in a show of sympathy.

Netta is facing away from him, so he can't really gauge how she reacts, but she doesn't pull away, so he takes it as a sign that he can continue.

Now she is saying that lately she has felt alone in their relationship, that she believes that she has borne the greatest burden in the family and had to play the part of the villain in every domestic drama for several years. She says that doesn't matter to her, she doesn't mind being the villain, but it would be nice if she at least had her partner's support now and then.

As she says this she turns towards him for the first time since she started talking. It's no doubt totally inappropriate of him, but he can't help noting how sweet she is when she cries. She really is what he would call an attractive weeper. When Netta cries her face isn't contorted into something unrecognisable, like it is with some women, but all her features are maintained and the weeping is concentrated in her eyes, like when people cry in films. The tears seem to run slowly down her cheeks, no runnel of snot under her nose, no dark smudge of make-up under her eyes or red patches above her eyelids. Unlike Mary, Netta's tears transform her into someone you want to take care of, someone you just have to support, someone you're prepared to go along with in whatever her heart desires.

The embrace that follows comes spontaneously. It's not in order to make Ulla think he's good to open his arms and pull Netta to his chest, quite the contrary. It's instinctive, and Netta doesn't resist. With a big sigh she sinks against him, and instantly it's as though she has run out of words. A stillness descends, not only between him and her, but over the whole room. The kind of stillness that Netta almost never has. They sit like that for a while, motionless together, and he can feel the beat of her heart against his own. At one point he looks up and meets Ulla's eye. She nods again, this time with an expression he guesses is caused by being moved herself, but he quickly drops his gaze. It feels odd to be looking at Ulla while he's hugging his wife. He lowers his eyes to Netta, kisses her hair, whispers that he's sorry, he didn't know, that it goes without saying they'll sort this out.

'Of course we'll figure this out, won't we? I love you.'

When he starts the car and turns out of Ulla Eriksson's street, he believes that both he and Netta know that this will be the last time they're here. They don't need a therapist. All they need is each other, and they have that already. From now on he will be better, he promised that solemnly and he intends to keep that promise. Netta will be better too. She is going to talk to him about how she feels and help him to understand before things boil over.

Next to him in the front seat Netta looks content. She lays her hand on his thigh, in the place where she always used to rest it when they were out in the car together in the past. When they're on the E20 and he can drive with only one hand on the wheel, he lays his hand on top of hers and squeezes it in return. They sit like that for several kilometres, silent beside each other in the front seat. Sometimes she strokes his groin, gently runs her finger down the crease where his crotch meets his thigh, and his body reacts in the same way it did before. Out of the corner of his eye he can see she's proud when she realises her touch still works, that she still has that effect on him. She carries on teasing for a while but stops when she realises he's having difficulty concentrating on the road.

They continue their journey in silence. The air between them is clearer now, he can feel it distinctly in the car. This has been the start of something, it's hard to say what, but something better at any rate. He believes that they can both sense that. And at least he knows what he's going to do with her once they're back at the farm. The only question is whether they do it in the stable, for a change.

Mary

She should probably put him on the spot, or at least ask why it's suddenly so important to accompany Susanne on her dog walks several evenings a week, but she can't be bothered. She already knows what he would say if she did. He would point to his stomach and say he needs the exercise, would add that it's always nice to have a bit of company, then would imply that she might benefit from some activity herself. He would never confirm Mary's observation that it shows by a mile that he likes Susanne best of all the neighbours, and that he might have peered a tad too deeply down her cleavage at the crayfish party in August. He's a decent man. A decent man who just at the moment needs the exercise he gets by accompanying Susanne on her dog walks pretty much every evening. Whatever his motive, Mary intends to humour him. If truth be told, it's actually been pleasant to have the house to herself while he's been out.

Only when Gaby comes to visit does the atmosphere around Rolf's walks become a little strained. Gaby really wants to go with Rolf when he goes out walking. And she doesn't notice, or pretends not to notice, that Rolf tries to put her off. It sounds marvellous, she thinks. She absolutely *adores* the forest, she says, starting to put on her outdoor clothes.

Mary registers Rolf's resigned look as he stands by the door, but she doesn't know what she can do to help him. She has never managed to stop her mother doing what she's made up her mind to do, and she very much doubts this evening would be a first on that score. Besides, Gaby seems to prefer Rolf's company to her own. Over the last few days she's spent more time out in the workshop with him than up at the house with her. In all probability he reminds her of the life she herself had for so long. Gaby has always esteemed careers in aviation more highly than any other. She never tires of talking about her years as a young stewardess when she succeeded in snaring her very own pilot, as luck would have it the most dashing of them all. Even tonight, as she accompanies him through the door, she is talking about the airline industry as if it were their own private concern.

When Gaby's voice has receded along the path that links Rolf's garden with Susanne and Jocke's, Mary replenishes her glass and sits down at his computer in the office. She opens the email program, keys in her username and password and waits. When the little beachball has stopped spinning on the screen she discovers she has new mail in her inbox. The message is difficult to read, since all the accented vowels have been replaced by question marks and exclamation marks, but after spending some time deciphering the text, she sees that a certain Vivianne Berntsson in Hässleholm wants to purchase not one, but two of the dog beds she's placed adverts for in the local dog club's newsletter.

When she clicks on the little button in the corner to reply to Vivianne's message, she scarcely dare breathe. She has never received an order from one of her adverts, has never posted something she herself has made to an unknown person at the other end of the country, has never answered an email from a customer. This is… really something, isn't it?

She formulates her response professionally. At the bottom of the message she pastes in a piece of text about the return policy, which she's saved in the file of documents on how to sell goods by mail order. The pasted section is of a different font size to the text in the rest of the message. She struggles for a while to try to solve the problem, but nothing works. It will have to do. She taps the key with the arrow and hears a ping as the message whisks away. She goes back to the mail containing Vivianne's order and reads it again. And then again. This is a cause for celebration.

When Rolf returns from his walk with Gaby and Susanne, he is stony-faced. This Saturday evening has obviously not provided as pleasant a walk as usual and he clearly regards it as Mary's fault, at least indirectly, for when she leads him into the living room and shows him the table laid with cheese and champagne glasses, he mumbles that he doesn't fancy it and disappears into the toilet in the hall. He's in there for a long time, so long that Gaby comes in and starts to help herself to the Gorgonzola, crackers and slices of pear.

'That's wonderful, darling,' she says when Mary shares the news about the order from Hässleholm. She takes another cracker, another slice of pear and a substantial piece of cheese, before she continues.

'Oh, but what a lovely woman that Susanne is! Don't you agree? And such beautiful dogs! Have you seen them? Incredibly dainty!'

At least Rolf's congratulations are warmer than her mum's.

'Wow! That's fantastic! Congratulations!' he says, once he's come out of the toilet and given her a hug beside the sofa. He insists he's full and doesn't really feel like champagne or cheese, but he'll have half a glass anyway, for Mary's sake, if nothing else. Of course she must raise a glass to her first order.

They toast each other, Gaby from the sofa and Rolf and Mary from the end of the coffee table. 'Yummy,' says Gaby. 'Mmm, very good,' says Rolf, before congratulating Mary again and then asking how much she charges for a dog bed.

For a second Mary weighs up whether to lie, or at least exaggerate, and say that they cost more than they actually do. But when she reminds herself that he can easily check her figures with a few clicks on his computer, she gives him the truth instead. Two hundred kronor apiece. Or one hundred and ninety to be precise. Plus twenty-five for the postage. So nearer five hundred in total. Well, four hundred and fifty, anyway. Her reply causes Rolf to scratch his head, still tousled after the walk in the wind.

'So...just over four hundred kronor for... How many hours work, did you say? And the cost of materials? Does it really add up, this thing?'

Mary is just starting to explain her thinking on her pricing model, when Gaby shoots up from the sofa and almost runs out into the hall. Mary has only come as far as justifying her decision not to take any payment for her own time to begin with, in order to put herself on the map and be able to compete on price, when Gaby's voice interrupts them. Waving her finger vigorously in the air, she shouts from the door between the living room and the hall.

'Darling! I just had a brilliant idea! What do you say if *I* buy two of your dog beds and then I can give them to Susanne as a present? She has two dogs, hasn't she? Wouldn't that be absolutely fantastic? Let me see… I'll go and get my chequebook. Was it four hundred? Have you time to make them tomorrow, do you think? Then I can give them to her as a surprise on the walk tomorrow evening. Oh, I can't wait!'

Gaby's back is swallowed up by the darkness in the hall and she's gone. In the living room Rolf looks at Mary in irritation and mouths: 'Bloody hell! Wasn't she supposed to be going home tomorrow?' Mary does what she can to nip her mother's notion in the bud, shouting with as much determination as she can muster into the hall that this won't work at all, she can't possibly make two dog beds in a day, she doesn't even have enough fabric at home to make two more beds, and besides Susanne's dogs are far too big, this type of dog bed is only suitable for small dogs.

'It was a great idea, Mum, but I'm afraid it's not going to work…'

Her mum shouts back from the hall.

'Nonsense! Everything works if you put your mind to it. Here you are, I found a five-hundred note. Take it, so you'll have a bit extra as well!'

JOHN

It feels quite formal to be sitting at the dinner table this evening. It's not often that all the children are at home at the same time nowadays, and even less frequent for them all to be at home without Fredrika and Netta at daggers drawn with each other, or else Fredrika and Victor. Sometimes it's Fredrika and Jenny, but that seldom manifests in anything other than them sitting in silence and avoiding eye contact across the table. Fredrika has a tendency to be implicated in most of the conflicts that smoulder under the surface in this family. She's also the one to be absent most often in the evenings. But tonight she hasn't even been nagging for a lift after dinner to Ola's flat in town, which he regards as something of a miracle. He'd really like to ask if anything's happened, but he's too apprehensive. He doesn't want to risk spoiling the atmosphere when it seems to be so good and everyone's at home together.

For the same reason he doesn't want to dive straight into the sausage stroganoff steaming in the pot on the table. Netta isn't sitting down yet and he wants to wait for her. She was about to join them at the table a little while ago when the phone rang and after she'd told the caller – presumably Mary – that Victor and Fredrika would ring back later, she decided that she had to fetch something from the hall before she could start eating.

He remains at the table with the children, who already seem to be tired of waiting and have started to help themselves to rice and hot stroganoff. He carries on waiting. It feels the nicest thing to do.

When Netta comes in and sits down opposite him, she has a little package in her hand. The package is rectangular, the shape of a large matchbox, the kind they use for lighting the boiler in the basement. The little box is shiny and looks as though it's been wrapped in aluminium foil. Netta's face is full of anticipation as she pushes the package across the table towards him. The children watch him as he picks it up and weighs it in his hand. Christ, he's thinking, have I forgotten our wedding anniversary again? At the same time he tries to work out what date it is.

With relief he confirms to himself that he hasn't missed an anniversary, or a birthday or a name day. He breathes out and starts to peel off the aluminium foil from the little carton, saying 'Ooh!' and 'What can this be?' while stripping off layer after layer of shiny paper. The box in his hand weighs almost nothing. So it can't be a new pocketknife, which was his first guess, or a small torch, which was his second.

He speeds up and rips off the last bit of foil. In the little box there's a white paper strip with a blue handle. On the white part of the strip there are two red lines running across. He gazes at the strip in the box for a few seconds. He knows what the two lines mean, understands their significance in theory, but he dare not say anything. Not before he's confirmed that she's not making fun of him.

Opposite him Netta's expression has changed. Her artful smile has evaporated and now she's sitting with tears in her eyes and a very different kind of smile. Unable to decide what sort of tears they are, he instinctively reaches forward, takes her hand in his and, although he really doesn't have to ask, he does, 'Is it true?'

She doesn't need to nod for him to know it's true, but she does anyway, and after the nod she starts to laugh, and that acts as a signal in the room for the children to start shrieking 'Congratulations!' and to hug them, and the commotion in the kitchen is a fact.

Fredrika laughs and says he's going to be a 'really old dad', then says the baby can have her room as she'll be leaving home soon anyway. Jenny looks as though she's crying too; she hugs her mum from behind and whispers something he can't hear, because now Victor is standing behind him and thumping him on the back, saying, 'Great, huh? You didn't see that coming, admit it,' and John doesn't know how to respond, because he hasn't had time to feel anything, but he thinks the feeling is that it's great. Simply a little unexpected.

He and Netta gave up on the baby front several years ago. They tried for a couple of years in the beginning, but when nothing happened, they called it a day. Now he's almost old, nearer fifty than forty, and in the hubbub around the kitchen table he doesn't really know what he ought to think about it.

All the same, it is what it is, obviously. And everyone around him at the moment seems thrilled. Even Fredrika is grinning, and she's not someone who normally grins. As a matter of fact she looks genuinely happy for them.

Not to mention Netta, who is still laughing through her tears when he looks at her, and who has kept her little hand nestled in his large fist beside the plate. Yes, he thinks, he is happy. He is really happy. Dammit! He's going to be a dad again!

After he's gone round the corner of the table and taken Netta's face in his hands, and they've kissed, and her tears have wetted his cheeks, he holds her away from him. He looks at her intently for a few seconds, before he says,

'OK... Let's do it then? One more lap?'

Netta laughs through her tears.

'Too bloody right! At least one more lap.'

Mary

By the end of the second day the smell of sweat is coming from her armpits. It's not a very marked odour, definitely not as repellent as the old men outside the off-licence in the city centre. Up to now it's been barely noticeable. She's only really aware of it when she lifts her arms up to reach the topmost fabrics on the shelf or when she bends down to pick something up from her store of provisions under the kitchen sofa. When she reaches for the crispbread, or the wine, or the water can or the nuts, she catches the whiff, which serves as a reminder that it's only a matter of time before she has to interrupt her stay in the cottage. To fill the water can, if nothing else. It's going to have to happen soon, and it's bothering her, because Rolf is off work for two more days and she doesn't want to speak to him at the moment. She'd rather not see him at all. Best of all would be if she could just stay here for good.

He insists on coming out every now and then and knocking on the door. He gives a cautious tap and tries the door, which is always locked. Then he sometimes starts talking to the door. He speaks softly, not wanting to attract the neighbours' attention, when he asks her how she is, says she 'must eat something, at least', wonders if she'd like him to go out of the house for a while so that she can have it to herself for a few hours.

Mary doesn't reply to any of it. She just turns the radio up and lets the music speak on her behalf. She has absolutely no need to talk to him at present. Nor any need to 'eat something, at least', or to go up to the house to be on her own for a few hours. She's on her own now. She has peanuts in the bowl, water in the can, wine in the kitchen cabinet and cigarettes to last several weeks. She can knit and sew and listen to her radio. What more could she need? Besides, she's relatively sure that she's doing everyone a favour, herself included, by not seeing anyone at the moment.

That they would end up at this point sooner or later is no surprise. However, she hadn't expected it of Rolf that he would go behind her back and involve Gaby. And now she's locked in the sewing workshop with two bills she can't pay, and her mum and Rolf in secret cahoots to try and teach her a lesson.

She's been aware of Rolf's view for quite a long time. It became increasingly clear during conversations at the dinner table in which he has pretty much explicitly criticised her for a variety of actions and personal characteristics he would like to see her lose. He thinks she's extravagant, squandering money she hasn't earned herself, that she's elusive, spending more time in the sewing cabin than with him, that she's naïve not to have created a 'sustainable budget' for her business and in addition that she's practically an alcoholic for occasionally having a glass of wine when he chooses not to.

She should have realised last autumn when he threatened to hold back his contribution to their joint account and give her cash instead every time she went out shopping. Dinner that day had ended with her getting up from the table with a force that sent the carbonara flying halfway across the cloth. Rolf hadn't helped to clean it up. Instead he stayed calmly where he was and didn't even raise his voice when he asked her to simmer down and come back and discuss it with him 'like an adult'. She shouted back from the terrace that it was impossible to speak to him like an adult if he seriously considered giving her pocket money as if she were a child. Since that time there's been no more discussion of her meal ticket. But obviously the matter wasn't closed, and Mary blames herself for not picking up on the signals. They've been there to see all the time. It's been evident in his eyes every time she's opened a bottle of wine at dinner, every time there's been a delivery of fabric from the wholesaler, every time she returns after one of her stints in the sewing cabin. It's the disappointed look he's given her, the one that says, 'I thought better of you.' Why didn't she grasp where it was heading?

She of all people ought to know that look of disappointment. She's been on the receiving end of that look her entire life. If her mum was the first, then John was the second, but he was far from the last. After John came the children, then Hans and now Rolf.

Over the years she's learned the best way to deal with the look, or so she thought. For as long as possible the look should be met with a smile, a nonchalant expression that indicates cool indifference. The look should never be met with an apologetic question, which provides the recipient with the opportunity to verbalise their criticism. 'Is there something wrong?' is forbidden, as is, 'What are you thinking?'

If, on the other hand, you meet the disappointed look with an unconcerned smile, more than half the time it ends right there. With pointed looks exchanged in the hall, or the kitchen, or any one of the many places you bump into one another when you share a home. She knows from experience that few people are seriously prepared to face the consequences of following the dialogue through to its conclusion. John wasn't and she didn't believe Rolf would be either.

But it turns out she was wrong. Because when both her mum and Rolf, only a week apart, firmly informed her that unfortunately they would no longer give her financial assistance, it all became quite clear. Her mum would no longer help her pay the company's bills, and Rolf didn't intend to shoulder the household and food costs alone from now on, she was told. They had conspired behind her back, and however hard she tried to work out when exactly it had happened, she drew a blank. Both Gaby and Rolf strenuously denied it. Both maintained there was definitely no connection, that each for their part and in all good faith just wanted what was best for her. They both emphasised that they weren't doing it to be mean to her, quite the reverse. They just wanted her to feel good about herself. That was exactly what they said, and it made no difference what she attempted to say in her defence.

Immediately after the separate but almost identical messages from Rolf and Gaby, Mary locked herself in the sewing cabin. And after that she stopped answering when her mother rang and Rolf came down with the phone. It will soon have been two days and it hasn't been particularly difficult. She can have a pee behind the lilac bush and she can keep ignoring Rolf for a few more days. He's going to Thailand the day after tomorrow – she can certainly hold out until then.

It's beginning to get dark outside the cabin windows when he knocks again. She's on the point of shouting through the wall that he can go to hell, has just drawn the breath into her lungs to utter the first words of the day, but he gets in first.

'I'll leave the phone here,' his muffled voice comes through the door. 'It's Fredrika, she says it's important.'

At her daughter's name Mary leaps off the sofa where she's spent the afternoon. She puts the empty wine glass on the chest, before – on legs that are more unsteady than she'd expected – creeping up to the door. Without opening it, she hisses at Rolf to go back up to the house, and she doesn't unlock it until she hears the clatter of his wooden clogs on the terrace and then the familiar click of the patio door. She opens it a crack, just enough to stick her arm out and scoop up the telephone. The evening air outside is cold on her bare skin. She holds the phone at arm's length while she closes the door and clears her throat. She ignores the sour taste of phlegm on her palate and swallows it, before putting the receiver to her ear and saying in her cheeriest tone, her most dependable Mum voice:

'Hi, sweetheart. Sorry you had to wait! I'm just doing a bit of sewing down here in the cottage. How's my little darling?'

If Rolf had been able to see her now from the house, if, for example, he'd been standing at the kitchen window with a little pair of binoculars and she hadn't drawn the curtains of the only window in the cottage facing the house two days ago, he would surely have been relieved by what he saw. He would have seen

Mary listening intently to her daughter's voice on the phone, and first her eyes and then her entire mouth widening at Fredrika's news. Shortly after that he would have seen Mary clapping her hands to her lips to smother what initially looked like a sob or a guffaw; it would have been hard to decide which in the first few seconds. He would probably have kept on looking and seen her roar with laughter after she'd hung up. He couldn't have heard what Fredrika's news was, but he would have both heard and seen that the manner in which Mary laughed was spontaneous and resounding, a way he had never heard her laugh before. If the binoculars had been particularly sharp he would also have seen her eyes filled with tears from all the laughing. If he'd seen that, he would probably been relieved. How nice, he might have thought, she seems to be in a good mood again. Maybe we can put this stupid argument behind us.

But Rolf sees nothing of what's happening in the cottage. He has no binoculars and Mary has drawn the curtains. Instead he's leaning back on the sofa in front of the television, wondering when he should go back across the lawn to retrieve the phone. His attention has been caught by something on the news, maybe it's the hockey, and he decides to leave the phone where it is. He has another one in the office, after all. And, he thinks, it will probably do Mary good to speak to Fredrika. He knows how much Mary misses the children when they're not with her.

It will be the following morning before he steps across the wet grass and finds the cordless telephone in the middle of the lawn. It will be on a level with the hall window in the cottage and when he sees it, he'll scratch his head, in the way he always scratches his head when he's thinking, for the life of him not able to understand how and why the telephone has ended up there. He won't have heard or seen her laughing hysterically when she's finished the call, or opening the window and slinging the phone out with a howl. Nor will he have heard the thud when the phone landed on the lawn after a silent bounce, or the crash as she banged the window shut. When he finds the phone there the next morning, he'll scratch his head and wonder, but he'll never know for sure, because she'll never tell him why she threw it, and when she does come to repeat what her daughter told her, she has totally forgotten why she thought it was all so hysterically funny. She'll use her normal voice, slightly nonchalant, low-key, casual, as if it doesn't matter. Fredrika and Victor are going to have a little brother or sister, she'll say, and then they won't talk about it anymore, because they'll have more important things to talk about. But not today. It will be another twenty-four hours before she comes back up to the house.

John

Something simple with the family, they'd said, but when the time comes to celebrate his birthday, they still have to book a long table at the Akropolis restaurant in the centre of Eskilstuna to accommodate everyone. Fredrika wanted Ola to come and Jenny brought Gustav, so that made seven with just them. When Hasse and Gunilla asked if they could come too, they could scarcely say no. The more the merrier, they reasoned, and phoned the restaurant to increase the number for the booking.

When they meet up in the entrance they hug and laugh at how unusual it is to see each other dressed in something other than work clothes. Netta is wearing her red dress and black high heels, Hasse has on brown chinos with his shirt tucked in, Fredrika has jeans without holes in the thighs and Jenny is wearing a tie-neck blouse with puffed sleeves. Victor is wearing an off-white rib-knit sweater and John himself has put on one of his suits from the years when he still had the occasional reason for dressing up. He almost changed his mind before they set off, there was something about the way it was sitting on the shoulders and it also felt slightly too dressy to wear a Boss suit for a dinner to celebrate a perfectly ordinary birthday, but Netta managed to convince him to keep the suit on.

'Doesn't it look a bit too big?' he asked, staring into the mirror in the bedroom.

By 'too big' he was referring to the space between his stomach and the jacket, which must have become larger than he remembered it during his days in the office. He turned in front of the mirror and wondered if he'd lost weight. Did he really fill this suit once? Didn't he look a bit odd?

'God, no. You're sexy as hell. People just want to eat you up,' Netta had said, giving him a hug from behind, which was enough for him to give in and keep the dark grey suit on.

The evening at the Akropolis begins with champagne. At least for the majority of those around the table. Victor, who's too young, and Netta, who's pregnant, and Gunilla, who's driving tonight, have to make do with Pommac, but you can't tell, as they too are drinking from champagne glasses. They make the first toast standing around the table.

'Here's to our beloved John, who's forty-eight today!' Netta says from the end of the table.

John shushes her, while raising his glass and nodding to the assembled company.

Hasse and Gunilla start laughing at his embarrassed shushing and say forty-eight is no age at all, he has nothing to be ashamed of, just look at them! Nearer seventy and very happy about it!

And yet he is. Ashamed. He can't escape the feeling that there's something embarrassing about sitting in a suit that's too big for him on his forty-eighth birthday with a distinctly pregnant younger woman at his side. He felt the same at the maternity clinic when they did the ultrasound test last week. He felt ashamed when he greeted their midwife, who was called Caroline and didn't look markedly older than Jenny. When he shook the midwife's hand, he couldn't help wondering if deep down she thought he was too old for all this. Doesn't he realise he'll be over sixty when the kid leaves school, he imagined her thinking as she directed him to the chair beside the examination table on which Netta was lying propped up.

Netta had been both businesslike and determined in the car on the way to the clinic, when she explained to John that there was 'some risk' that the baby would have a chromosomal abnormality because she was over thirty-five, but she definitely wanted to keep the baby regardless. John, who hadn't given any thought to the risk of a chromosomal abnormality or the possibility of terminating the pregnancy if that proved to be the case, was horrified at her words. In the car he asked Netta to explain exactly how great the increased risk was, but she couldn't. It was just something she'd heard, she said, that older mothers ran a higher risk than younger ones. But, she went on, everything was sure to be fine and whatever happened, they would work it out together.

'We're going to love this little one no matter what, aren't we?' she says, squeezing his thigh, and John had nodded and said, yes, of course they would love their child. Just over half an hour later they received a reassuring message from Caroline and that put an end to that anxiety.

Since that day they've called the baby the Pearl. It began as a private joke between him and Netta but soon spread through the rest of the family. Now they all call the baby the Pearl and, as it transpires at the restaurant, obviously the name has reached Hasse's and Gunilla's ears, for Gunilla asks at the table how the Pearl is doing today.

Netta strokes her bump and answers that the Pearl is doing absolutely wonderfully, thank you for asking, and then lays her hand on top of John's, as if to demonstrate that it would be appropriate for him to stroke the Pearl's outer layer of protection too, since they're talking about her. He takes the hint and does as he's told, stroking the red fabric at the top of Netta's stomach and saying that they will be at the halfway point by the end of this week.

'It's incredibly exciting,' Gunilla says.

'You'll have your work cut out for you now,' Hasse chuckles.

'I can't wait,' says Netta, lacing her fingers with John's on top of her stomach.

If it weren't for her stomach, you would hardly notice that Netta is expecting. He doesn't understand what happens on a purely physical level, but she's as active today as she was before she became pregnant. Almost more active. There's still choir on Mondays and dog club on Thursdays. And then the constant chauffeuring of children who have to be taken to riding lessons and boyfriends and football training and mates' houses. In addition, she takes care of the both the animals and the farm in a way that makes him ashamed that there's so much he doesn't manage to do.

He tries to make her rest, tells her again and again that he has nothing against doing a bit more, especially now she's getting bigger every week, that even if it takes him a shade longer than her – it's his back that's bothering him again as usual – he would really like to help. She laughs when he says that and maintains that she can't sit still, so she might as well do something useful while she waits. She says that manual work has always made her feel good, that she has loads of energy, especially now, when she's so happy.

It's difficult not to believe what she says. It's obvious she's feeling good by the atmosphere at home, by the almost complete end to the arguments between her and the children. It's obvious in the way she chats to the animals, laughs more, teases him affectionately again. And above all it's obvious in the way she wants to have sex with him all the time. Several times a day, if she has the chance. Of course it's not always possible, but he tries to make himself available whenever he can, even if he is quite tired some days.

It's hard for him to admit he's tired, particularly as she's the one who has a right be tired at the moment, not him. He tries to grit his teeth, stand up straight and keep on working at his usual pace. He does his stretching exercises in secret in the bedroom after Netta gets up, and they help to a certain degree. Yet he can't claim to feel as fresh today as he did when Mary was expecting Fredrika. At that time it was Mary who was in a bad way, not him. He remembers her lying on their tangerine sofa on Tallvägen and complaining, from start to finish. Her hips ached, her stomach ached, and you couldn't get within a mile of her breasts. There was always something that stoked her self-pity. If it wasn't what a bore it was not being able to smoke, it was what a chore it was to move at all. Or go to work when she was feeling so ugly, and heavy, and fat. Sometimes she moaned because there was nothing interesting happening at the weekends, but when he tried to organise something she was too tired anyway and backed out at the last minute. There was no question of a sex life, none at all during either of her pregnancies and scarcely any afterwards.

Even so, he can't recall finding it annoying at the time. He remembers it as a period when he rose to the occasion when it was required: he cooked and shopped, did the washing-up and laundry, and later, when the babies arrived, he was the one who tended to them at night, without any complaint. He must have been a stronger man then, but it has been almost two decades. It would be pretty strange if his physical condition hadn't changed.

All the same, it's irritating to see how rusty his machinery has become. If it's not his back, then it's his stomach, or a fuzzy head for which the only remedy seems to be an extra hour's sleep in the morning. Last week he had a temperature that appeared from nowhere. It came on without warning in the afternoon and disappeared just as abruptly after two painkillers and a short rest. Netta fussed over him, despite him telling her to keep away in case he was infectious. She brought water and vitamin tablets, laid an extra blanket on top of the duvet and massaged his temples. She made a few phone calls the same day and now he has appointments with both a physiotherapist and a general practitioner at the beginning of next week. It wasn't his idea at all. If anything, it makes him feel like an overwrought hypochondriac, running to the doctor with a sudden temperature that's lasted a few hours. Something that would only preoccupy a weakling, in his opinion, but Netta was stubborn and wouldn't listen to his protests. She wants to take care of her little old man now he'll soon be a father again, she says.

Fredrika orders a glass of wine to go with the main course.

'The house red,' she says urbanely to the waiter, without asking John or Netta if it's OK. It's still a few months until she's eighteen and permitted to order alcohol in the pub, and when John leans across the table to remind her discreetly of this, she laughs in his face.

'You know I'm here every weekend, huh? The staff never check ID. Me and my friends, we've been coming here since we were, like, sixteen.'

He knew nothing of the kind. And he doesn't know how to react to his daughter's nonchalant attitude towards his concern. Even Ola seems to squirm uncomfortably in his seat at Fredrika's unexpected confession that she's been drinking alcohol in the pub since she was sixteen. Rules are rules, John feels like saying, and besides it's him, not Fredrika, who'll foot the bill in the end. As the person with legal responsibility he might reasonably have something to say concerning his daughter's order, and she should understand that. But plainly she doesn't, since she tilts her head to one side, strokes his cheek and says, 'Dear old Daddy,' in the same tone she employs for talking to a horse in the stable. Then she turns back to Ola, who's ordering a steak pizza and a large beer from the waiter. Disconcerted, John leans back in his chair and tries to catch Netta's eye for some support in any potential conflict over the wine issue, but she's busy talking to Jenny's new boyfriend, Gustav, and doesn't look in his direction. On the other side of the table the waiter has reached Hasse, who asks if he can recommend the veal schnitzel this evening. John gazes around the motley crew who have assembled to celebrate his birthday and decides to let it go. This time, he thinks. But just one glass, and that will be it.

Mary

They're no longer arguing when they drive Mary's belongings to Gaby's overnight flat in Stockholm's Gärdet. Quite the reverse. For the last few weeks the atmosphere between Rolf and her has been better than for quite a long time. It was as though they'd both become calmer and more peaceably disposed towards each other after they'd agreed to separate. Once the decision had been taken, neither of them could really understand why they hadn't reached it earlier. It was all so obvious. It was never her finances, or the sewing cabin, or the wine. The problem was simply that they're not compatible, and when they'd established that, it seemed to be a relief for them both. Everything was suddenly so clear. She had needed a reason to get away from her job and back to Sweden, and Rolf had needed company and support during the final phase of his divorce. He had a large house and she needed somewhere to live. She was good at cooking, and he was good at eating. It was actually never more complicated than that.

For this reason it wasn't very difficult to end it either. It had only taken one conversation the night she finally caved in and returned to the house after several days' exile in the sewing cabin. It took no more than an hour to come to an agreement. They would go their separate ways but still be friends, and all they needed to do was sit down together and draw up a plan, a plan that included a new place to live for her and practical help with the move from him, and then everything would work out for the best.

Naturally Gaby had been opposed to the idea of a friendly separation, but as the plan involved her overnight flat, they were obliged to bring her onboard. It had required painstaking effort over a number of intense weeks, a task that funnily enough had only brought Rolf and her closer together in the end. Suddenly they had a common adversary who needed to be manoeuvred and persuaded and they entered into the exercise wholeheartedly, now as a team and not as silent enemies. Among other things, they had invited Gaby to come and spend a long weekend in Kolarvik. The pretext was to demonstrate what good friends they intended to remain, but during the weekend they also showed her the action plan Rolf had helped Mary to produce. In the plan, which in practice was a printed sheet with a list of bullet points, Gaby could see in black and white how her daughter intended to wind up the business and find a proper job. Mary had even made a CV, which Rolf had helped her design and write. On the same list she could also see that Mary was prepared to sell her car to pay off the company debts and that as soon as she found a job in Stockholm, she planned to hand the flat back to Gaby for her own use again. Not that she uses it very often. She's more comfortable in Båstad and Tenerife. But still she was reluctant to give Mary the spare keys and her blessing to borrow the flat yet again.

They set off straight after breakfast. In the first trip they take Mary's clothes and sewing machines, in the second all the fabrics and yarns. Between trips they stop to eat at a burger restaurant and treat themselves to a double cheeseburger and dessert. As they walk across the car park afterwards Rolf pats his stomach and wonders whether it will shrink now he won't be eating her food anymore. She laughs and says she doubts it.

'Just say, and I'll come over and fill the freezer,' she adds.

'Don't make too many promises, now,' he says, and they both laugh again.

They've finished before it gets dark, both with each other and with the move. Rolf stops for a short tour of her mother's cramped flat before they say goodbye in an awkward embrace in the hall. When their bodies move apart he holds her at arm's length and looks at her with a concerned frown.

'Look after yourself now, promise me,' he says, before letting go of her arms.

'You too,' she says, 'and drive carefully.'

When she turns the key behind him, the sound of the door echoes in the stairwell. The echo is sharp and almost masks the sound of his steps, which fade as he descends the steps. Still in the hall, she lays her ear to the door, incapable of venturing inside the flat. She wants to wait for the bang of the outer door before she turns to begin her new life, but as his steps grow fainter a wave of unexpected sadness mounts.

What if that was the last time she would ever tell him to drive carefully? she thinks, after the door finally slams shut downstairs. What if I never tell anyone to drive carefully again? she thinks, clasping her hands together behind her back in an effort to suppress the urge to unlock the door and rush after him. Will no one ever drive carefully for my sake from now on? she thinks, and meanwhile she doesn't run down the stairs, doesn't catch up with him on the pavement outside, doesn't shout: Wait, I've changed my mind, I'll come back with you, can't we just sort this out instead?

Rolf is kind, he would certainly let her go back with him. Maybe it's not vital for the separation to happen today. But seconds pass and she's still standing in the hall with her hands behind her back, and when there's been sufficient time for him to get into the car and start the drive back to Enköping, she forces herself to go into the living room, literally willing her legs to move. In there, bags and boxes are spread across the floor. Her mum's flat is only thirty-two square metres. There's very little floor space left.

She takes a few steps into the room. Opens a box but closes it again. Doesn't know where to start, or in what order to do everything. Most of all it feels as though she needs a break.

It's been a long time since she thought about Mona and Irene, but when she navigates between the boxes on her way to the kitchen, she misses them both intensely. It's been years since the friends last spoke to one another, but it feels as though it would be the most natural thing in the world to ring one of them this evening and have a chat. And a bit of a moan. Laugh at her woes together. Another failed relationship. Ha ha. Hopeless, that's what she is.

But now she can't. After Irene died of breast cancer at the end of Mary's six months in Denmark, her contact with Mona fizzled out too. They had made a few attempts at the start, after Mary had come back home. They tried to have a book club meeting at some point, spoke on the phone now and then, but that became less and less frequent until it petered out completely. Whatever the reason, she can't ring Mona today. She doesn't even know which of the boxes contains the address book with her old contacts.

After a quick glass of wine in the kitchen, she decides to save the boxes until last. It seems easiest to start with the bin bags. The knot in her stomach eases slightly as she works; it feels good to be doing something with her hands, but the sense of failure lingers. Almost forty-seven and all she owns can be fitted into eight bin bags and six cardboard boxes. She hasn't managed to keep hold of anything in her life. Not her career, or her relationships, scarcely even her children. When she tries to ring them they're never at home. She hasn't had a chance to tell them that she and Rolf are separating, not when she would need to do so via Jeanette, who seems unable to stop talking about her pregnancy at the moment. It will be better, she thought, to tell them when she's in. Once she's settled, maybe with a new job, when she has at least a little bit of good news from her side too.

She unpacks her clothes and stows them away at the top of the wardrobe in the hall. The patterned dress with the coffee stain on the front is at the bottom of the last bag and she has the feeling it's laughing at her as she squeezes it into the cupboard. She does it quickly, banging the wardrobe door shut. The dress will definitely be creased, but it doesn't matter, she never means to wear it again.

She switches room. Goes into the alcove where the bed is with her sheets and towels, squashing everything that fits into the brown chest of drawers next to the bed. A pale blue cloth handkerchief falls onto the floor when she opens the top drawer. Her dad's initials are embroidered on the handkerchief in scrolled stitching. She picks it up and holds it to her nose. She sniffs for a scent, but finds none. The thought of her dad hurts unexpectedly. She'll have to take another break, another glass of wine, another cigarette under the extractor fan in the kitchen. It usually works.

But it doesn't work today. The ache in her stomach is still there, she still feels sad, is still playing with the idea of phoning Rolf and telling him she's changed her mind, asking if she can come back. She misses his large kitchen, the soft sofa, the comfy double bed, the sewing cabin. Her sewing cabin. She looks at the clock above the kitchen door. It's only forty minutes since he drove away. He probably isn't even home yet. If he's not in a hurry. He might be driving really fast to be in time for another dog walk with Susanne tonight.

She places the sewing machines on the small table in the kitchen. Together they occupy almost the entire surface; it's going to be difficult to use the table for anything other than sewing. That doesn't matter either. You can always eat on the sofa, she thinks, while she takes another break, another glass, another cigarette.

She gazes out of the kitchen window. Dusk is starting to fall over Gärdet and the view from the kitchen window is remarkably familiar. This at least hasn't changed over the years. Not so many years ago she would stand here every other Friday. She stood in exactly this spot when she flew back to Stockholm from Copenhagen, waiting to usher in her weekends with the children. She would have a cigarette by the window then too and look at the mint-green clock above the kitchen door. Back then she was waiting for the moment she had to meet the children at the metro.

Back then – or at least this is how she remembers it today – when she stood here, she was always excited. She and the children would be spending a weekend in her mum's flat, and in her memory Fridays felt like holidays. They always spoiled themselves a little. On rainy days she took the children to the cinema and when the weather was fine they would walk across Gärdet to one of the museums below the Kaknäs tower. Victor loved the Police Museum and Fredrika the Museum of Science and Technology, or it may have been the other way around. In the evenings she cooked their favourite meals and they watched films on her parents' tiny TV. She never repeated the previous year's Eurovision blunder. When the film ended, Fredrika and Victor could choose the sleeping arrangements. One of them slept on a mattress on the floor and the other two in her mum and dad's bed. More often than not Fredrika ended up on the mattress and Victor and Mary in the bed. But sometimes, if Fredrika was upset and wanted to be close, they would swap. She could always be close if she wanted to. As Mary remembers it, both her children loved coming here. It was a happy time. But the flat has a different feel today. Barer, pokier, more confined.

Outside the kitchen window the Kaknäs tower flashes in the darkness like a lighthouse. Mary has ended up on the sofa with her cigarette, has already given up her initial plan only to smoke in the kitchen under the extractor fan. She's sitting comfortably, her legs up, waiting for the effects of the third glass. Soon the bad thoughts will fade away and leave room for a different, better feeling.

The last box has been emptied and now the place doesn't look as messy. She wonders if it's too late to play some music. If the neighbours in this building are the touchy sort these days. If she doesn't try, she'll never know.

It will have to be Miles Davis. It's the first record she recognises in her mum's little collection under the TV. She settles back down on the sofa. Her cigarette has gone out in the saucer on the coffee table. Miles Davis' trumpet rocks her and now it comes, the better feeling. She knew it would.

No matter if it was the last time she told Rolf to drive carefully, she thinks. It's not her job to ask him to do that anyway, not anymore, it never really was. From now on he can drive as carefully or recklessly as he likes, and if she knows him as well as she thinks she does – after all, he's a kind man with beautiful eyes and a steady pay cheque – there'll be someone else telling him to drive carefully before too long. Let that be the case, she thinks. She wasn't right for that relationship either. It might simply be better if she lived alone. When you think about it, it's totally obvious.

She laughs out loud at this sudden insight.

She's a person who is best suited to being alone. How come she's never realised it before?

If she's alone she can do what she wants with her days, and she'll have more time to devote to what really matters. Her craftwork, for example, her sewing projects, all her pretty yarns and fabrics. Her creative streak will thrive. Not to mention her relationship with her children. If she's on her own without a man she can be there for them in a better way. The timing couldn't be more perfect, actually.

Fredrika and Victor are certainly going to need their mum a bit more now, with a new baby on the way at the farm. If she's alone she'll have both the time and the energy to focus on being just that – their mum. The realisation makes her so elated, it sparks her imagination. It's been a long time since she's known something as surely as this. She can see the future and the flat with new eyes now. Both are full of potential when you look more closely. If she can get hold of a spare bed and make a curtain to hang between the sleeping alcove and the living area, it will almost be as though the children have their own flat. How many teenagers have that? She could have duplicate keys cut for both of them tomorrow. Post them in a padded envelope with a loving message. *You're welcome here whenever you like*, it will say at the end. *I miss you. My door is always open.* The whole thing is nothing short of perfect.

What she needs to sort out now is the flat. The curtain to begin with. She laughs when she remembers she already has the material she can use. It has to be the Italian velvet in burgundy that she used along the children's bunk beds on Svalgången. She knew there was a reason for keeping it after she sold the flat. Her mum's one-roomer will be transformed into a practical two-roomer in a flash. She's so delighted she can't sit still any longer. She goes dancing around the flat, digs out the fabric in the hall and holds it up to the living-room wall.

Indeed it is perfect, both in texture and colour. She measures the height of the alcove, taps cautiously on the ceiling, fetches a piece of paper from the drawer and writes down the long list of things she's going to need to buy in order to put the curtain up. She's going to have to get hold of a drill as well. And she mustn't forget to go to the shoe repair shop by the metro to get her mum's keys cut. She has a lot to do tomorrow, but now it feels like fun. There was meaning to this whole situation after all.

JOHN

In the lift in the Mälarsjukhuset clinic they hold on to one another. Netta's head is against John's chest and she's weeping silently. Her bulging stomach and swelling breasts are pressed against his body as he wraps his arms around her, stroking her hair, whispering that everything will be all right. He catches a glimpse of himself in the mirror. It looks romantic, the way they're standing. They look like something out of an American film, two quite handsome and relatively young people who love each other truly and deeply. Not at all like two middle-aged Swedes who've just received a cancer diagnosis at Mälardalen's hospital in Eskilstuna.

'We'll sort this,' he whispers into her hair.

In reality he doesn't need to whisper. They're alone in the lift, were alone in the waiting room too, no one can hear him whisper or see Netta soak the front of his jacket with her tears.

When the lift doors open the moment is past. Netta dries her cheeks with the back of her hands, takes a step away from him and walks ahead down the hospital corridor. In silence they pass the kiosk, the florist and the information desk. They don't start speaking until they're back in the car park.

*

'What do we do now?' Netta asks as they make their way between the rows of cars to their own.

He's walking a few steps behind her and it takes him a moment to reply, because he doesn't know what his answer should be. He's never been given a cancer diagnosis before in his life, doesn't know anyone else who has either. He doesn't know what they have to do now, and nor does he know precisely what Netta meant with her question. What's more, she sounded almost irritated. As if deep down she thought it was his own fault he'd gone and got sick. From his position behind her he can only see her back, but he notices that her steps are still brisk, despite her stomach growing bigger. Her long strides make her backpack bounce as she walks. In it there's the information booklet the doctor sent them away with. On the front cover there's an elderly couple in an embrace and above their heads the words *Receiving a Cancer Diagnosis*, in the county's standard blue font. The doctor suggested that they read the booklet together in peace and quiet this evening, preferably with the children. And they were more than welcome, the doctor stressed, to get in touch if they had any questions afterwards.

'I don't want us to tell the children anything,' John says, when they've reached the car.

Netta, who is bending down at the passenger side to put the backpack on the back seat, straightens her back and stares at him across the dusty roof. It's obvious she thinks he's joking, so he tries again.

'I mean, the doctor said the prognosis is good. Can't we just deal with this without making a fuss about it? Do the children and the neighbours really need to know that it's…cancer?'

The theatrical pause before the word was unintentional. For a millisecond he was caught off-guard in the sentence, seeking another word in his head to use for what was apparently growing in his bladder and would need to be quickly removed. Netta keeps staring at him across the car roof as if she's having a problem interpreting what he means. Her eyebrows are slightly raised, she's waiting for him to carry on, so he tries again. Can't they just call it something else, he says, something that doesn't sound so ominous and unpleasant?

On the other side of the car Netta takes her eyes off him. She opens the passenger door, sits down in the front seat and shuts the door again with a loud bang. Baffled by her reaction, he follows her example. He sits behind the wheel and fastens the seat belt, listening to Netta puffing as she does the same. When she's finished, she leans back in the seat and looks at him again, this time with a milder expression on her face. She reaches towards him, takes his hands in hers and then holds them steady in the air above the gearstick. When she finally speaks, she does so slowly.

'My dear old man. You don't have cancer of the brain, do you? Of course we're going to tell the children, and the rest of the family, and some of the neighbours as well. We'll tell them, and then we'll get through this together, like we always do.'

The same evening they gather the children in the kitchen and announce that their dad has cancer of the bladder. They don't have long to wait for their response. It's like a chain reaction, beginning with Fredrika howling, 'NOT CANCER' and then crying convulsively until she has to gasp for air, followed by Victor sitting motionless on his chair and staring at the table, and ending with Jenny leaping to her feet and rushing out of the kitchen.

She disappears out through the hall, across the yard and down to the stable. John and Netta haven't even had time to reach the good news part, that the prognosis is good and over 90 per cent of people with this particular cancer recover within a year, before she's gone. When they find her, she's sitting in the corner of one of the stalls with her head in her hands.

There are more tears to deal with before the day ends. The same evening he listens to his mother's stifled sobs on the telephone and immediately afterwards it's Anneli's turn. It's well after eight by the time all the necessary calls have been made. When the phone in the kitchen rings and they see that it's Mary, Netta gives him a meaningful look as she picks it up.

'Will you?' she mimes, pointing at the receiver.

He shakes his head, mouths a 'no' and starts backing out of the kitchen. He cannot face talking about his illness any more today, least of all with Mary. He doesn't have the strength for another phone call. Netta nods and gives him a thumbs up as he goes into the hall. What her thumb means, he doesn't really know, since he goes down to the boiler room to add some more wood and doesn't hear the rest of the conversation, but he assumes that she'll take care of it herself. Just as she usually does.

'It was a bit tricky,' she tells him when she finds him in the boiler room later on. 'She was completely taken aback. She said nothing to begin with and then she asked at least ten times if there was anything she could do.'

Netta had to comfort her and tell her that everything was fine, or at least soon would be, and in fact it wasn't an especially dangerous type of cancer that John had.

Bladder cancer can be surgically removed quite easily, she had to explain, just as the doctor had explained to John and her just a few hours earlier. She also had to say that the children couldn't speak just now, but they would ring back as soon as everything had calmed down. In the sooty air of the boiler room John holds his wife close and kisses her hair as his thanks to her for taking the call.

'All in all, it looks very positive.'

That was what the doctor had actually said. Those are the words both John and Netta will repeat from now on. They will use the phrase numerous times in the weeks to follow, both to each other and to the world outside, whose anxiety and concern feels as infinite as it is profuse.

And today too, in front of the boiler's flames, they repeat the doctor's words before they go back up to the children. All in all, it looks very positive. They will get through this together. Of course they'll get through this together. That's how they work, he and Netta. They are people who handle things together and, all in all, yes, it does look very positive.

Mary

She sends a basket of goodies to John and the children. A few days later she sends a parcel to Netta with some sweet-smelling creams that are supposed to do wonders for the skin during pregnancy. After that she takes a break from the welfare of John's family and tries to turn her attention to the flat instead. She puts up the curtain and buys a new bedspread. Treats herself to a better coffeemaker and makes some more cushions for the sofa. She cooks stews that have to simmer on the stove for several hours and rings Gaby, who enthusiastically tells her about the latest piano concert at a local bar next to her flat in Tenerife. She takes a walk after breakfast and sometimes a second one after lunch. Tries to keep herself occupied, and for the most part it works. Just once or twice in the evenings she finds herself picking up the phone and starting to dial the number for the farm again. She always hangs up before she's connected, reminding herself every time she mustn't get in the way, that now's not the time for her to pester them. Not at the moment, when they have so much to think about.

At least Jeanette sounded hopeful when she told her about John's cancer. She said that the children were upset, of course, but that would soon improve. She explained that the prognosis was good, that over 90 per cent of those diagnosed recover fully, that the doctors didn't seem unduly concerned and, what's more, that they had a clearly defined treatment plan. The plan involved radiotherapy and chemo and an operation, and obviously it would be a lot for all of them for some time to come, but it's going to be fine. Jeanette practically promised. Then she apologised that the children couldn't talk to her this evening. Mary said of course not, obviously there was a lot for Victor and Fredrika to take on board. But when a week passes and then another, and they still haven't rung back, it becomes a little harder to get through the evenings. More and more often she finds herself wandering aimlessly around the flat, back and forth between the phone in the kitchen, the sofa and the bed.

'You can't carry on like that. Get going with your own plan instead,' Rolf says when she rings him one evening. 'You know what you can do. Why don't you do that instead of hanging around waiting?' he says, trying to encourage her.
'But looking for a job is so tedious,' she says.
At the other end of the line Rolf laughs. His rumbling chuckle isn't mean, or contemptuous, it's the same old warm laugh he's always had, no more, no less, and it's reassuring to hear it.
'Of course it's tedious! Everybody thinks so. But you've already done half the job. I've helped you with your CV, now just make some copies and start applying. It's going to be great; you'll get whatever post you apply for. You're clever. And you need something to do, believe me. Living like this will drive you mad in the end.'

*

After they've hung up, she doesn't feel encouraged or clever. Nor does she feel inclined to look for a job. There's still a little money left from selling the car in Enköping; she still has enough to afford a life without work, at least for a while longer. It's something else that she needs, she can sense that clearly. She just has to find out what it is.

She decides to take a walk to Gärdet Field to clear her head, but regrets it as soon as she reaches the wide open space. It's windy and the grass is wet. She shivers and her feet get wetter and wetter every time she has to veer off the beaten path to avoid colliding with the pensioners and all their dogs. After only a few minutes she turns around and hurries home, feeling frozen. Back in the flat she still hasn't figured out what she wants to do and still doesn't feel like sitting on the sofa, staring at the telephone. So she changes her socks, chooses a different pair of shoes and goes out again.

This time she sets her sights on the pulsing beat of Valhallavägen instead of the biting wind on Gärdet Field. As she walks along, she looks into the shop windows lining the street. There are a good number of places she hasn't noticed before, despite walking past them so many times. The hairdresser next to the tobacconist, for example. How can it have been there adjoining the little hole in the wall where she's bought her cigarettes for the last few weeks, without her seeing it? The same applies to the restaurant at the crossroads between her mum's street and Valhallavägen. It has tables outside, with heated lamps and green blankets and dark green plants climbing up the façade. Collectively the details create the illusion that the restaurant is on a totally different latitude to any in Scandinavia. How strange that she hasn't thought about it before. She ought to go there and treat herself to a meal one evening. Maybe Gaby will go with her when she comes back from Tenerife.

Further down, the Fältöversten shopping centre towers above Valhallavägen. The signs on the outside of the building show up more clearly in the dark than in daylight and now she notices for the first time that there's a library inside. And a dental practice, a sweet shop and a job centre. At the far end of the building there is also a small hotel.

When she reads the red letters above the hotel entrance, she has an impulse she can't resist until it's too late. Not until she's standing at the Good Morning City check-in desk, talking to the friendly receptionist, who tells her in a soft Dalarna accent that they *most certainly* have several lovely rooms available tonight, does she give a thought to her personal finances. When she does, it's too late, she's already swiped her card and by then the thought doesn't help anyway. Instead she takes pleasure in the prospect of the night ahead. In her mind's eye she sees dazzling white sheets and fluffy pillows. International TV channels, a steaming bubble bath, maybe a minibar. The room wasn't even overly expensive, especially considering she was given an upgrade to a deluxe room on the top floor for the same price as a single room on one of the lower floors. The receptionist, who according to the name badge on her black waistcoat was called Katja, hands a key fob over the counter and wishes Mary a nice night.

'If there's anything, I'm here all night. Just ring or come down.'

'Thank you. I will,' Mary says, smiling at Katja.

Mary keeps smiling in the lift on the way up to the fourth floor, this time at her own reflection in the mirror.

She thinks she's really pretty today. Her cheeks are rosy after the walk and her eyes look unusually bright. Even her teeth look whiter than they did in the hallway mirror in Gaby's flat only a few hours ago. It must be something to do with the lighting in the lift. But even so, there's no denying it's nice to glance at your own reflection and get a pretty smile in return. And on top of that, she's soon going to be sinking into a bathtub where the shampoo and lotions are free and will certainly be smelling clean and fresh. There are no two ways about it, it was a brilliant idea to check in here, she has to give herself that.

John

It's not without some sense of victory on his part that the first round of chemotherapy passes almost without notice. All the warnings they received, all the side effects they'd prepared themselves for, all the nights they'd have to tramp up and down the stairs to comfort first one child and then the other, and then it was...practically nothing. A certain degree of fatigue during the days following the treatment, certainly. And a headache that came and went at irregular intervals. And a feeling of simultaneously freezing and sweating that was hard to describe. And a kind of numb tingling under the skin on his hands. Some small ulcers in his mouth. But all the same. It hadn't been worse than a bad bout of flu. He could eat throughout the entire period and didn't vomit once. Just that alone. He'd been prepared for much worse.

Today, only eight days later, he's down and working on the farm again. Almost as if nothing has happened, but with Hasse for company because recently they've been forced to change places to some extent.

Netta has finally accepted that she needs to start taking it easy. She's too big now. The least exertion makes her breathless and she has contractions whenever she moves quickly. Her pregnant body put its foot down in the end, and about time too, at least according to John. If anyone needs to learn how to wind down, it's Netta. She can still drive, and she does that a great deal, as her primary responsibility for the present is to act as the family's chauffeur. She drives the children around, and these days him too, since he needs to go to the hospital several times a week. She'll be entering week thirty-four of the pregnancy on Sunday. Her stomach, however, looks as though it's about to burst right now. That's something that has to be avoided at all costs. She has to wait at least five more weeks so that he can go through the operation and recover afterwards. For that reason, she now has to stay in the house and let him and Hasse and the children look after everything else, whether she likes it or not.

It's plain that she has difficulty delegating, because unless he tells her bluntly not to, she waddles down to him and Hasse, even though it's clear she's in discomfort when she moves. When she reaches them she smiles innocently and says she just wants to see how they're doing.

'I was just...' she begins, and then inserts whatever it was she was just going to do this time. It's usually check on the hens, or the sheep, or the horses. And if she doesn't walk down herself, he can be sure she'll stand on the doorstep and shout her reminders to him and the children so loudly that her voice echoes between the farm buildings. There's an awful lot they mustn't forget while they're down there.

'Don't forget to switch off the electricity in the fence when the last horse is in,' she says, when he and Jenny go down to the stable for the evening feed.

'Don't skimp on the measure of concentrated feed,' she says to Fredrika's back, when she's heading in the same direction.

'Remember to rub the liniment well into their hocks!'

'Take another look as Julle's eczema at the base of his tail. Put some more on if it's worse.'

And on she goes. Sending out reminders in every direction, writing lists of what they need to buy when they go to the shop, asking John to write down a timetable so she knows when Hasse's available. She rings the neighbours in the village to see whether they can cover if something unforeseen should happen. Such as a baby coming too early or him being worn out by his treatment, for example. He has only one round left and then it's time for the operation. But Netta thinks you shouldn't get ahead of yourself. Just because the first treatment went smoothly doesn't mean the next will be the same. When he jokes and says it's only sissies who succumb to cytotoxic drugs, she gets really angry with him.

'You can't damned well say that!' she says, and he feels ashamed because he knows she's right. But he was only joking.

When Netta comes down to the stable and he sees that she's in pain, he sends her back up. He repeats, for surely the hundredth time, that he and Hasse have everything under control and the only thing she needs to think about is having a rest. None of the animals are off colour and Hasse is nearby around the clock if they should need him. John isn't on his own working the farm, far from it, the children are also more involved in the farm work than they've ever been before.

Even Fredrika is at home nowadays. She really only disappears to stay with Ola at the weekend and returns to the farm on Sunday evening, a little green around the gills after what John assumes were Saturday night parties, but nothing that prevents her doing her bit on the early Monday morning shift.

After a break of two weeks it's almost time for his second round of treatment, and when it's over there's only another month before he's admitted for the operation. That day he is looking forward to. To wake up afterwards and know that the tumour has gone, know from that moment on he can put all his energy into recuperating and subsequently be able to focus entirely on gathering the strength required to receive the next family member, that's the goal. And now it's getting close.

The timing could certainly have been better. Especially given the estimated delivery date is less than two weeks from the date of his surgery. But by and large they seem to have everything under control. It could have been worse. They have friends and family who pitch in where necessary, and basically all they need to do is follow the plan and everything will work out in the end.

Mary

There's a man called Costas who works in the Greek restaurant on the corner of Valhallavägen. That's probably not his real name, but it's what she calls him in her head. He looks like a Costas at any rate. The name would suit him admirably.

She thinks it's Costas who owns the restaurant. He's some kind of manager at the very minimum. He's at least twenty years older than the girls who are serving, who for their part seem to be called Cissi and Jennifer and appear to be about Fredrika's age, the whole bunch of them. But not Costas. He is somewhere in the attractive borderland between fit forty and mellow fifty. No wedding ring on his finger, but a discreet gold chain around his neck. The little cross catches your eye when it falls into the thick hair on his chest sticking up above the top button of his shirt. Costas is always wearing a well-ironed shirt, even at the end of the evening.

While the young girls go from table to table with plates, bills and menus, Costas stands quietly at the bar – at the corner of which Mary will be sitting most of the time, on the side facing the door – and surveils operations. Fiddling with something behind the counter, the coffeemaker, the beer taps or the wine cooler. Polishing the surfaces with a cloth now and then. In between, he looks at her. Oh, how he looks at her. It's one of those looks that makes it clear he would have absolutely nothing against sleeping with her, but at the same time he would never suggest it himself. Costas is not a man to beg, he *observes*, and then gets back to work. His gaze is attentive and polite, always within the bounds of propriety, but for all that he's patently interested.

Sometimes Mary will play a little game with Costas. It happens mostly at the end of the evening, when she's mustered sufficient courage to meet his gaze and hold it for a little longer than is customary. Sometimes she'll raise her glass to him. The precursor to an invitation, a private toast between her and him that none of the other customers notice. He nods back with a twinkle in his eye and after a few seconds returns to what he was doing, now with a smile on his lips that nobody other than the one who's been watching him carefully for several weeks can catch.

She hasn't decided exactly when it will happen, but she feels relatively certain that he's going to go home with her one night soon. It's actually a necessity for this to happen, because she's started to fantasise about Costas in a way that's become embarrassing for her on a day-to-day level.

More often than feels appropriate, when she goes to bed, she thinks about the skin under his arms and she thinks about the strands of hair that protrude above his shirt. She fantasises about undoing the top buttons of his shirt and running her fingers through the hair, which she's sure covers his entire chest and probably lower down his stomach too. She's never been with a hairy man. All her men have had bare chests and patchy facial hair, presumably as a direct effect of her father looking like that when she was growing up. They've maybe had a single strand of hair beside the nipple, possibly a thin line between the navel and the top of their pants, otherwise nothing. They've all looked more like boys than men, even when they've reached middle age. She'd believed it was a subconscious choice on her part, that hairy men frighten her, but now it turns out that's not true, because she's being sent almost crazy at the mere thought of Costas and all his hair.

The other day it even happened during a job interview at the little bakery at the end of Banérgatan. Just as she was about to give an account of her professional experience in customer service he popped into her head – what's more without any clothes on – and she lost concentration and started jabbering incoherently.

The bakery hasn't been in touch and by this stage she can deduce that she didn't get the job. For all intents and purposes, it's Costas' fault. It feels increasingly as though it would be in everyone's best interests for them to just get on with it and sleep together as soon as possible. To get it over with. So she can stop applying her energy to wondering what it would be like. Because now it's time, time to move on, time to draw a line between the past and the present. She wouldn't exactly be the first person to move on in life after sleeping with Costas.

It had only been five weeks since she left Rolf's and then a woman called Berit answered when she rang him at home. What an old-fashioned name, she thinks now. Not precisely the same pazazz as Costas. Berit sounds like a pensioner from her voice, and had Mary not been acquainted with Rolf's mother and been well aware that she was called Inger, she would have assumed it was his mum on a visit, not his new lady. But Berit answered and sounded like a retired school mistress when she said that unfortunately he wasn't at home, but she would ask him to return her call as soon as he was back. The instant she said that, Mary remembered what day of the month it was and that of course Rolf was in Bangkok. With a woman called Berit alone in his house. How significant.

The news she was intending to share, about John and Jeanette's newborn baby, who'd been given the name Eva, seemed like the non-news of the century from Rolf's perspective. Why would he care that Mary's children had a new half-sibling when he and Mary don't even live together anymore? He had barely bothered about her children when they still did. And now he was apparently living with a new woman, a certain Berit, who had made herself so much at home that she answered the phone in his house when he wasn't there. Why would he care in the slightest what his ex-partner's ex-husband got up to in the forests outside Eskilstuna?

The idea seemed so preposterous she couldn't for the life of her remember what she'd been thinking when she dialled his number. She told Berit it wasn't important, she didn't need to leave a message for Rolf, and hung up. While she was at it, she pulled the cord out of the phone and flung it on the floor. It's been lying there ever since. Today is Friday and she hasn't the slightest interest in receiving a call from Rolf to tell her that, as it happens, he's met someone new. Knowing him, he'll keep trying to reach her all next week, then time will pass and he'll forget her and devote himself to his new life and his new Berit instead. By all means let him. Mary can easily take control of the situation by leaving the telephone unplugged until she needs to use it. Personally, she can do just as well without a phone. Gaby's calls are coming less frequently, anyway. She appears to be fully occupied with her piano-playing in Tenerife, and when she does ring, she barely asks how Mary is.

It's time for last orders in the restaurant. It's a quarter to eleven and most of the dinner guests have already gone home. Ever since she started coming to the restaurant, it's felt as though evenings here have a habit of flying by.

The first time she visited, she splashed out on dinner too. She still had money left over from the sale of the car then and thought she deserved to celebrate her first weeks in Stockholm with a meal out. On that occasion she was given a table immediately to the right of the toilets by one of the young girls, but it didn't take many visits to discover she felt much happier at the bar with Costas. Since then, that's been her regular spot. It's cheaper that way. Admittedly the food at Costas' restaurant is very good, but it's far too expensive. The wine is much cheaper. Costas doesn't even have to ask what she'd like, as it's always the same. The house red, sometimes with a little bowl of olives on the side. That's all for now, thank you.

Tonight he puts the bowl out with her last glass, without even asking first if she'd like them. For a second she debates whether to say that won't be necessary, thank you, but she doesn't get the chance, because Costas says, 'On the house,' and smiles in that unequivocally attracted way again. She raises her glass to him across the bar and he responds with his classic nod, his classic smile.

She takes tiny sips of the wine to drag it out, while pondering how she's going to present the proposition that he goes home with her after closing time. Should she just say it straight out, or wrap it up in some kind of pretext to take a walk together after the restaurant has closed? Her pulse starts racing at the very thought of it. So humiliating to have to be the one making such a suggestion to a man. But times have changed, that much she understood. Nowadays women are expected to do the asking as often as men, it's just that she hasn't kept up with that development. That's why she's still sitting here. With a bar between her and the man she wants to ask out, or in, or however she prefers to phrase it. If he hadn't been the restaurant owner and she one of his patrons, she'd like to believe the situation would have been different. Then she could almost have put money on him asking her out. But as things are, he doesn't. And therefore she has to pluck up the courage.

When the lights are turned out in the restaurant she still hasn't plucked up the courage. She looks around and discovers she's the last one left. The waitresses are nowhere to be seen, having evidently had the time to clear the tables and set them for the following day's lunchtime session. The only one remaining is Costas, who is standing by the cash register and seems to be counting money. The bright light from the fluorescent tubes in the ceiling hurts her eyes and in front of her, right behind the olive bowl, is a bill that she didn't notice anyone placing there. She adds a generous tip to the little leather pouch. She'd really like to point out that the tip is for Costas, and not for any of the young girls, but she dare not do that either. She's not sure her appearance is at its best in the strip lighting at this time of the night. Nor is she sure she wouldn't slur if she started to speak now.

The floor swims slightly when she tries to focus on it in order to make a graceful descent from the bar stool. She stumbles when she stands up, the footrest is in the way, but she straightens with a feminine, 'Whoops-adaisy,' which she hopes Costas will find charming. Over by the till he smiles as he waves and wishes her a good night. She thanks him and says, as if in passing, when she's already on her way to the door:

'You too! See you around!'

It sounds a strange thing to say. As if she's suddenly going to go away and stop coming to his restaurant every night. Not at all as mysterious and seductive as she'd imagined her ideal response in her head. It was weird, in all honesty. What normal person says that immediately before leaving a place everyone knows she's going to go back to the following day? She feels ashamed when the bells above the door jingle, once as she opens it and again as it shuts behind her.

Out in the street the pavement is covered in golden leaves. It's already autumn in Stockholm. She's lived here now for just over two months. Two months and not very much has happened. The hill up to her mother's flat is of course darker tonight than the first night she walked up it, when it was summer and still quite mild. Now it's autumn and cold. The puddles are a reddish brown with all the flattened leaves.

As she unlocks the door to the flat, she wonders whether she could do with a break from Costas' restaurant. Both to save money and to give him a chance to miss her. A break of a week, maybe even two, might be what they both need to move on in their relationship. And meanwhile she could concentrate on searching for a job. She could use the time she would otherwise be spending in Costas' restaurant to check out the hotels around Östermalmstorget and Karlaplan. She's always thought that working in a hotel sounds really quite enjoyable.

In the kitchen she takes her diary out of her handbag to mark a date. The date she circles will represent a boundary, after which she can go back to Costas' restaurant. Definitely not before. In her diary she has to flick through the pages for August and September to reach today's date. It's clearly been a long time since she used her diary.

When she's finally found the right week, she freezes. Circled in red pen under today's date is Fredrika's name with a little red heart. After the name: the number 18. Mary screws up her eyes to focus. The pleasant humming in her head is dispelled in a flash. She is totally sober and her blood runs cold as she thumbs between the entries to check that she's found the right week. She turns the page over and then back to make sure what she's seeing is correct. Ends up back on the entry for this week. The letters are still there. The number as well. And the heart.

She has forgotten to congratulate Fredrika on her eighteenth birthday. Her daughter is eighteen today and she hasn't rung to wish her a happy birthday. She didn't send her anything in the post and she didn't get in touch to invite her over for dinner any time in the preceding weeks. She's had the telephone unplugged for most of the week, and if Fredrika has tried to ring her, she won't have got through.

'Fuck,' she says, into the silence.

She will never be forgiven for this, never.

JOHN

It may not be the liveliest gathering that has ever occupied the restaurant at the hotel in Eskilstuna, but it's definitely the happiest. If it hadn't been for Ola, they would never have managed to surprise Fredrika as thoroughly as they did in the end. Without Ola's help they wouldn't have been able to secure a private booking for seats under the heated lamps in the hotel garden, or have managed to organise a surprise in the form of all her friends showing up during the course of the evening. The idea of this kind of celebration for Fredrika came from Ola, and he is also the one treating her to a night in one of the hotel suites when the party's over.

The idea of the mobile phone, on the other hand, has come from John. He assigned to Victor the task of finding out how much they cost and how they work, an exercise Victor tackled with gusto. Almost too zealously, because before they were finished Victor had managed to persuade both him and Netta to buy one each and negotiated one for himself. By this point it would have seemed unreasonable not to give Jenny one too, in particular as she's now planning to go to the USA to work as an au pair, so in the end Fredrika's eighteenth birthday provided both a financial setback and a technological boost for the entire family. Now they all have a mobile phone, with the exception of Eva, but given she's just over a month old, they've decided she can wait a while.

When Fredrika enters the hotel garden and sees her family at the corner table under the patio heater, she clasps her hands to her mouth and starts to cry. The others stick to the plan, shouting 'Surprise!' in unison and then starting to sing.

At first Fredrika stands still, not sure whether to turn and hug Ola or run up to the rest of the family at the table, but by the end of the song, just as they're all shouting 'Hurrah!', she chooses the latter. Neither John nor Netta manage to stand up and move towards her – he's still on crutches after the operation and Netta has Eva in her arms and is breastfeeding – but they don't need to. Fredrika hugs them both in their seats, and her arms around his neck combined with her wet cheek against his own speak for themselves. The birthday dinner is a success before it's begun, and her friends haven't even joined them yet.

Fredrika beams at Ola when she returns to him and continues to beam for the rest of the evening. At least for the part of it that he himself can cope with. He, Victor and Netta drive home just before nine, about the time the music is turned up and Eva starts grizzling and his lower back aches too much for him to sit still for much longer. When they're about to leave Fredrika comes up to him and gives him another hug. By now a little drunk, she says she loves them 'so bloody much', all of them. John is so moved he has to hold back a tear. All in all, it's been a very successful evening.

What doesn't go down so well is the doctors' considered opinion that the pain is taking longer than they'd expect to reduce after the operation. They're now investigating a slipped disc and arthritis, and he is being passed back and forth between different floors and departments in the hospital on the outskirts of town. The doctors don't think he should be so sore two months after the surgery, and the current theory is that his pain is totally unrelated to the cancer.

Related or not: it hurts all the same. So much so that some days he can't do much more than walk around the ground floor of the house a few times. And with Eva literally fastened to Netta day and night, since Netta refuses to give Eva the bottle yet, the farm is starting to become a bit of a problem. They can't accept Hasse's services forever, and that's a fact.

'The chap's nearly seventy and has his own farming to see to,' he tells Netta, but she turns a deaf ear.

'He says he wants to help. What can I do?' she says, turning her back on him and already heading across the garden.

If Netta would at least consider calling a halt to the breastfeeding, it would be easier for him to look after Eva when she's working on the farm. He can have Eva in the pram inside the house, can walk around with his crutch and the pram while he's getting her to sleep, he can warm the formula milk in a pan, and he can actually manage to change a nappy. Sometimes it seems as though Netta doesn't really trust him. As if she's forgotten that he has in fact done this not once, but twice before. Twice as many times as her, frankly. He points to Victor and Fredrika and reminds her that both of them were raised on formula.

'And see,' he says, 'they survived.'

But Netta won't give in. Eva will be breastfed, and when she's not feeding her, Netta works in the stable, carrying her around in a kind of papoose that she fastens across her stomach. All the while he carries on hobbling around the house. Irritated with the pain, dosed up with medication and generally frustrated by the health service, which is taking forever to ascertain what is causing him so much damned suffering.

At least he'll be going to Danderyd hospital in Stockholm next week. There they'll do an MRI of his back in a department specialising in orthopaedic problems. If they find a slipped disc, there may have to be another operation, his consultant at Mälarsjukhuset said at his appointment last week. At the same appointment John opposed the idea; he thought that he simply didn't have time for another operation, but the more the pain intensifies, the less opposed he feels.

Operate on me then, if that's what's needed, is more his attitude today. Just fix me. I have a farm to look after and a family that needs a dad and a whole life to take care of. I really don't have time for this.

Mary

The answerphone message at the farm has gone. Mary doesn't know when it went, and it surprises her that she misses it as much as she does. No jaunty encouragement from Jeanette to the caller to seize the day, instead a dry automated voice advises the caller to please leave a message after the tone. Mary has done this, several times, but no one ever rings back. Neither of the children appear to have time to speak to her just now, either on their mobiles or on the house phone. Fredrika did ring to thank her for the birthday present, which arrived a week late in the post, but since then there's been silence. The only one who can sometimes be bothered to answer his mobile in Victor, but she gleans limited information from him.

As Mary understands it, they're in the process of selling the farm on account of John's illness. What the condition of that illness is, Victor doesn't really seem to know. 'A sarcoma,' he said, and something about metastases in the hip bone. No clear prognosis, but obviously bad enough for the family to have to sell the farm. For his part, he has a girlfriend from Nacka called Ellen. When he told Mary that, she tried to invite them both over to hers, and at the time he did indeed accept, but up to now hasn't been able to give her a date. 'Sounds good. We can talk about it,' he finished with. As terse on the phone as his father. Mary had said she understood and he should get in touch when it was convenient, and since then they haven't spoken.

The other day she tested a new strategy. Instead of directing her words at the children on the answerphone, she now spoke directly to Jeanette. It felt peculiar to be talking like this and she was so nervous while she waited for the automated voice, she managed to choke on her own saliva as she began to speak. She had to cough and start again, beginning with Jeanette's name to make clear that she was the one the message was aimed at. After that she tried to talk to Jeanette as if she was actually there on the line, a conversation between one grown woman and another. A grown woman who would really welcome the opportunity to help. She emphasised that it wouldn't be any trouble at all for her if they thought of something, anything at all, that they needed help with, while they're going through such a stressful time.

'I can cook,' she said to the answering machine, 'or help with packing, or perhaps cleaning, or driving the children around. Anything at all...except maybe looking after the animals,' she said, in an attempt at a joke which she deeply regretted the moment she hung up.

This is absolutely not the time for joking, that much Mary is well aware of. It was only because she was so nervous that it came out like that. Perhaps that's the reason no one rings back. Or their answerphone has broken. It's hard for her to say, since they don't ring back.

The consequence of her not getting hold of them is that the days pass more slowly than ever. Now that she has a probationary period at Good Morning City she can't even spend her hours job-hunting. The mornings consist instead of restlessly walking up and down in the flat. Sometimes she sits down at the sewing machine and tries to sew, but she seldom manages to; she can find no inspiration, everything is just ugly and boring and the fabrics clash. At a quarter to eleven she can at least put an end to the misery. She leaves home then to clock on for her shift at the hotel a quarter of an hour later.

Depending on the occupancy – there's always more to do on weekdays than at weekends – she finishes the cleaning some time between two and three. At that time, she's allowed to eat free of charge in the hotel restaurant on condition she has changed into her normal clothes and there's food left over after the paying guests. The free meals are a perk, she's been told. Her new boss Nadja was at pains to point out that very few hotels offer their cleaning staff any such thing. Mary tries to show her gratitude, complimenting the chef when she's finished and making sure she smiles and waves to the reception staff when she leaves the hotel for the day. She quickens her pace up the hill, on no account stopping at Costas' restaurant, not even walking past slowly as she did in the beginning. Instead she goes straight home to see if one of the children has rung back, or maybe Jeanette, or even John. Up to now it hasn't happened.

She spends her evenings in the flat soaking in the bathtub or watching TV. In the bathroom cabinet there's a bottle of the kind of sleeping tablets that Gaby's been taking for as long as Mary can remember. Mary was no more than fourteen when her mum first gave her one. It was during the year they lived in Nairobi, in the flat that was boiling hot in the daytime and ice-cold at night. One night she couldn't sleep because she was worried about a science test at the British school she attended then. For reasons that she can no longer recall, she chose to confide her fears in Gaby, who came straight back into her bedroom with a little tablet and a glass of water.

Mary slept so soundly she didn't hear the alarm clock the following day. When she woke both her parents had left the flat. She missed the first half of the test and received a fail for the first time in her life. Her mother had been so upset when she heard about it, she grounded Mary for the whole of the following week.

These days Mary is well versed in both the strength and the quantity she can take. She usually allows herself half a tablet straight after the nine o'clock news on the TV and the other half when she turns off her bedside lamp an hour later. Until that moment she still harbours hope and wants to be alert if anyone rings from the farm. After she's taken the first half she has just under thirty minutes before she gets ready for bed. Sometimes she'll read an article in one of the magazines she's smuggled out of the hotel reception, on other days she doesn't have time to start before she's overcome by sleep, and then she'll generally stay asleep until dawn, when she wakes and the restless pacing begins again.

It's over a month since she last visited Costas' restaurant. For the first few days it felt a real effort not to go in, she would even go past it on her evening walks and drag her feet in the hope he would come out into the street and invite her in for a glass of wine, but then something remarkable happened. As the days passed it became harder to remember what she'd been doing there in the first place, and more difficult to justify the hundred-kronor notes that an evening at Costas' can cost. It's still a few weeks until she receives her first wage from the hotel and she certainly doesn't dare ask her mum for a sub, not when she's living in her flat free of charge and they speak so seldom. She gets lunch at the hotel and it's not difficult to take a roll of toilet paper from one of the rooms when she's there cleaning anyway. The same goes for shampoo, conditioner and shower gel. And the small sachets of instant coffee that are next to the kettle in the deluxe rooms on the fourth and fifth floors. It's impossible for the management to know if it's her or the hotel guests who help themselves. It doesn't even feel like stealing. More that she's taking something for herself that someone else has paid for and has chosen not to take.

Anyway, she has a plan for the remainder of the money in her account. She wants to save it for train tickets and a hotel when the children or Jeanette ring and ask for her help. She wants to be flexible when they ring, wants to be able to get on the five past five train the same afternoon, has already checked which hotel is nearest to the farm. She's also planned what she'll say to work when she rings in sick. She can be off for a week without a doctor's certificate according to her contract, and if she hasn't misread it, that applies to the probationary period as well.

The only thing that's missing is the phone call from them and the invitation. She can't for the life of her understand why they don't do it. She's here, she's been all set for months, with an extra pair of hands that would like nothing more than to work on something other than changing sheets, scouring toilets and vacuuming fitted carpets for anonymous hotel guests day in, day out. It's only a matter of time, at least she hopes it is, before they realise they need help and pick up the phone. Then she'll be here. Ready to jump on a train. Ready to help where it's really needed.

John

He bids farewell to the farm when Netta is out. He does it when she's at the children's health centre with Eva, when she meets the surveyor to inspect the townhouse they've purchased, when she drives the car out of the yard with the trailer full of all the stuff they need to sell or give away before the move. His leave-taking happens in bursts, it takes up several weeks of his time, but it's important for him to do it properly. And it's important for him to be able to do it in peace.

He doesn't want Netta to see him break down and weep like a child when he strokes his first tractor, the green one he bought on Hasse's advice the summer they moved here. He's in too much pain to climb up into the driver's cab, but he pats the engine hood and the tyres. The large ones at the back and the smaller ones at the front. Sentimental tears well up obstinately in his eyes, despite him repeating his perpetual mantra: *They're only things. Things aren't important. People are important, not things.*

When he's finished with the farm vehicles he moves on to the henhouse on the other side of the yard. He goes slowly, not used to walking much with the crutches yet, and they chafe his hands. The blisters sting every time he puts his weight on one or other of them. Netta has taped orange foam rubber onto the handles, but it slips around, ends up at an angle, making the crutch feel unsafe to lean on, as if it might slide out of his hands at any moment and disappear into the middle of nowhere. So he walks slowly. But he makes progress.

He kneels down in the henhouse, despite the pain in his hip as he bends making everything turn black before his eyes. When the worst has subsided and he can focus his gaze again, he calls to them. He calls to them all, the Skåne Flower hens and the Lohman Browns that Netta bought as a surprise the first summer and then were allowed to roam free in the garden because the henhouse wasn't ready. Only the oldest one comes forward. Frida has always been his favourite, the hardest-working of them all, infallibly laying one egg a day and never leaving her box filled with droppings like several of the others persist in doing. Today she lets him stroke the feathers on one side of her neck. She stands still at first then she carries on doing what hens do. She pecks at the straw around his wellingtons and then moves meekly on when she realises she's cleared the surface of edible seeds. Next week she and her friends are going to move to Eriksson's farm in Södra Valla, but they don't know that yet. There's no point in telling a hen a thing like that.

'We shall hope for the best and prepare for the worst.'

That was what the doctors had said this time and it was also what Netta and he repeated in the evening when they gathered the children in the kitchen for the second time in less than six months to deliver some more bad news. When they shared the diagnosis that the cancer had spread to the bones, Netta was very keen that they should quote the doctor's exact words to the children, because it was important for them to know what the situation was. They needed to understand why the family would have to sell the farm so quickly, that their help would be indispensable for some time to come. Above all they too needed the chance to process the information. This was Netta's belief and also that of the hospital counsellor, who had been assigned to them immediately after they were informed about the metastases. He didn't have the strength to argue this time. Instead he focussed on looking as calm, strong and pain-free as he could for the time they were sitting together around the kitchen table later the same evening.

This time none of the children started howling. No one stood up and rushed out of the room either. The mood was different. It was more hushed around the table, almost reverent. Some of the children cried, but quietly this time, with no hysterical outbursts. As if all three had matured several years since they last sat here together, even though it had only been a few months. Even Eva was quiet on her baby mat sprawled between the kitchen units and the table. She babbled from time to time, but she didn't cry or scream.

Each time he comes back up to the house after his private goodbyes to the farm, the answerphone in the kitchen is flashing. There are lots of people ringing them at the moment. His mum, of course, and his sister, and some of the neighbours. Even old friends from Stockholm have started to get in touch again. And Mary too, who tries to reach them nearly every day but he can't bring himself to return her call.

'That back will be the death of you,' Mary used to say when they still lived together. She didn't mean it literally, obviously he knew that. It was just a phrase she would use when she thought he was walking around for too long with the children in his arms at night, or when he complained after a long drive to the mountains, or when he insisted on carrying both their suitcases when they were setting off on holiday or on their way back. She said it out of concern, he knows that, but the phrase echoes in his head each time he sees that she's telephoned. That's probably why he can't face ringing her. Because if he speaks to her, he'll have to tell her where the metastases are, and the fact that they're partly in his back feels like a defeat, as though she was right all along. And he can't handle that. Not at the moment. Not when there's so much else he has to deal with first.

He has to get through two more rounds of treatment before the move takes place. And then a car journey to Stockholm where the medical team at Danderyd will gather to give their verdict on how his body is responding to the treatment. And he must find the strength to be there for Netta and the children throughout all of this worry. And secretly have time to say goodbye to the sheep. And to the horses, and the stable, all fourteen stalls he built himself four summers ago. He mustn't forget the forest behind Lindvallen. The marsh where he shot his first elk. The haystack he'll never be able to climb up, but he has to resign himself to that. He can pat the ladder instead. The main thing is that he includes as much as possible.

Mary

When Hans enters the hotel lift, Mary hasn't thought about him for a long time. But she knows it's him before he's stepped out of the shadowy hotel corridor and into the bright fluorescent light of the lift. There's something about the outline of his body that gives him away instantly. The slight slope of his shoulders, the way his coat sits on either side of his neck, perhaps also the shape of his head. She instinctively lowers her head to the white towels on the cleaning trolley as he comes in. He doesn't appear to recognise her in the way she recognises him and gives a brief nod before positioning himself beside the trolley that separates them. He nods, presses the button for the ground floor and turns his body towards the mirror behind the panel.

As the lift descends she examines his profile out of the corner of her eye. He looks the same, and yet different. The first thing she notices is that his hair is thinning. The hair that used to stick up, bushy and dark brown, even before she'd raked her fingers through it, is now sparse and looks as though it's been slicked down to one side. The second thing she notices is the way the sharp line that a few years ago showed a clear demarcation between his chin and his neck has blurred. It's become a gentle slope from his face to his chest, as if his chin is sliding into his neck and then disappearing under the collar of his brown coat.

When the number two on the display panel scrolls past and is replaced by a one, she bends her head towards the trolley again. She looks at her hands around the round metal handle, notes that the back of each is more chapped after the day's shift. As usual she's been careless about wearing rubber gloves and the disinfectants have made them dry and turned them almost grey. Veins wind their way across them like pale blue earthworms. In her head she tries to recreate the picture of Hans' hand when he pressed the lift button. Was it as soft as it used to be, or have his hands also become older, uglier, greyer? Was there a wedding ring? She doesn't recall. All she can see before her are his hands as she remembers them from before. The long fingers, the short nails, the strong grip when he squeezed her breast underneath her blouse. The smooth gold band that always felt colder on her skin than the rest of his hand.

She's heard the robotic woman's voice announce, 'Lobby, front desk,' thousands of times, but she still jumps. Hans seems to react too, either to the voice or to her abrupt jolt, because he suddenly turns towards her. It's a natural movement, she's standing nearest to the doors facing reception and it's in her direction that he will head on his way out of the lift, but she feels herself freeze in panic.

She doesn't want to be discovered by Hans, not like this. Not when he's a guest at the hotel where she's employed to clean. Not when she has such veiny hands and no eye make-up and a tired old bob haircut with grey streaks growing out. Now he is standing right in front of her and despite her bending her head so low over the trolley that he can't possibly see more than the tip of her nose, she senses how close to disaster she is.

When the door opens she backs out without raising her eyes. She gingerly pulls the trolley over the little sill in the gap between the lift and the lift shaft. The wheels clatter when they go from one surface to the next, but the trolley quietens down again on the soft carpet in the lobby. She backs out of the lift, out of his field of vision, begins her swing to the left to allow him to pass on the trolley's right. This way he can go straight to reception without needing to pay her further heed. She swerves discreetly out of his way, positions the trolley against the wall and then puts her hands to work. Her fingers twitch as she pretends to be busy counting the remaining clean towels.

At the reception desk Hans attracts the staff's attention with an exaggerated cough.

'Number forty-six would like to settle up again,' she hears his familiar voice say, and even though she can't see him in front of her, she's pretty sure he's smiling while he says it.

'Absolutely,' Katja chirps from her side of the desk. 'Was everything OK? Did you sleep well? Everything to your satisfaction this time too?'

He says he's slept like a prince, 'as always,' at which they laugh together. His laugh sounds the same as it did before too. The low timbre she recognises from lunch breaks at Arlanda is in stark contrast to Katja's laugh, which is more discordant, higher, more noticeable. Compared to Hans, she sounds practically hysterical.

With her fingers still going through the pile of terry towels, Mary asks herself if she's ever heard Katja laugh like that before. She didn't sound like that the day Mary checked in. She sounded warm, friendly and professional then, but she didn't laugh. Nothing Mary said made her burst into that octave. She and Hans sound more like old friends than receptionist and hotel guest. Two old friends, sufficiently comfortable with each other to have no qualms about asking if they've slept well and breaking into laughter when they meet in the morning.

Once upon a time it was Mary who was that friend to Hans. It was with Mary he would chat at the coffee machine or joke with at the conference dinners, and it was Mary who might sometimes laugh unnaturally loudly at his comments in their meetings about finance or logistics. It was she who fell for his softly spoken charm and his shapely hands and bushy hair and in the end started having sex with him in the staff toilet. It was her then, it's Katja now. It could be, at any rate.

Not until she hears Hans' gentle voice say, 'Thanks for now,' and Katja's rather more shrill reply urging him to have a really good day and to promise to come back soon, does Mary dare look up from the towels. She sees the sleeve of his brown coat wave as he walks towards the entrance, sees Katja wave back while she shouts her last goodbye, sees the automatic doors slide apart to let him out onto Valhallavägen. And then, with no time to react, she sees him turn and look in her direction.

The eye contact that follows is as inescapable as the instant feeling of being busted. She stands rooted to the spot behind the trolley, locked in his gaze, certain she's been caught. She's ready to start laughing in confusion, shout out words of surprise and amazement. Any moment now she'll have to come out from behind the trolley and hug him. *God, Hans, it's you*, she'll say, *long time no see*. She can already feel the muscles in her face start to twitch, feel her eyes prepare to widen, feel her expression take on mounting surprise.

But nothing else happens. Hans sees her from the street, hesitates just a second, then turns back, carries on walking and the moment is past.

When the doors behind him shut, everything calms down again. The sound of traffic subsides, the jazz music from the speakers in the lobby accompanies the tapping of Katja's fingers on the keyboard again, and Mary too is quiet. Her eyes are still on the space left by Hans, fixed on the spot where he was standing just now, turned towards her, as if he were still there. As if he'll soon come back, say sorry, he recognises her now. As if everything she's imagined will still happen.

'Mary?'

Katja's voice has regained its normal tone when she calls out from the reception desk. There's no giggling or shrillness when she asks Mary if she could see her way to clean number forty-six, where the guest has checked out a little late.

'If you have time? You can do it tomorrow otherwise, we don't have a booking for tonight. He's so cute I usually turn a blind eye to his lie-ins.'

Mary looks at the clock on the wall behind reception. She should actually be finishing work in four minutes. Still, she's not in a hurry to be anywhere else. She takes hold of the trolley handle and starts to push it back to the lift.

'Of course,' she says, and presses the button just as the robotic voice again says, 'Lobby, front desk,' and the doors open.

'I'll take care of it,' she says, as the wheels rattle across the sill.

'You're a star,' says Katja, and her totally normal voice resounds in the lift as the doors close behind Mary.

John

Straight after breakfast Netta wheels him into the living room and helps him into the newly purchased leather armchair in front of the television. On the glass table next to him Netta puts out crisps and water, orange juice and Coca-Cola, a bowl of fruit and a nutritional drink.

'What a treat you'll be having,' she says as she lays them out.

She doesn't say anything about the empty bucket, though. She just places it on the other side of the armchair and pretends nothing's amiss. They try to avoid talking too much about the sad fact that she has to carry the bucket and empty vomit out into the toilet every so often. It is what it is, they reason. Not very dignified for him, not much fun for her, but there's not a great deal they can do about it. Besides, it's only like that on the worst days. Today isn't one of those days and hopefully the bucket will remain empty. With any luck he'll find something interesting to watch while Netta's at the dog club committee meeting.

'I'll be home again in an hour. Promise you'll ring if there's anything?' she shouts before she goes out into the hall.

'Don't forget to put the wheelchair away,' he shouts back.

*

They only use the wheelchair when the children aren't at home. Netta stores it away in the garage just before they come home from school. He spends the rest of the day in front of the TV in the new leather armchair, which they jokingly refer to as the robot chair as it has so many functions it resembles a machine more than a seating preference. If the kids look into the living room, they make an effort to act as if he's sitting there because he's interested in the programme, and not because he's in too much pain to move. Sometimes one of them sits down and watches with him for a while, and on those occasions it's especially important for him to grit his teeth. There's no reason to let them know how much pain he's in, not when they've had so much to cope with. It's enough that he and Netta know.

When the children are beside him he tries to breathe as carefully as he can. Deep breaths affect his back in ways that are unpredictable, and so he tries to breathe lightly. As high up in his chest as possible. It makes his voice sound a little strange, but it's worth it. The main thing is that the children don't become more anxious than they already are. Under the circumstances, it's the best solution: to sit still and keep his eyes on the TV and only talk about what's on the screen.

Another thing that works quite well is to direct attention back to the children themselves. He can ask about their day at school, for example, or if they have any homework they'd like him to help them with. Then they usually withdraw in a matter of minutes. Before they disappear they tell him they've got it covered, there's nothing they need help with at the moment, everything's 'cool'. He's not sure that is the case, but he's relieved when they go on their way. It's simply too exhausting to spend time with them at the moment.

Since they moved into the townhouse two months ago he must have watched more TV than he'd done in his entire life up to then. There's not much else he can do while the treatment is ongoing. While his body aches and he vomits at the slightest exertion, and the skin on his hands is flaking off and his mouth is dry like sandpaper and he has ulcers on his lips and his legs are covered in bruises even though he hasn't bumped into anything. Then it's best to sit still as much as possible.

He often falls asleep in the armchair. The robot chair is good in that sense. There's a small remote control that puts it into a reclining position without him having to strain more than the muscle in his thumb. Some days that's as much as he can manage. With the TV control in one hand and the armchair remote in the other, he sits and adjusts the backrest while he flicks between the channels. He takes his medication according to a specific schedule. Must never skimp on the morphine, it just doesn't pay. He talks to Netta when she comes in and wants to chat, talks to the children the same, waits for night-time and when it comes lets Netta push him into the bedroom. But never before the children have gone to bed. It's too upsetting for them to see him in the wheelchair. He doesn't want to subject them to that.

In the townhouse you can reach the heated garage via the laundry room on the ground floor. It's practical, considering the wheelchair. On this floor there's a bedroom for him and Netta and Eva, a living room, kitchen, two smaller guest rooms of which one serves as a study and the other will be Eva's nursery when she's older.

In the basement there are two further bedrooms, both with narrow windows at ceiling height, and a den with a second TV and a grey fitted carpet on the floor. Unfortunately that's all he can remember about the basement, because he's only been in it once. At the house viewing he could still use stairs and he was a big fan of the basement. After the viewing he argued all the way back to the farm that it would be fantastic to buy an old pinball machine and put it in the corner of the den. Netta had laughed at him, teasing him for calling the basement a den, and he had spent most of the journey home explaining that it was an appropriate term, and not just something he'd thought up. By the time they arrived at the stable, they were as one. Netta had agreed to calling it a den and buying an antique pinball machine.

When they moved in he could no longer climb the stairs and they never got around to buying that pinball machine. It seemed more sensible to give Victor his own computer space instead. There he basically sits twenty-four hours a day, playing his games. Netta suspects he sometimes sleeps on the sofa next to the computer, but Victor strongly denies it.

Fredrika hasn't come off too badly in the basement either. She has her own bathroom adjoining her bedroom and as a consequence her arguments with Netta have virtually ceased. There's no one queuing outside for the toilet and rattling the handle, and she can take her time in front of the mirror. Fredrika was also given the largest bedroom downstairs, almost twice as big as Victor's. Which is only right as she's at home so much since she finished with Ola, and for his part, Victor goes to see Ellen at the start of every weekend. In the basement Fredrika can have as much privacy as she likes. Netta has put a gate at the top of the stairs so that Eva doesn't get it into her head that she can go down. Since she started crawling, no floor space is really safe.

*

He wasn't aware he'd dropped off, hadn't even put the chair into sleep mode, but when the telephone on the glass table rings he gives a start and opens his eyes. Pain shoots through his spine at the sudden movement, spreading out through his lower back and hips, making him scream out loud before he works out he's in his usual corner of the living room. The sound surprised even him and the echo of his cry hangs in the air. His voice sounded so high. It's definitely changed over the last few months. Less masculine, it seems to him. There's absolutely no difference, according to Netta. It's just the medication, the doctors say. When he reaches out to pick up the phone from its position between the fruit bowl and the bottle of water, it stops ringing. He leaves it where it is. Rests his hand on the soft armrest and closes his eyes for a little while longer.

The moment the front door opens, Netta's voice comes from the hall.

'Hello-are-you-OK?'

She's starting saying it every time she comes home. When they're together during the day she acts as if she's not worried, she chats and jokes with him almost like she did before, but when she comes back after she's been out somewhere, she gives herself away at once. Her voice is shrill, demanding an instant response. He always tries to answer quickly when she shouts like that, as he does today.

'All fine here! How was the dog club?' he shouts, as cheerily as he can.

From his position he can hear, but not see her stifle a sigh of relief and roll the buggy over the threshold. She pushes it all the way into the kitchen, where she parks it in its usual place by the window, loosens Eva's blanket and opens the kitchen window a fraction. Then she goes back into the hall and hangs up her hat and coat. When she comes into the living room and asks him how he's been, she's adjusted her voice, which sounds relaxed and normal again now.

'Fine,' he says, and hopes it's not obvious he's been asleep. 'I saw a documentary about bees that was really interesting.'

What he says is almost true. He has actually seen a documentary about bees that was unexpectedly interesting, though it wasn't today. Netta sits down in the armchair next to him. She turns it in his direction and wrinkles her brow, as if trying to tell whether he's lying or not. He meets her eye with confidence, ready to start describing the specific tasks each bee has in its hive, but Netta doesn't want to talk about that.

'Mary rang on my mobile while I was at the club,' she says.

She narrows her eyes at him across the glass table separating them. At least that's how it seems to John, who feels his grip on the remote control tighten.

'Did you know she hasn't spoken to either of the children for over a month?'

'How should I know? They have their own phones now, they take care of that themselves.'

'Well...clearly they don't. She's pretty worried, you know.'

'About what? The children?'

'For God's sake, John, what do you think?'

Netta looks irritated as she stares at him from the other side of the table. When he doesn't say anything, she carries on.

'She's worried about the children, worried about you. She doesn't seem to have any idea at all what's going on here!'

He sighs and turns his gaze back to the television. Starts pressing the buttons on the remote control to give his hands something to do. At the same time he thinks about the calls he hasn't answered, the call he didn't answer a little while ago, the ringing that woke him abruptly from his sleep. The fact that it was probably Mary who was phoning then. He hits upon an American news channel and sighs again.

'OK. I get it. I'll speak to them.'

Netta doesn't appear to be satisfied with his answer, because on she goes.

'Good. But you need to talk to Mary too. And you and I can drop by her flat in Stockholm after the appointment at Danderyd next week. It's hardly a detour at all. So you can both talk. It feels like it's about time.'

Netta stands up. The conversation is apparently over, because she's on her way to the door and into the hall by the time he raises his voice and shouts after her.

'What? I'm definitely not doing that! That was the stupidest bloody idea you've ever had!'

He stares angrily at her when she stops at the door and slowly turns towards him. As she does so, he can see her smiling. It's her tired smile, tired but determined, the smile that's told him hundreds of times over the years that he's lost the battle and there's no point in arguing.

Mary

Before John and Jeanette's visit she bakes two racks of saffron buns. Advent hasn't even started yet, but she couldn't resist. There's something about the change of seasons that always makes her very productive. Last week it was even snowing a little when she walked home from the hotel. And John has always loved her Lucia buns. Back in the day, he could get through a trayful in less than twenty-four hours. They used to laugh when he tried to blame the children whenever she asked what had happened to all the buns. He could eat upwards of five in a row without getting stomach ache or putting on any weight at all. They used to laugh about that too. She certainly hopes he'll be pleased to have something tasty today as well.

When the doorbell rings it's four o'clock and the flat is filled with the smell of baking. The racks are ready in the kitchen and she hurries through the living room to the hall. Exactly according to plan, she opens the door wearing her pink linen apron and exactly as planned she uses the greeting she's been rehearsing ever since the phone call with Jeanette last week.

'*Hello*, guys! How *great* to see you! You both look radiant.'

*

She regrets her words the second she utters them. In the shadowy doorway she sees a couple who don't look in the least radiant, quite the reverse. Behind her misted-up glasses Jeanette looks pale and bloated. Her puffy eyelids point to lack of sleep and her blonde hair, stuffed into a black knitted hat for today, is definitely not as shiny as the last time they saw one another. The bits sticking out at the side look matted. More mousy than golden.

As for John, he's…grey. It's the first word that comes to mind when she sees him, and the more she tries not to think about it, the clearer it is that everything about him has gone grey. Or black-and-white. He looks like a sepia photograph in the entrance-hall lighting. The skin tone in his face is ash-grey, but more yellowish under his eyes. His knuckles – also grey – look as though they're about to push through his skin. There's no denying he's lost weight and the skin under his cheekbones doesn't obey when he tries to smile back at Mary.

'Long time no see. And even longer since I was here,' he says, as he crosses the threshold and, leaning on Jeanette for support, comes into the hall.

Mary finds herself laughing nervously at his remark. He's right, she says, it really *was* a long time ago. But, she goes on, everything in Gaby's flat is much the same, as he'll see, she hasn't done a great deal to the décor as the idea is she'll move before long.

'Not that I'm unhappy here,' she continues, gesturing around Gaby's living room. 'It's close to work and it's a really lovely area, it's just that it's short of a couple of rooms, well, you'll see for yourselves…'

The last thing she says is directed at Jeanette. She's keen to include both her guests in the conversation while also wanting to suggest that nothing at all is wrong, nothing at all about their appearance was a shock, *definitely not*. Jeanette *definitely* doesn't look tired and worn-out, and John *definitely* hasn't lost weight and colour and become black-and-white.

They take their time in the hall. As Jeanette helps John off with his jacket, their movements together are careful, synchronised as though they're performing a slow dance they've been practising for a long time. Only after John's coat is hanging on the hook and he has recovered his crutch with the foam rubber on the handle, does Jeanette turn to face the flat and reply to the last of all Mary's nervous questions.

'Eva's down in the entrance, asleep in the pram. There wasn't room in the lift,' she explains, gesturing towards the door. 'So I thought I'd take a walk with her down to Gärdet Field and she can have some more sleep. And you two can talk a bit on your own, it's been a while.'

When she turns to John, she lowers her voice.

'Will it be OK if I come back in an hour?'

'Of course,' he says, still facing the coat rack. 'Or earlier. Just come when she wakes up.'

Jeanette stands on tiptoe and gives him a kiss on his cheek. Mary stays in the living room, not knowing what to do with herself, so she waits, for the kiss, for the door, for John to turn around and start to move towards the room. When he finally does, it happens slowly. He holds his neck straight as he rotates, without turning his head, and therefore he can't see Mary waving her arms between the armchair and the sofa, and asking where he'd prefer to sit, in the armchair or the sofa? Or should she bring a chair from the kitchen?

'The one that's tallest would be best,' he says, in a high voice she doesn't quite recognise.

Mary starts pushing the armchair across the floor to the end of the living-room table, while from the doorway

John confirms that the flat really does look just as he remembers it. He's quite right. Both the furniture and the arrangement are the same as in the eighties, when Gaby and Sven used the flat for their visits to Stockholm and John and Mary sometimes went to them for coffee with the children. John can hardly be expected to notice there are new curtains at the windows and a velvet drape dividing the living room from the bed alcove.

The armchair, which is without a doubt higher than the sagging sofa that's always been in the flat, needs to be moved a bit. More precisely, from one end of the table to the other. She pulls it slowly across the floor to avoid scratching the parquet, as John moves forward on his crutch. It looks as though every movement hurts, he flinches at the end of each step he takes and stands for a few seconds before starting on the next. Mary pretends not to notice his stifled moan when he drops into the chair. To mask the sound of the deep sigh that escapes his lips when he settles, she fills the hiatus with asking if he'd like some coffee.

'Or maybe some tea?' she asks on her way to the kitchen.

'Water will be fine,' John says from the armchair.

'Water coming up,' she shouts over her shoulder, rather more jauntily than she'd intended.

She prepares the tray on the kitchen counter. Places two small plates, two warm Lucia buns and two floral serviettes beside a jug of water. While she's busy with her hands, she chats to John in the living room. When he asks how Gaby is, she tries to make him laugh by telling him that she suspects her mum has found a new man in Tenerife, because she's almost impossible to get hold of nowadays, and it's been several weeks since she last rang.

'Gosh, but maybe that's nice for you,' John's new voice says from the living room, and Mary laughs even more. Laughing rather too much, she says, yes, it is nice, in fact, nice but unusual.

When she goes from the kitchen into the living room balancing the tray, she notices that her knees are shaking. The sight of John together with the artificial small talk has made her nervous. She wonders how they'll continue their conversation, which one of them will introduce the subject of the children, whether she should mention how ill he looks, or how strange his voice has become, but John forestalls her. The moment she puts the tray down on the table, he starts to speak.

'I want to apologise that we've been so hard to reach recently. It's been a bit much with everything, I guess you could say…'

He nods towards the crutch leaning against the armchair. Mary's gaze follows his nod. The movement of his head indicates that it's been too much with the crutch, the crutch itself is the reason that he and the children have been almost impossible to reach in the last few months, the crutch's fault, the whole lot, not what it symbolises.

'I understand if you've been worried for the children, that was mostly what I wanted to say.'

'Yes…a little bit,' she says, relieved that the conversation has at last focussed where it was supposed to and she doesn't need to chat about things that aren't important. 'How are they?'

She pushes the water glass across the table to the place nearest to him, followed by the plate of Lucia buns and a serviette. John keeps his eyes on the movements of her hand. He sits with his back straight, keeps his upper body still, takes a few short breaths.

'Er... The children are doing well, under the circumstances, I think,' he says, after she finally sits down; it seems an eternity since she posed the question.

She smiles and nods encouragingly, waiting for him to elaborate.

'Of course, it's been really tough. Fredrika's started going to see a psychologist because she's having difficulty sleeping at night. She says it feels good to talk to somebody who's not family. And she's applying to that school in London that she wants to start at in the autumn, you know, she's told you about it?'

'Yes, that one. How exciting,' Mary lies. She hasn't heard about the psychologist or any school in London. She hopes he'll say more, let slip what the school's called, what it specialises in, when they thought she might go, but he changes subject.

'And then there's Victor. Well... He is what he is. Doesn't say much. Spends most of his time in front of the computer in the basement, and sometimes he goes to see the girl he's met in Nacka...'

For the second time Mary nods and waits for more, but there's no more to come. John falls silent, swallows and fixes his eye on the glass of water on the table in front of him. When he leans forward in his chair and his face twists into something that she can only interpret as severe pain, she responds instinctively. She launches herself forward, reaches the glass before him, picks it up and hands it to him. It's only when he takes it that she considers the risk that he might react to the incongruity in the situation, of her almost taking from him the possibility of lifting up his own glass of water, but he doesn't say anything. He takes the glass, has a few sips, and then lets her repeat the manoeuvre in reverse. Her action is clumsy, the bottom of the glass bangs against the teak tabletop, a few drops of water spill over the edge. She dries them with her serviette, keeping her eyes fixed intently on the table to summon the courage for her next question.

'And you, John, how are...you?'

She didn't mean her question to sound so dramatic, but when the last word comes out as more of a whisper than normal conversation and at the same instant John reaches out his hand to her, the moment takes on a solemnity that makes her wish she hadn't asked. She doesn't need to know how things are with him. She can see very well how he is. He's not good, and he doesn't need to embarrass himself by telling her. Now he's sitting there, his hand outstretched, and it looks as though he's in pain, frowning and supporting himself with his free hand on the chair's armrest. She takes his hand in hers and their clasp is a cross between a handshake and an endearment. They stay like that for several seconds without either of them speaking.

'Sorry,' she says after a moment. 'You really don't have to sit here and give me a...'

'Between two and four months, if the worst comes to the worst. That's what they're saying. The children don't know. We think we'll wait until after Christmas.'

His grip on her hand tightens as he speaks, but otherwise nothing in his face betrays the seriousness of what he's just said. He keeps his eyes fixed on hers, watches her quietly as his words sink in, gives her time to assimilate the significance of each sentence into a whole. His fingers around her left hand are cold. Two to four months, she thinks. Two to four months... Oh, God.

'We'll wait until after Christmas and New Year,' he goes on, 'and then we'll see. There's one type of chemo we haven't tried yet, but it's not certain my body can withstand another round of treatment. Not the way things are looking at the moment, anyway. The metastases are everywhere, mostly in the hips. No further prognosis, they say.'

When John stops speaking he lets go of her hand and her gaze and he looks straight ahead, at the wall on the other side of the living room. He doesn't see her raising the hand he was holding in his to her eyes and wiping her cheeks with the back of it. Instead he stares at the wall on the other side of the room and at the antique wall clock that Gaby bought at Bukowskis auction house in the mid-seventies and on numerous subsequent occasions tried to give to Mary and him because she thought it would go so well in their living room on Tallvägen. In the silence of the room the second hand sounds like a hammer.

'John, I'm so sorry...' she finally manages to say.

'I know,' he says, his eyes still fixed on the wall, 'so are we. Anyway, we'd like to ask for your understanding, because we'd rather keep them at home over Christmas this year.'

Mary is just in the process of telling him she understands – of course she understands, of course the children have to stay home with him and Jeanette, it's no problem at all as far as she concerned – when the doorbell in the hall gives a shrill ping and she loses track of what she's saying. She gets up to open the door, but there's no need, because before she's managed to squeeze out between the sofa and the table, Jeanette comes into the hall. This time accompanied by a visibly displeased Eva, who's flailing around in her arms.

'Hello there,' Jeanette calls from the door between the hall and the living room. 'She woke up so I thought I might just as well come back. She's in a vile mood, as you can see.' She nods towards a red-faced Eva, who is angrily flinging herself back and forth in Jeanette's arms and whose evident objective is to remove her own hat.

'How's it going here?' she says, above the noise. 'Do you think you're nearly finished, or shall we come in for a little while?'

Mary's eyes dart between Jeanette and John, who is already halfway up out of the armchair and says it's fine, they've finished, can Mary please hand him his crutch? Mary does as she's told. She gives him the crutch and stands ready while he rises to his feet, then she stays behind him as he makes his way slowly across the parquet.

In the hall Eva's bawling intensifies the closer her dad comes to her. Jeanette holds her daughter against her hip in a firm grip and uses her free arm to take John's coat down from the rack.

'Are you tired, darling?' she asks John, who appears to be suffering from the racket at least as much as Mary is trying to pretend she isn't.

Jeanette seems to interpret his expression in the same way, because she opens the door and quickly backs out into the entrance.

'Sorry about the chaos! It was nice to see you, Mary, and how cosy you've made it here!' she shouts, waving into the flat.

Mary waves from the living-room door. She wonders whether it's appropriate to offer them a bag of Lucia buns to take home for the children, but she doesn't get the chance to ask, because after she's said it was nice to see them too, and John has thanked her for the coffee, which he didn't drink, and the chat, which had hardly begun before he had to leave, they close the door behind them and the moment has passed.

Eva's screaming echoes in the entrance for a few more seconds, until there's sudden silence and the lift door shuts. Mary returns to the living room, where she puts the glasses back on the tray, takes the Lucia buns with her into the kitchen and in the end, after a moment's hesitation, throws them into the bin under the kitchen counter.

John

In the car on the way back from Stockholm Netta presses him on the details of his conversation with Mary. *How did it go? What did she say? What did you say? Did she start crying, did you decide anything, what did she say about Christmas, did you talk about that thing with the children?* She wanted to know everything. In the passenger seat John becomes increasingly irritated by all her questions. He's already answered them once, and he doesn't think there's much else to say.

'But what do you mean? Was that *all* you said? That she can't see Fredrika and Victor this Christmas? It sounds a very strange conversation, if you ask me. Weren't you going to talk about the children and what happens next, if... Well, you know?'

She stops short, because she's well aware that on no account does he want to talk about what happens next, if, well, he knows. And actually, she doesn't either. All the same, the tone of her voice reveals that she's not very pleased with his contribution to the conversation in question, that she wishes he had touched on a number of the issues that are related to the eventuality of what they don't want to talk about happening anyway.

He shrugs his shoulders angrily, for nothing, since she can't see him in the dark. The movement is painful and, as an unwelcome side effect, makes him even more irritated with his wife than he was before. He actually wants to rest, not talk about Mary all the way back to Eskilstuna. Why can't she just let it drop? Why must she drive him around on visits he doesn't want to make? Why doesn't she grasp that the only thing he needs is rest, nothing else?

'What did you think I should say then?' he snaps. 'Christmas was the important thing, wasn't it? Or was there something else you and Mary had decided behind my back that I should talk about?'

His sarcasm is more aggressive than he intended and he regrets it immediately. He and Netta have finished their fight about this, after all. It's several days since they made up after the quarrel that ensued when she went over his head and decided that he and Mary would meet. Netta has already apologised and he's already forgiven her; they have kissed and cuddled and said they love each other a number of times since then. What's more, he's proved her right, which makes his sarcasm even less appropriate. He reluctantly admitted to Netta that he has shied away from speaking to Mary, and since then he's also promised to try and help make things right between the children and her. That's why he's ashamed now. And he hopes she won't be annoyed by his snarky comments and defend herself on the grounds she only wants 'what's best for everyone'. He decides to pre-empt any response to his pointless grouchiness.

'Darling, I'm sorry, that was a stupid thing to say. I'm just so damned tired. I really did my best in there. It wasn't easy to give her that news and say she can't see the children at Christmas. It just seemed like it was enough. Can't we drop this now? And I'll talk to her soon on the phone? I feel as though I really need to shut my eyes for a bit.'

Netta's hand on his leg tells him she accepts his apology. She strokes his thigh, not playfully as she once did, she does it more softly now. She knows he's in pain, knows he did what he could, and that's the most important thing.

He lays his hand on hers and leans back against the headrest. The lights in the buildings under the bridges in Södertälje twinkle in the darkness. There's still an hour of the car journey left, probably a little more. With a bit of luck he can fall asleep here, with Netta's warm hand under his cold one, and not wake until they come to the roundabouts outside Eskilstuna. An hour's sleep will make everything feel better, he's almost sure. It usually does.

He closes his eyes and welcomes the sleep that will soon erase the echo of today's agonies from his consciousness. He closes his eyes, lets his head fall gently to the side and tries not to think about anything at all. Not the doctor's words or the metastases. Not Mary's eyes when she waved to him and Netta as they were leaving. Not Netta, who still refuses to give up hope of his recovery, despite the doctors' words, and definitely not Eva, who's asleep in the back seat behind him. He doesn't think about any of it when he finally falls asleep in the front seat next to Netta, because it does no good to think like that. Such thoughts will make no difference, will make things neither better nor worse. He lets the hum of the engine rock him to sleep instead. When the sharp drone stops ringing in his ears and starts to melt into a comfortable background murmur, he knows he'll succeed.

Mary

On Saint Lucia's Day she works with tinsel in her hair. The crinkly thread leaves red marks on her forehead when she's covered with sweat from vacuuming the hotel-room floors, and the long tail down her neck keeps slipping forward when she leans over the toilets with her disinfectant spray and cloth. She swears out loud to herself a number of times during her shift. When she's finished the last room, she has a good mind to pull the tinsel off and throw it out with the rest of the rubbish, but at the last moment she abandons the idea. She doesn't intend to let Nadja have a go at her for a second time today.

When the senior management team announced at the monthly meeting that hotel staff were expected to adorn themselves with tinsel 'as usual at Lucia', Mary assumed it didn't apply to her. Reception staff, she could understand, and the team in the restaurant, definitely, but a cleaner? That would be ridiculous, Mary thought, and therefore she didn't attach any particular importance to the request and for the same reason didn't take any tinsel with her to work that morning. That turned out to be a mistake, because when she passed reception she was stopped by Nadja, who pointed out through pursed lips that Mary had surely forgotten something.

'Didn't you hear what the exec said?' she said. '*Everyone* has to wear tinsel today.'

Mary apologised and said she'd misunderstood, whereupon Nadja gave her a metre or so of her own tinsel and across the reception desk helped her tie a tight knot behind her head. Then she waved Mary away with a cheery, 'Have a nice shift!'

On the way down from the last floor of uncleaned rooms, Mary can't help wincing at her own reflection in the lift. It looks so undignified: a middle-aged woman with drooping eyelids and greying hair, dressed up like an ageing handmaiden in some kind of Lucia procession for hotel guests. It's only children who wear tinsel, she thinks. Surely not even Fredrika uses it nowadays? At any rate, it's years since her daughter sent her any pictures of herself with all the regalia.

At the thought of Fredrika, the smile leaves her lips. Following John's visit Fredrika has only answered one of the many calls Mary has made, and even then the conversation was short. Mary, who didn't know how she should broach the subject of John's illness, had begun far too tentatively. She'd asked Fredrika how she was, to which Fredrika had replied, 'Totally fine,' and then said she was in a hurry and had to go.

'Let me know about your wish list for Christmas,' Mary had managed to get in before they ended the call, and in answer to that Fredrika had said, 'Definitely, I'll be in touch,' and hung up.

That was more than a week ago now. Christmas Eve is fast approaching and without knowing what the children would like or when there'll be an opportunity to see them, the question of Christmas presents has been hard for Mary. With the help of a contribution from Gaby, she's purchased some bits and pieces in the Fältöversten shopping centre on her way home from work, but nothing she's bought really feels right. She's not sure if it's appropriate for a mother to give her eighteen-year-old daughter make-up, and if so, she's even less sure what kind of make-up Fredrika uses. If anything, it's more difficult with Victor. Mary knows nothing about the video games John maintains Victor spends his nights on. Last week she went into a games shop on Grev Turegatan and asked which game was the most popular, but the green-haired girl on the till just glared at her and said it depended on who you were and what kind of games you liked. Mary had walked out with a football game and a war game and decided that she'd go back to the shop as soon as she'd got hold of Victor. But he hasn't been easy to reach lately either.

She takes off the tinsel in front of the reception desk and asks, half in jest, if Nadja would maybe like it back? Nadja doesn't want it back; she picks it up between the tips of her finger and thumb and with an expression of disgust drops it into the wastepaper basket under the desk. With that she goes back to tapping on the computer.

'Don't forget to come in earlier tomorrow, we're planning the staffing cover for Christmas,' she says, as Mary approaches the doors.

Mary nods and smiles at her boss. She makes an effort to hide the fact she's offended, both by the disgusted look on her face and the fact that Nadja speaks to her as if she were a senile old woman whose memory is unreliable.

'Of course, see you tomorrow,' she says as she goes out.

'Have a nice Lucia,' says Nadja, typing away.

Back in the flat there's a letter waiting on the mat in the hall. Mary doesn't need to open the envelope to know who the sender is. It's several years since she last received a letter from Fredrika, but evidently she hasn't lost her distinctive way of writing. Her handwriting slopes alternately forwards and backwards and in the four short lines on the front of the envelope, she's achieved the feat of writing her a's in no less than three different ways. She's put the stamp in the left corner instead of the right. It could easily have been a ten-year-old who'd sent this. Mary smiles when she prods the envelope in her hand. Judging by the weight of it, there's no Christmas card hidden inside, it must be the wish list her daughter has finally put together and posted. Mary hurries into the living room to read what Fredrika has written.

The sofa is covered with Christmas paper, tape, string and sticky labels from the previous day's present-wrapping. Mary gathers it all up and moves it onto the coffee table. She's aware that she's perspiring even before she's opened Fredrika's letter, partly because she's so eager, and partly because she's still wearing her coat and scarf. She did have time to take her shoes off before she ran in, so she permits herself to put her feet up on the sofa. She opens the letter as carefully as she can. She uses the scissors from the present-wrapping so that she doesn't damage the envelope more than necessary, already knows before she reads the letter that she'll keep it in the box of personal mementoes in the wardrobe in the hall.

Dear Mum,

Please don't be sad, but I need to ask you to leave me in peace. Like...forget me a little bit. The thing is, right now I can't cope with having a bad conscience. I see every time you ring and I've listened to all your messages, but I get an ache in my stomach every time I'm going to ring you back, and then I can't sleep all night. It's like a stress I can't handle just now. SORRY!!! You haven't done anything wrong and the birthday thing really doesn't matter, I promise. But I think I need a break, because otherwise it feels as though I'm going to fall apart for real. I hope you understand.

Loads of kisses,
Fredrika

P.S. It was my psychologist who said I should write this.

Mary reads the letter twice. After reading it for the second time, she turns the piece of paper over, to see if there's any more. There isn't. The back of the paper, which looks as though it's been torn out of an exercise book, is empty. Mary lays the letter on her lap; she doesn't know what to do with the sheet of paper or herself. She remains sitting on the sofa for some time. When she tries to go over Fredrika's words to understand the meaning, she fails after the very first sentence. She picks the letter up and reads it again. And again. And yet again. Then she puts it on the coffee table, on top of the Christmas paper and the tape and the scissors and the string and the notebook with all the half-finished rhymes, and she stands up.

As she puts her shoes on in the hall she doesn't really know where she's going. Costas or the hotel, the hotel or Costas, it has to be one or the other. She has nowhere else to go. She can't stay in the flat, anyway.

She runs down the stairs to the entrance.

It'll have to be Costas.

She prays he's working tonight.

JOHN

The kids' faces when he comes into the kitchen and sits down at the dinner table are priceless. All three do a double take, stare at him as if they've seen a ghost, before they rearrange their expressions and try to act as if everything is normal. Netta helps with the seat cushion before propping the crutches against the wall. She is in a particularly good mood as well, positively oozing with pride when she presents the evening meal. She has every right to be, since the chicken stew with coconut milk smells heavenly. Victor doesn't express it in that way, but at least he does say it smells good. Adding, after he's sniffed the air, that the smell reminds him of 'Grandma's sun cream', which makes everyone around the table laugh, including Netta, even though she has never met Mary's eccentric mother and can't possibly understand the reference. John himself laughs at the unexpectedly uplifting thought of Gaby and her extensive use of sunscreen products, and it's only when he's been laughing a little while that he realises he doesn't need to be quite so wary about his stomach muscles today. The pain has diminished considerably of late. If he's not miscalculated, he's down to 150 milligrams of morphine a day, and that, as far as he's concerned, is nothing less than a triumph.

When they start eating he wonders how long it is since they last ate together at the table. It seems that at least one or two of the others are thinking the same thing, as the conversation is slightly stiff and occasionally forced. It's been a few weeks, anyway, maybe even a month. He spent most of November in bed. The first half of December too. It was from a horizontal position that he played his part in the final planning for Jenny's forthcoming trip to Texas, where she's going to work as an au pair at an equestrian centre. The same applied to Fredrika's application for the school in London.

It was plainly a good decision on the part of the doctors to put the brakes on after the latest round of treatment. It took much more of a toll on him than the previous rounds. His bloods were alarmingly low at the last check-up at Danderyd, while the metastases hadn't reduced appreciably. Therefore, he and Netta, together with the doctors, agreed that his body needed a break over Christmas and New Year, to give it a chance to recover. If he has lots of rest over the holiday, they said, and can avoid undue infection, there is at least a theoretical chance of starting the new type of chemotherapy by the middle of January. Since then the family has entered a quarantine of sorts, to protect him from the risk of infection. Fredrika and Victor have been given permission by their schools to study at home for the last week of term. Jenny's part-time job at the riding school entails only contact with horses, and scarcely any people. Netta goes shopping early in the morning when the supermarkets are still empty, washing and sanitising her hands carefully afterwards. All visits by family and friends have been called off this Christmas, and everyone who's received the message appears to have taken it well, under the circumstances. The family's combined efforts seem to be working already, because today he can sit on a normal chair – albeit furnished with an ergonomic seat cushion that looks suspiciously like a toilet seat – and they can all eat dinner together. It feels good to be back. The children smile at him across the table.

After dinner, unfortunately, the fun's over. The children say thank you for dinner and disappear down to the basement, Fredrika to study and Victor to do 'his own thing', whatever that may be. Something on the computer, if he knows his son. Jenny vanishes into the office to ring a friend and John remains at the table, alone, while Netta clears away. Eva crawls around her feet; she tries to pull herself up at the kitchen cupboards, but falls down and tries again. In between, she utters little squeals, which are swiftly followed by words of encouragement from Netta. He reaches forward cautiously for one of his crutches. He congratulates Netta on the food as he gets to his feet, and then he walks slowly towards the living room and the robot chair. He doesn't really have any desire to be in there, but doesn't know where else to go. It's far too early to go to bed, especially after such a happy evening. All the same, it's probably best if he sits in front of the television.

On his way across the hall he stops and glances at the staircase leading down to the basement. It looks long and steep. He can hear a familiar sound coming from the den, a jingle from a video game that Victor loves, but John has never managed to master. The ding-dong noise travels up the stairs. Netta's voice comes from the kitchen, rising above both the running water in the sink and the music from the game in the den, to remind him it's time for his medication in a quarter of an hour. He says he knows, promises not to forget. He mobilises his body to carry on its path to the living room, but something makes him change his mind. Before he has actively considered it, his body has altered course. It's just a matter of following.

He veers away from his original route and steers his feet towards the stairs. He walks slowly and very cautiously. He creeps to escape Netta's notice, in as much as it's possible to do so with thick socks and a crutch. One step at a time. Left leg before right. Then stop. He can feel it in his hips. The crutch in his right hand, the bannister in his left. One step more. And repeat. It works. He goes softly down the stairs to say hello to his children and see what they're up to down there. He still has a few surprises up his sleeve. There's still a bit of kick left in the old boy.

Mary

It turned out Costas didn't want to go home with her. It turned out he wasn't called Costas either, but Miroslav. Mary still breaks out in a sweat every time she thinks about how the evening at the restaurant ended. At the vulgar way she'd offered herself, and, to make matters worse, that she'd done so right in front of both his staff and some of the clientele. At the fact she'd left her purse in her handbag and her handbag in her mother's flat and had consequently been obliged to ask if she could put everything on a tab, after she'd already humiliated herself. At how then, when she was leaving, she'd slipped on the pavement outside and Costas, that is to say Miroslav, had had to come out and help her up onto her feet. At how he'd insisted on walking her back to the flat entrance. At how he'd gripped her arm, not in an amorous way, but as if he suspected she couldn't stay upright by herself.

Most of all she's ashamed when she thinks about how, when he was about to go, he'd hugged her and said it seemed as though she needed a friend. And when he said that, she'd started crying in the most undignified of ways. She must have made an awful mess of his white shirt and have woken some of the neighbours, when she told him between howls about the letter from Fredrika, about Victor never getting in touch, about John's illness and Rolf and her job and God knows what else. She doesn't remember all the details, but for that she can only be thankful. That was the least the six glasses at Costas', or Miroslav's, restaurant, could bestow. In every other respect they were just a source of pain. She should most certainly not have gone there that evening. The memory of it still makes her hyperventilate, she's so deeply ashamed. She doesn't believe she has ever behaved in a more undignified fashion in her entire life than on that Thursday evening. All concentrated into less than three hours.

One week later she still hasn't paid Miroslav. It's not that she can't afford it, but her legs won't seem to take her down the hill. It's as if the shame has taken up residence in her muscles. Each morning she makes up her mind to do it, but it's as if her body won't obey when she goes out. Her legs take a detour to work, whether her head consents or not. As a result her walk to work has become longer, but it doesn't really matter. It's not as if she's in a hurry to go anywhere. Or as if anyone wonders where she is.

Last Friday she came close to taking sick leave for the first time since she started at the hotel. She did go to work in the end, and she wasn't late, despite the detour. It was the thought of staying at home, in the same flat as the letter, and where the telephone still doesn't ring, no matter how much she wills it to, that had finally made her get up and go out.

Once there, she went into Nadja's office and offered to work extra hours over Christmas and New Year. Nadja seemed pretty indifferent to her proposal, but in contrast, some of Mary's colleagues were delighted.

Katja was jubilant about squeezing in an extra day with the family, and Musse in the restaurant gave her an impulsive hug as thanks for her sacrifice. It was decided then. She'll fill in as needed and this will ensure she's not at home for too many hours at a stretch over the holiday. At the same time it gave her a valid reason to put a stop to Gaby's constant nagging about bringing the children down to Båstad.

Four days before Christmas Eve she goes into the post office in Fältöversten with her parcel. She has the opportunity to regret her decision several times in the half hour she spends queuing at the counter. She's far from the only person trying to post Christmas presents today and it's hard to think straight in the mêlée. Trying to determine whether it can be interpreted as disrespectful to send the parcel, despite Fredrika's wish to be left in peace, seems an impossible task. Whatever she does will be wrong.

She can stop getting in touch, if that's what they ask her to do, but surely they can't take away her right to send them Christmas presents? Surely she still has the right to carry on loving them, even if they don't seem to love her back very much at the moment? At the counter she notices that perspiration is dripping from her brow. She should have taken her hat off when she came in, now the sweat rolling down the side of her face and making her fingers wet when she touches her cheek. The woman at the till looks at her with distaste when she asks if she needs to borrow some tape to seal her parcel. She hadn't thought of doing that before she left home. She apologises, thanks her for the offer, and at the last minute takes the little tags with the Christmas rhymes out of the parcel.

The cashier sighs and says that maybe she should have thought about the tags before. Mary apologises and says she'd completely forgotten about them. She stuffs the tags with the rhymes into her coat pocket. Something tells her this is not the time for her rhymes. Besides, she can't stand the thought that the children would read them out loud to John and Jeanette. Even worse, that Fredrika would refuse to read hers so Victor had to read them all. It will just have to be pre-printed tags on the Christmas presents this year. What's on the stickers will have to suffice. With a short postscript for what matters most:

Merry Christmas,
From Mum, who loves you

John

Fredrika receives a sum of money corresponding to the student loan she would otherwise have had to take out for her first term at the school in London. Victor receives a new computer with an integrated modem and sufficient performance for all the games he wants to play, and more besides. Jenny receives a return ticket between the USA and Sweden, so she can afford an extra trip home during the spring when she's working at the equestrian centre in Texas. Netta gets nothing, though she's really the one who deserves everything.

It was impossible for him to find a way of thanking her for all she's done. For rousing him from his lethargy and with loving care making him part of a new family, this family. Not to mention the farm, the animals, their life in the country, the hunting licence, the new friends, all the harvests, everything they've experienced together. He has her to thank for all of it. Everything that turned out well in the end was her doing. How can you thank someone for something like that?

He would like to thank her for her ceaseless energy, for her intractable stubbornness. For everything she does and has done throughout his illness. And everything she did before it. For never giving up. For finally agreeing not to tell the children that the doctors have switched to palliative care. Even though she was reluctant, she agreed. He'd like to thank her for that.

And he wants to thank her for promising him she'd help the children in their relationship with Mary, for promising in the same breath that she would always regard his children as her own, always love them as unconditionally as she loves Jenny and Eva.

Most of all he wants to thank her for Eva. Little Eva, who became the bond that links them all together. Everyone in the family is related to Eva. And all that comes from Netta. Without Netta: nothing.

That's why Netta deserves everything, but in the end will receive nothing. He grew too sick, it came too fast, he couldn't manage it. There's an empty space under the Christmas tree for her this year.

And yet she's sitting here. Unswervingly present, the eternal fixer, who has already cleared away after Christmas lunch and put an elf's hat on Eva's head. She joins in the children's present-opening, seems genuinely happy when they look pleased, gives an extra-loud whoop of appreciation when the parcel comes from Mary.

He looks at her and can't for the life of him understand how she can do it. He looks at her and wants to carry on looking for the rest of the day, for the rest of his life, but he doesn't have the strength.

He falls asleep on the sofa, in the middle of the present-giving.

He falls asleep to the sound of his family opening gifts.

The living room smells of mandarins and mulled wine.

It is all exactly as it should be.

He's grateful when he falls asleep, grateful for everything.

Epilogue

When they glimpse the two church steeples rising up side by side on the other side of the river, the light is already beginning to fade. Only a few hundred metres separate them from the large brick church, but they still have to cross the bridge. And they're running out of time. Gaby's new limp was not something she'd mentioned when they'd made arrangements over the phone to go together. Instead, she used the train journey to recount the details to both Mary and the rest of the carriage. This same limp was the reason the walk through the centre took longer than planned, and now they're almost too late. Mary quickens her pace and shivers in the wind. With her eyes fixed on the clock on one of the church towers, she tries to warm her hands in the thin pockets of her jacket. A dark winter coat would have been more suitable for a day like this. Or a real fur, like the one Gaby's wearing.

At the entrance to the church she nods to the verger, while scanning the area behind him. She prepares herself mentally to open her arms wide and express her deepest sympathy, but none of them are to be seen behind the wooden door. No Victor, no Fredrika, no Jenny, and no Jeanette holding her little baby. Only the elderly verger, who in a low voice and with a discreet gesture into the church, informs them that they are free to sit where they wish. Mary takes her mother's arm and steps inside.

The rectangular church, with its double spires and vaulted brick ceiling, is one of the largest buildings Mary has ever been in. After the door has closed and her eyes have become accustomed to the dim light, she can see there's enough space to accommodate several hundred visitors, but it's only in the front half of the rows of pews that the black-clad mourners are sitting, spread out in little clusters. Right at the back, where she and Gaby are standing, it's completely empty. All the others are already seated. That's how late they are.

Although there's a maroon carpet running down the stone floor in the centre aisle, Mary thinks her heels are echoing between the brick walls when she and Gaby make their way forward through the building. She adjusts her gait, putting her weight down on the balls of her feet, moving almost stealthily towards the middle of the church. The distance between her and the white coffin at the altar still seems a mile long. The portrait at the front of the coffin looks no bigger than a postage stamp, so small it's impossible to distinguish the person it portrays. The man in the picture could be anyone at all. They might easily have come to the wrong place.

The further down the aisle they go, the more hesitant Mary's steps become. Free to sit where you wish, the verger at the door said, but what does that mean in her case? Mary glances over the pews in the hope of deciphering a pattern, finding some kind of clue as to where it would be best for her to sit down, but all she sees are people's backs. In row after row deep into the church loom the mourners' silhouettes, some of them tall, others short. Some with their heads bowed, others staring straight ahead. But none of them seems familiar, and none of them tells her where she belongs today.

Surely there must be a system, she thinks, casting her eyes over the rows of pews, for this kind of occasion? It should at the very least be self-regulating, so that the closest of the bereaved naturally occupy the front rows and those at the periphery of the deceased's life stay further back? It was like that at Irene's funeral anyway. She and Mona sat somewhere in the middle then, and it felt quite normal. The same system applied when they buried her father in Båstad. That time she sat at the front with Gaby and the children, and the whole thing seemed obvious. But today she can't work it out. She doesn't understand her place in the system, doesn't know whether she should sit at the front, given her history with John, or if she ought to stay further back.

Perhaps, she thinks, as she walks forward, they should sit down right in the middle. Somewhere in the neutral ground between those who were close and those who were a little more distant. But the middle rows look crowded. There seem to be many who've decided that's where they belong today. She's not certain they'll find a space there, not one wide enough for them both.

Gaby's wheezing has quietened down since they entered the church, but she's still breathless. When she comes to a stop and starts tugging at Mary's arm, Mary assumes she's tired of walking, needs to sit down and catch her breath. For a second, she hopes Gaby might have caught sight of someone familiar. Perhaps there's someone sitting in the darkness, waving to them, someone who knows them and is asking them to sit down? When she turns to her mother she can see it's as she first suspected. Gaby needs to rest. The row she's aiming for is empty. It's also a long way back.

In the row her mum is pointing to they would have plenty of space. They wouldn't draw attention to themselves when they sat down, and they could easily slip out directly after the ceremony. They could stand outside the entrance to the church and meet Fredrika and Victor there for a warm hug of condolence. And maybe, Mary now thinks, this is exactly where she belongs. Considering how late they arrived at the church, and also considering how many years have elapsed since she and John went their separate ways. Perhaps the distance that arose between them as time passed doesn't entitle her to a better place than the one Gaby is pointing to now. Furthest back, furthest away, furthest down in the gathering's hierarchy. Maybe this is exactly as it should be.

Yet something makes her stay in the aisle when Gaby lets go of her arm and shuffles into the row she's selected. There's something about the distance that troubles her. From this distance it's still not possible to see the portrait on the coffin. Viewed from here, the funeral could be anybody's. Not the man Mary lived with for over a decade, not the man who was the father of her children. From here she can't see them either, the children they had together. Only the backs of their heads, right at the front. She can see Fredrika's tight bun at her neck and Victor's dark mop beside her, but that's all. She can't see how they're feeling. She can't see how they're breathing, *that* they're breathing, or if they're weeping. Nor can she see if they're holding hands, if they're taking care of each other, if they're maintaining their composure or falling apart.

In the pew next to her Gaby is struggling out of her fur coat. She grunts audibly to emphasise how tight it is, how stiff she's become, how tired she is after the hurried walk. How useful it would have been, quite frankly, to have had a helping hand from her own daughter at a moment like this. Mary sees her glowering mother in the pew. She meets the querulous look, notes the furrowed brow, registers the upturned palms which wave to underline her point.

'For God's sake, are you ever going to *come*?' Gaby finally says in a hiss, loud enough to be heard above the organ.

But Mary doesn't come. Instead she takes her eyes off her mother and turns her back to her. Her steps are cautious to begin with, but when she becomes aware that her shoes no longer echo, her tread becomes much steadier. The notes from the organ have increased in intensity since they've been in the church, the organist is pressing several keys at once now; Mary can calmly put the weight back on her heels and as she does her speed increases too.

The man in the portrait stands out more sharply with every step she takes. The photograph on the coffin, she can see now, is of John. A middle-aged John leaning against a barn, dressed in blue overalls. It must be summer, because his skin is suntanned, and his greying hair is bushier than she's ever seen it, but his smile is the same as it was before. His sly smile, one corner of his mouth going up and the other sideways. In his hand he is holding the handle of something that looks like a farm implement. It might be a pitchfork or a spade, it's impossible to say, since the photo ends just below his hand, but he looks strong, anyway, standing there.

Skilful and competent. At peace, in the prime of life. At home, in a way.

Mary is a long way down the aisle by now. There are only a few metres between her and the priest, who has positioned himself behind the microphone stand, ready to begin the funeral as soon as the organ notes fade away. But Mary doesn't look at the priest. She doesn't look at the priest, because she's in the process of turning. She turns towards the pew at the front and now, finally, she can see her children. She sees Fredrika in profile: the pointed nose, the smoky eyes, her gaze resting steadily out into the air next to the coffin. Victor sits next to her, and she sees his smooth cheeks, defined jaw muscles, the dark hair, combed to the side for today. She can see how they breathe, *that* they breathe; can see Fredrika's chest rising faster than Victor's, but neither of them is crying, neither of them is breaking down, not right now. Victor's left arm rests on the back of the pew behind Fredrika's shoulders. Her own arms are crossed in front of her chest. Jenny sits on her left and Jeanette nearest the aisle, with little Eva on her knee. They sit close together, as if it were a tight squeeze, though there are several metres of empty pew next to Victor. As if somebody were missing.

Two steps separate Mary from their pew. She takes a deep breath and keeps the air in her lungs while she leans forward, lays her hand on Jeanette's armrest and accidentally touches her arm. She holds her breath when Jeanette turns towards her and when the children instantly do the same. She doesn't breathe when she meets their eyes, one after the other, first Jeanette and then on via Jenny to her own children. Only when her eyes are on Victor and Fredrika does she dare to breathe again. When she lets the air out, the words come too, of their own accord.

'I'm sorry,' she says to Victor.

'I'm sorry I'm late,' she says to Fredrika.

'I would really like to sit with you,' she says, and then it's over.

No more air, no more words, and now it's up to them.

A NOTE ON THE AUTHOR

CAROLINA SETTERWALL was born in Sala, Sweden, and is the author of *Let's Hope for the Best*. She studied Media and Communication in Uppsala, Stockholm and London, and has worked within the music and publishing industries as an editor and writer. Setterwall lives in Stockholm with her son.

A NOTE ON THE TRANSLATOR

DEBORAH BRAGAN-TURNER is a literary translator from Swedish. Her translations have been longlisted for the Booker International Prize, the Dublin Literary Award and the National Translation Award in Prose, and shortlisted for the Bernard Shaw Prize and the Crime Writers' Association International Dagger.

A NOTE ON THE TYPE

The text of this book is set in Linotype Sabon, a typeface named after the type founder, Jacques Sabon. It was designed by Jan Tschichold and jointly developed by Linotype, Monotype and Stempel in response to a need for a typeface to be available in identical form for mechanical hot metal composition and hand composition using foundry type.

Tschichold based his design for Sabon roman on a font engraved by Garamond, and Sabon italic on a font by Granjon. It was first used in 1966 and has proved an enduring modern classic.